PAPER GIRL

CINDY R. WILSON

Entangled Publishing, LLC
2614 South Timberline Road
Suite 105, PMB 159
Fort Collins, CO 80525
rights@entangledpublishing.com

Entangled Teen is an imprint of Entangled Publishing, LLC.

Visit our website at www.entangledpublishing.com.

Edited by Lydia Sharp and Stephen Morgan
Cover design by Juan Villalobos
Cover images by
Wayne0216/Shutterstock
phonchai/Shutterstock
pixelparticle/Shutterstock
stuar/Shutterstock
SmartPhotoLab/Shutterstock
Interior design by Toni Kerr

ISBN 978-1-64063-187-8
Ebook ISBN 978-1-64063-188-5

Manufactured in the United States of America

First Edition December 2018

10 9 8 7 6 5 4 3 2 1

To my daughters,
who cheered me on as I chased my dreams.

1.

BlackKNIGHT: We've been playing chess for three months now.

Rogue2015: Very astute. Your turn.

BlackKNIGHT: That's a long time in the chess world. In fact, that's a long time in the real world.

Rogue2015: Thank you for pointing that out. Why don't you take your bishop out for a stroll? He can't hide back there all day.

BlackKNIGHT: He likes it back here. It's strategy. Three months, Rogue.

Rogue2015: Why do you keep saying that?

BlackKNIGHT: Because I think after that amount of time, I should know your real name.

Rogue2015: While you were busy reminiscing, I just won the game. Checkmate.

BlackKNIGHT: Ouch.

Rogue2015: I told you, you should have taken your bishop out.

BlackKNIGHT: I'll forgive you for beating me if you tell me your name.

Rogue2015: No.

BlackKNIGHT: Please?

Rogue2015: Double no. Do you want to play again or admit defeat?

BlackKNIGHT: I just want your name.

2.

ZOE

Zoe King. That's my name.

Sixty-two inches of seventeen-year-old female living on the thirtieth floor of the Safe Zone, otherwise known as my family's penthouse apartment. It gave me a view of approximately seven of Colorado's peaks over 14,000 feet—none of which I'd seen up close because I hadn't left my house for 392 days.

That's right. I was *that* kid. The one my parents weren't expecting. The younger sibling, the baby, the one who should have demanded all the attention and made my parents laugh. The one who should have taken the world by storm.

Instead, I built paper art in the study and pretended I cared about my sister's cheerleading squad. I pretended to watch my mother's YouTube videos as she addressed the world like they were all her closest friends. I pretended to want to see my grandparents when they came back from their visits to Japan with Hello Kitty purses, thinking my sister and I were still five years old. I pretended to be able to breathe as the world closed in on me.

When there were two kids in a family and one kid couldn't

leave the house without her chest clamping tight in panic like a bear trap, then you really only had 1.5 kids because .5 of one kid was defective.

That was me. Living as half the person I wished I could be.

My therapist claimed it wasn't literal when statistics said the average American family had approximately 1.5 children. I told her, when she came to my house because I couldn't go to her, "Welcome to the average American family."

3.

JACKSON

The mobile blood collection bus was parked outside of the Denver Public Library today. They handed out orange juice and chocolate chip cookies once you'd had your blood drawn, but I wasn't eligible until I turned eighteen, and I didn't have parental consent.

Dad wasn't likely to be awake this time of the morning, let alone capable of putting pen to paper to give me permission, so I continued on without juice or snacks, even though the gnawing hunger in my stomach wouldn't go away.

Some things in life are guaranteed, but food isn't one of them.

I walked past the strange rock sculpture that reminded me of a futuristic Stonehenge and around to the entrance of the library, where they had just opened the doors. It was usually the same group of people, most with backpacks or suitcases because they didn't have anywhere to stay during the day. Homeless.

I was more discreet and left my belongings in the trunk of my car. All except for my backpack.

Inside the library, I waved to the guard and went for the

holds on the main floor first. I gathered my items from the shelf: an astronomy study guide, three CDs, two sci-fi novels, and a book on chess techniques, because Rogue2015 was kicking my ass.

Then I rode the escalator to the second floor and entered the non-fiction section. My usual spot by the window was open, and I dropped my backpack there before nodding at Dale. He stocked the shelves with a monotonous *swish* and *thud*, settling books into place as he had every Saturday for the past year.

He never said anything, only continued the swish-and-thud motion until he reached the end of the shelf. Then he'd walk over, deposit something on my table, and move on to the next aisle.

Today, it was an apple and a book. *Free $ for College for Dummies.* I glanced up, but he'd moved out of sight.

I was pretty sure Dale knew I was homeless — though not in the traditional sense. Not like those guys who sat at stairwells on the 16th Street Mall to collect what they could from business people as they rushed to the Cheesecake Factory for lunch, or scrounged for leftovers from the groups that stopped to play on the stone chessboards lining the street.

No, I was homeless in the sense that I'd lost everything that symbolized home for me. And the place I had left…wasn't for me anymore. Dad and I had an agreement. I'd stay out of his hair if he'd let me continue to use his address and mailbox for important things like school and my cell phone bill. Basically so the state didn't shove me into a foster home.

Of course, I wasn't sure how much of that agreement Dad remembered, since he'd made it while working toward an epic high on heroin.

Being homeless was a small price to pay for the peace of uninterrupted sleep. For the consistency of quiet instead of yelling. For my own memories of Mom instead of Dad's.

I sat in the chair next to the window and ate my apple. Outside, I could see my favorite sculpture, one with far more whimsy than futuristic Stonehenge. This one was called *Yearling*—which was, incidentally, its actual name, not the one I'd given it:

Horse on Chair.

It was a twenty-one-foot-high red chair with a tiny horse on it. You could read about the history of the sculpture, right here in the library, by the man who'd created it, but I preferred to think he'd been inspired by the lack of oxygen in our Mile High City and had chosen to build something fun in his air-deprived stupor.

I opened my backpack and shuffled around for my laptop, one I'd gotten secondhand from my friend Robert. I shoved aside the case with the toothbrush, toothpaste, and a bar of soap. I'd find an empty bathroom later and clean up.

My computer connected to the library's wifi, and I brought up *Chess Challenge*. The scoreboard appeared on the right, a running tally of how many matches each gamer had won. Rogue2015 was still at the top, with BlackKNIGHT settled at the number four position. Damn, that girl didn't give an inch.

I used to play with all sorts of other people, even people in other countries. But once Rogue and I started a running dialogue along with our matches, I rarely played anyone else. According to her profile, she was only a year younger than me. I had no idea where she lived, though, at present, her location said Justin Bieber's house. Last week it had been 1776, NYC. Despite her clear sense of humor, she played the game like her life depended on it and had a penchant for telling it like it was. I admired her focus.

I needed that same kind of focus for college. I knew where I was going, I had a plan, but anxiety filled me every time I realized how easily it could fall apart. I cringed every time I had to lie and write down my dad's address on scholarship applications even though I didn't live there. I only forced myself to go back to check the mail. But it was a choice I'd made over a year ago. No going back now, even though I'd had to lie on my college application, too.

And it wasn't just college stuff. I was lying to every single person in my life—except Rogue. She was the only one I could completely be myself with.

A message box popped up on my screen.

Rogue2015 has initiated a match with you. Would you like to play?

I smiled, feeling my shoulders relax. Right now, playing with Rogue was the best escape I could think of. I *needed* this. Someone who didn't judge me and someone I could tell my secrets to and never have to worry about the consequences. If I didn't have Rogue, I wouldn't have anyone I could really talk to.

I'd focus on college stuff later. I clicked the *Yes* box and studied the screen before making my first move. Two months until graduation, which meant I had plenty of time to work my way up the scoreboard.

That and line up a slew of other jobs for the summer so I could pay the college fees for my first semester. I had to do this. Otherwise, I wasn't just letting my mom down; I was losing my dream as well.

4.

BlackKNIGHT: That wasn't your best move.

Rogue2015: You won't be saying that when it's checkmate.

BlackKNIGHT: So…Rogue? Is that an *X-Men* reference?

Rogue2015: You're stalling. It's your move.

BlackKNIGHT: You like comics, don't you?

Rogue2015: Your turn.

BlackKNIGHT: Don't you?

Rogue2015: Yes.

BlackKNIGHT: Comic lover and chess player. Cool. What other awesome things were you born to be?

Rogue2015: I was born to be a lot of things.

BlackKNIGHT: Like what?

Rogue2015: Maybe I didn't phrase that right. I meant I was born to be a person who does a lot of things.

BlackKNIGHT: Sounds like you already do.

Rogue2015: I wish that were real life. In real life…I'm scared of almost everything. The computer is safe. Chess is safe. The real world? Not so much.

BlackKNIGHT: I get that. You can be yourself when you're anonymous, but in real life you have to answer to who you really are. And sometimes, that's the scariest thing of all.

Rogue2015: Exactly. Now, it's your turn.

5.

ZOE

It was Monday in the Safe Zone, which meant 12,222 steps around our apartment because I needed my exercise and then crappy math makeup homework from my online class before I got to finish creating Saturn.

Before I left my room, I studied the messages on the door of my closet. Red sticky notes went on top because they were the most urgent. Yellow went next, and then blue below that because water was at the bottom.

I wrote on a red sticky note, *Remind Mom to get more paper,* and stuck it on the top row of my closet door. I was almost out of red and brown, since I just finished making Mars. I'd need both for a few more planets, but especially brown once I got to the asteroid belt.

I left my room at 7:15 a.m. I walked past the door to my sister Mae's bedroom, through the gigantic living room, and toward the kitchen where I'd circle the island. Approximately 143 steps in one circuit through the apartment (passing by my study and my parents' bedroom), which meant close to 89 circuits to reach my goal.

Outside the huge bank of windows in the living room, it

was a clear and sunny day. Warm for March. But my choice of leggings and a T-shirt worked for any weather because I wouldn't be going out today.

I glanced in the study as I passed, admiring my paper wall. It took me a week to make Mercury, forty-seven sheets of gray and white copy paper, folded just right to create the planet closest to the sun.

My footsteps slowed as I neared the kitchen again and heard voices. Mom and Mae. My stomach clenched when I heard my name.

Damn. Not going through the kitchen messed up my circuit. I checked my phone, which had an app that catalogued my steps, and walked by the bank of windows in the living room again before heading back to my bedroom.

They were talking about me. I knew it. Another pass through the living room.

My heart raced, even as Dr. Edwards's voice echoed in my head. *It's not all about you.*

But my next pass by the kitchen confirmed it.

"…but it's only two months away," Mae was saying. "What if she doesn't come?"

"She will," Mom answered, voice low.

My stomach clenched and nausea kicked in. Another circuit down the hall and then to the living room. They were definitely talking about me. Mae was graduating this year. In *two* months. Mae had school functions and events she invited me to all the time, and I hadn't gone to any of them since I was a sophomore—a whole year ago.

But this was graduation. A *huge* deal. And I'd already promised her I'd go. Sure, it was back at the beginning of the school year, when I thought I'd have a ton of time to get to where I needed to be. And sure, I figured it was far enough away I wouldn't have to deal with it for a while. But I'd promised.

Graduation. I swallowed, but my throat didn't want to be moistened. Hundreds of people I didn't know. My heart beat faster. Mae's friends. They'd wonder why I even came. They'd look at me the same way they looked at me when they visited our house. Like I was an alien. Like I didn't belong.

It made me want to vomit. Just like all those times Dad had made us star in his Car King commercials. All those eyes on me…

I did another circuit and stopped by my room to write another sticky note and slap it on my door. Remind Mom to get paper.

The next circuit, I wrote the same note and brought it to the study. I added it to the note board by the door, aligning it perfectly at the end of the row.

Mom and Mae were gone from the kitchen. They probably went somewhere else to talk about me. When I walked to my bedroom again, Mae appeared in the hallway with her backpack.

"See ya," she said. She wore her cheerleader uniform, a pleated skirt too cool and cheerful to be friends with my black yoga pants.

Mae made life seem so easy, and school was a breeze for her. Even homeschooling was a challenge for me, and it wasn't what I really wanted. At school, junior year waited for me like a prize I knew I'd never win. That, and maybe Mae's friend Jackson. The same one I used to watch play basketball, willing him to come sit with me on the bleachers and talk like he sometimes did.

I'd love to see him again. Instead, he was just another reminder of all the things I'd lost when I got trapped in my house.

Hadn't I said something to him once about living life to its fullest? And now look at me.

"You have practice after school today?" I asked.

"We have that new routine we're learning. I can help you with your math when I get home."

"I don't need help," I grumbled, though I did.

Just not Mae's help. I swore the answers magically popped into her head without any effort at all. She never had to show her work because it wasn't *work* for her to get the answers.

"Whatever," she answered, heading down the hall without even glancing back.

"Bye."

Yeah, she had definitely looked at me funny. She was mad at me.

Mom met me in the living room, barefoot, her shiny black hair already combed and styled. "Don't forget Dr. Price is coming today."

Therapist #6. Dr. Edwards asked if I wouldn't mind seeing someone else for the next few weeks, and I'd agreed even though I didn't think seeing *another* new therapist was going to help.

"Okay," I said to my mom. I wouldn't forget. It was on a yellow sticky note on my bedroom door. And the note board in the study. And my phone. "Mom?"

"Yes?"

"When you go to the store, can you get some more paper?"

She ducked back into her bedroom, voice muffled when she said, "Sure, when I get a chance. I have to make a week's worth of freezer meals first."

I did another circuit, convinced Mom was mad at me, too. Hopefully she'd still get my paper, though.

Just to be safe, I wrote her a note. Because without my paper, what else did I have?

Mae's graduation. *That's* what I was supposed to be working toward. Not more paper planets. And that was the reason for my new therapist. To make progress. But having a new therapist just gave me one more thing to stress about. I'd have to start all over again with someone I didn't know, and someone who didn't understand how terrified the outside world made me. If I couldn't even meet a new therapist, how in the world was I supposed to be able to leave the house for graduation?

6.

JACKSON

It sounded like a black hole in here. The washers and dryers made a whirring and whooshing noise that reminded me of those NASA videos I watched on YouTube. Sometimes I could picture myself way out there in space, away from everyone and everything, and I wondered if I'd even miss being here.

I closed my astronomy book when the cycle finished and stood to pull my clothes out of the dryer. This was my favorite laundromat. It was close to school and everywhere else I liked to go. Someone always left their old *National Geographic* magazines on the counter by the bulletin board. They were good late-night reading material when I hunched down in the back seat of my car and couldn't sleep.

I used to consider poking holes in the upholstery of the roof to make the shapes of the constellations so I'd have something to stare at, but I'd probably end up making the Big Dipper lopsided. If I had any fraction of an artistic bone in my body, like my mom, it might have worked. Mae's sister, Zoe, was like that, too.

I remembered her shoes.

My phone buzzed as I pulled out an armful of socks. I

took it from my pocket and peeked at the screen. Robert. His message said: Basketball @ school @ 5:00?

I mulled this over as I folded two T-shirts, my favorites. One was frayed at the bottom, and a little hole graced the collar. I probably had more clothes at home—unless Dad had decided to sell them for drug money or maybe to pay rent—but there was no way in hell I was going back to check.

I'll be there, I told Robert.

My fingers squeezed the phone, but I resisted the urge to check the *Chess Challenge* site for a move or a message from Rogue. I was almost out of data for the month. But Rogue... she was quickly becoming my new addiction. It wasn't so much that she was a chess master as the fact she made me feel normal. She didn't know I often played her from coffee shops or the library because I had no home. She talked to me like I was anyone else. A friend. Even better—she had no idea who I was, so I never had to worry about her even accidentally spilling my secrets.

I piled my clothes into my laundry basket and then stopped at the bulletin board by the door. I pulled a flyer for tutoring out of my pocket and tacked it to the board. If I didn't find something soon, I was going to have to get more creative. My biggest scholarship was riding on the number of community service hours I was getting through tutoring. I hadn't reached the amount I needed yet, and I *had* to get this scholarship. It was the biggest thing keeping me going, encouraging me to get to my dream. College.

I released a long breath. I could do this. My mom had taught me that much. Nothing was too hard as long as you didn't give up.

Outside in the sunshine, my car was parked in a corner spot. I glanced around before settling the basket in the trunk and dividing my clothes into piles to place them in the duffel bag. Then I pulled the bag of quarters from my pocket and put that in the basket as well, so I'd have them for next time.

It was close enough to five o'clock—I might as well head over to the school. I snagged a granola bar from my stash in the trunk, pulled on a baseball cap to block the glare of the sun, and hiked my backpack over my shoulder. Basketball at the gym meant free showers afterward. The day was already looking up.

I headed on foot in the direction of the school, trying to remember the last move Rogue had made against me on *Chess Challenge* so I could figure out a way to beat her.

The cheerleaders were in the gym as well, their enthusiastic claps echoing off the high ceilings.

Mae was with them, peppy with her hair in a high, messy ponytail. Her sister, Zoe, used to come with her a while back, always sitting with her notebooks and colored pencils, making me want to see what she was doing. Then she seemed to vanish off the face of the earth. One day I asked Mae what had happened, and her answer was a simple: "Zoe decided to be homeschooled instead."

I was pretty sure I'd answered with something like, "I'd rather cut off my own leg before being homeschooled," which I realized now was fairly insensitive.

But I'd been riding a ship through the shit storm of life with my father at the helm. My grades were plummeting, and I'd only stuck with basketball because it got me out of the house. That last day before I decided to leave for good, Zoe had come to watch Mae practice, and I'd caught her reading a book on chess.

I'd sat next to her, happy to brood in silence until she'd spoken to me.

"Zugzwang."

I'd glanced over. "What did you call me?"

She'd smiled and pointed to her book. "Zugzwang. It's the point in a chess game where a player is forced to make moves that are going to cost him pieces—and maybe the game altogether."

"Meaning the other player is probably going to win."

"Right. The other player being me."

I'd shifted to face her. "You're that good at chess?"

"I plan on being that good at chess."

"Zugzwang," I'd repeated, returning my attention to the basketball game. "You learn something new every day."

"That you do."

She'd gone back to her book. I didn't know what had possessed me to turn to her again. Maybe it had been her determination to do something so simple: be awesome at chess. Maybe it had been the fringe of black bangs she'd had to keep brushing out of her eyes, or the manga characters drawn in a rainbow of colors on her shoes.

Whatever it was, I felt compelled to say, "Maybe we could play chess together someday."

She'd nodded. "We should."

Like I'd known how to play chess. I'd been pretty sure I'd played it with my mom once years ago and referred to the pieces as "little horsey guy" and "castle man."

I'd known the pawns, though. I remembered them well because my mom had told me, "The pawns are the pieces you sacrifice for the greater good."

Sacrifice was something I was far too familiar with, and I hated that feeling, so I'd buried those thoughts of my mom along with all the other crap moments of feeling sorry for myself. My mom would have hated that, me feeling sorry for myself, so I wouldn't let her see me like that.

And then Zoe had said something I would never forget. The exact words my mom had said to me before she died. "Life's too short not to live it to the fullest."

Those words had stayed with me since then, propelling me to keep going even though life wasn't exactly full of rainbows.

Forcing myself to focus on the present as my basketball teammates piled into the gym, I grinned at them, and life was on an even keel for the most part.

I still thought about Zoe, though. Enough to sign up for matches online at *Chess Challenge*.

I wondered if Zoe still played chess. Or why she never came out of her apartment. Maybe Zoe's childhood had vanished just like mine, and we were both unfortunate adults now.

7.

BlackKNIGHT: I'm not going to lie to you. I'm pretty sure you're a robot.

Rogue2015: Because my chess game is flawless?

BlackKNIGHT: There is that.

Rogue2015: Because I say words like "compute"?

BlackKNIGHT: That, too.

Rogue2015: I just took your rook. Is that something a robot would do?

BlackKNIGHT: Absolutely. It might have something to do with your bionic leg, too. Like a cyborg.

Rogue2015: ☺ How did you know about my bionic leg?

BlackKNIGHT: Wild guess.

Rogue2015: Sometimes I wish I were more like a robot.

BlackKNIGHT: Why's that?

Rogue2015: Then you don't have to feel. To know when you're letting someone down.

BlackKNIGHT: Is that how you feel?

Rogue2015: I made a promise I'm not sure I can keep.

BlackKNIGHT: What promise?

Rogue2015: Just something I wish I wouldn't have said.

BlackKNIGHT: You're not going to tell me what it is?

Rogue2015: No.

BlackKNIGHT: You sure?

Rogue2015: You spend more time talking than playing, you know.

BlackKNIGHT: It's not every day you meet a robot.

8.

ZOE

I heard the elevator ding from down the hallway. Therapist #6. Probably another clone of Dr. Edwards and all the other therapists I'd had over the years. I ducked into my study when Mom told her to come back, and planted myself beside my desk. When she came in, her quick smile suggested she was perfectly comfortable walking into a strange place. Well, strange didn't even begin to cover me and my room. The proof? Her surprised expression when she realized she'd just entered the Milky Way.

Strewn about the room were paper planets, stars, moons, and hopefully soon a couple of constellations. I folded them, cut them out, and crafted them until they became art. They mostly lined the southern wall, but Jupiter was bound to leak onto the ceiling.

And therein lay 80 percent of my life. Paper art in these four walls.

Therapist #6 said, "Wow. This is…out of this world."

My cheeks flamed, and I gurgled out a laugh. It sounded so silly, so I kept my gaze averted. She didn't look like a therapist. In fact, she looked young enough to be Dr. Edwards's daughter, with her dark skinny jeans, a hip blazer, and a navy scarf with designs that reminded me of the galaxy above us. Her shoes were yellow—the same shade I used to make the sun. Did that mean she was inexperienced?

"Zoe, I'm Dr. Gina Price. You can call me Gina. Dr. Edwards mentioned I was coming when he saw you last week, right?"

I nodded. He'd sprung it on me after our session, right after we'd talked about compulsions and changing behaviors. We'd talked about how my parents were enablers, allowing me to stay cooped up in my large apartment with my own paper playground so I'd have no reason to want to leave. I wouldn't be surprised if he'd talked with them as well. My parents probably didn't know what to do with a word like that. Enabler. Martin and Yoko King weren't sure what to do with my therapy, either. They thought I was just "shy" and maybe "a little obsessive."

"This is really impressive," Gina said, staring at the ceiling. "How long did it take?"

I flicked a glance at her, surprised she asked. Dr. Edwards never asked about my paper art. My stomach clenched so tight, I thought I might throw up. I knew exactly what she was doing. Making small talk to get me to open up, feel comfortable. I kind of wanted to create paper dolls out of both her *and* Dr. Edwards so I could make them get swallowed by a black hole.

"A long time," I said, so quiet I was sure she hadn't heard me.

She stared up at Pluto, one of my favorite pieces. The dwarf planet and I were more alike than I wanted to admit. Both *not quite* what everyone thought we should be. It could be cold and lonely out in space.

"Are you comfortable talking in here?" Gina asked.

Talk? She meant assess me.

Though I was terrible at math, I loved numbers. There was always comfort in certainty. For example, I knew for certain Gina would use the words "cope," "panic," and "focus," at least once during our "talk."

"Sure," I said when she wouldn't stop staring at me.

I nudged a pile of comics farther under the desk and stood to block the computer. It was a chess match, and I'd used the King's Pawn opening because I was really starting to like BlackKNIGHT and I didn't want to beat him too badly. A message popped up on the bottom of the screen.

BlackKNIGHT: I know what you're doing.

I wanted to answer, but not in front of Gina. BlackKNIGHT spent just as much time talking to me as he did playing, and it was my secret addiction. I had lots of addictions, but everyone knew about the rest.

"You like music?" Gina asked, wandering to my wireless speaker.

I called it Cyclops because there was a symbol of an eye in the middle. "Yes."

"You listen to it while you make"—she gestured to the wall covered with paper—"all this?"

"Yes."

"It's pretty elaborate."

I shrugged, keeping my gaze directed at the floor. "Kind of like a part-time job."

"Hmm. A good coping technique." (Cope=1)

I winced. I clearly gave the wrong answer. When I looked at Gina again, she met my eyes. I tried to hold her gaze because Dr. Edwards said I should make eye contact. It was one of the steps for coping with the real world. But Gina was too sure of herself, and she didn't falter. I wished I could be like that. I picked up a pen from the desk, like I might start doodling right in front of her.

Which I would never do.

"So, you're in your junior year?" Gina asked.

I nodded.

"How's homeschooling going?"

I strangled the pen. Not well, considering I wasn't a math or science genius. I could measure and cut and fold thousands of pieces of paper, but the concepts for *real* math and science still eluded me.

"It's going fine," I said.

"Your mom mentioned you and Dr. Edwards were working toward getting out of the house more. You have a goal?"

"Mae's graduation. It's in two months. I promised her I'd go." There was no way I was going to let her down. I couldn't.

She started walking around the room, taking in all the components of my recyclable Milky Way. "Two months. That's good. It'll give you time."

"Time," I repeated dumbly. What was that supposed to mean?

"Sure. Time." She reached up and touched a palm-sized glittering piece of yellow paper. "How did you make this?"

It was a 3-D shooting star that stretched away from the wall and hovered in the air. There were seven of them altogether. Some were gigantic meteors that took ten sheets of paper, and others small shooting stars that I'd colored first.

"An X-ACTO knife," I said. "That's how I'm doing some of the constellations…and the mountains on the planets, too. I just have to—to be careful. You know, cut them just right so the paper doesn't fall apart."

A beep from the computer indicated BlackKNIGHT had made a move. There was too much going on in my little room. Too many things for me to focus on.

I wanted to be back with BlackKNIGHT, just us, in my safe space.

And I wanted Gina to leave. But when she asked me about my art, I wanted her to stay. No one ever asked me about my creations.

I wondered what Jackson would think if he saw my galaxy. One time I'd overheard him talking about a Discovery Channel special he saw on wormholes.

BlackKNIGHT wrote: Top that.

My fingers itched to answer him.

"That's really cool," Gina said. "Does it help you relax? Focus?" (Focus=1)

"Yes," I mumbled.

Gina faced me again. "Dr. Edwards said you were wary about trying some of his techniques for coping." (Cope=2)

I shrugged.

Gina leaned against the wall. I couldn't read her expression. I was pretty sure Dr. Edwards taught her that. Give nothing away. But…she didn't seem like Dr. Edwards. Or like any of my other therapists.

"Do you think…you could help?" I ask, keeping my gaze down. "With the graduation thing."

Gina smiled at me. "I think it's worth a shot. I have some ideas."

Oh no. "Like…what kind of ideas?"

"Other goals, other steps you can take. You going to prom this year?"

I almost choked. "No way." I didn't even go to school, anyway. Prom didn't apply to me.

"Are you worried something bad might happen at prom?"

"I don't know." Yes and no. Why was she even talking about prom anyway? I was supposed to be focusing on Mae's graduation—*that* was my goal.

"Are you worried about what to do if you start to panic?" (Panic=1)

Didn't she understand? I was pretty much always worried. That was why the Milky Way and BlackKNIGHT and 12,222 steps made me feel so safe.

Gina shifted, not waiting for me to answer. "Do you want to go to prom?"

Oh my God. What was her obsession with this dance? "You already asked me that," I muttered.

"No, I asked if you were going to go. Now I'm asking if you *want* to go."

Maybe if Mae stayed with me the whole time. Maybe if I didn't have to talk, or all the lights went out and I could just listen to the breathing all around me.

"I don't know," I whispered, when really what I meant to say was *no*.

Because I'd panic (2) at home before, and I'd panic (3) during the dance, and even if I tried to focus (2) on the fact that I wasn't the only nervous girl out there or the reality that no one was staring at me or talking behind my back, I still wouldn't be able to cope (4).

"They're steps, Zoe. Prom. Graduation. Even the smaller things like getting up in the morning and going for a walk. Everything has a purpose. What do you think?" she asked.

"I think I'd rather stay home," I said.

Gina nodded like I'd given the correct answer this time, which meant I'd said the wrong thing because that's what she expected from me. And what she expected from me was probably the same thing Dr. Edwards expected from me, which was that I'd do what made me comfortable.

Stay inside my four walls and cope (5) with life how I wanted to.

"I understand," Gina said, and I was afraid she did.

I was afraid she'd already learned more about me than Dr. Edwards had in the entire time he was my therapist, and I wasn't sure whether it gave me hope or scared me to death.

9.

JACKSON

After school, I played basketball in the gym for an hour with Robert and some of the other guys from the team. Mae and Kelly were there with the cheerleading squad, ruffling pom-poms and practicing dance moves.

I glanced to the bleachers where Zoe used to sit. I didn't know why I kept thinking about her. Probably because of the chess game. But I wanted to see her again.

Robert made the last shot and then scooped Mae into his arms.

"Ew!" she squealed. "You're sweaty! I was going to invite you over to my house, but I don't think I'd survive."

Robert lifted his eyebrows at her. "I was going to take a shower first. You can help."

Mae rolled her eyes. "You're delusional." She turned her attention to me. "We're going to my house to watch a movie. Would you like to come?"

Mae's mom always had cookies or something she'd made fresh sitting on the island in the kitchen. Their television was as big as my car, and their penthouse had the best view in the whole city. It was a real home.

Also, Zoe.

I nodded. "Sounds good."

Even better—I'd get a shower beforehand. A lot better than working to hunt one up.

As we rode to the penthouse, I thought about how long it had been since I saw Zoe. I'd been to Mae's house a handful of times, but hadn't glimpsed her even once. I wanted to uncover the mystery of her disappearance. Maybe ask her for chess tips so I could move up to number three on the *Chess Challenge* scoreboard. A little closer to Rogue.

Mostly, I just wanted to get to know her better.

Which meant I was going to have to work a little harder to see her.

My shoes squeaked on the shiny tile when I entered the lobby of their penthouse. It never ceased to make my jaw drop. I could have fit my entire home—my *old* home with my dad—in the lobby and still had space to move around.

I made the excuse of needing to wash my hands so I could look for Zoe. I left the others in the kitchen and took my time walking down the hall as they laughed and joked behind me. At the end of the hall was a bedroom, probably the master, and an office next door.

Music throbbed from the closed door of another room, and I paused outside of it, trying to hear what was playing. I could only pick up the murmur of words, soft singing, and drums that drowned out the rest.

Was Zoe inside?

Not like I could knock. I barely knew her.

Rather than stand like an idiot outside her door, I walked into the bathroom.

Mrs. King had set out bars of soap in a shallow bowl. They looked brand new. I wondered if anyone used them or if they were just for show. They even matched the towels. I bolstered a smile, trying not to remember that this wasn't my life. That I didn't have designer towels or soap. I didn't even have a bathroom.

Why hadn't Dad changed his life after what happened to Mom? Weren't things like that supposed to bring families together? I didn't need fancy bathroom accessories or even a clean house, I just needed a home.

I washed my hands without soap and dried them before I could lose my good mood. Moving on had done me a lot more good than dwelling.

When I returned to the kitchen, Mrs. King greeted me with a plate of sugar cookies. Her eyes crinkled deeply with her wide smile.

"Good to see you again, Jackson."

"How are the videos coming along?" I asked, accepting a cookie and sitting on a stool at the island counter. I wanted to take three more, my stomach grumbling at the fresh smell of sugar and spices, but I held back.

"Great. Two hundred new subscribers this week."

"And your camera equipment?" As one of my odd jobs, I'd helped her hook up her new recorder and computer so she could play back and edit her videos, and she'd paid me with enough money to feed me for almost a month.

"Great. It's working well. I just did a whole segment on how to get more Instagram followers. A big hit with the younger crowd."

"You're a regular celebrity," I said.

Mae rolled her eyes at me, and I buried a grin. Sucking up to her mom was one of my favorite things about visiting the King household. Sure, it was partly because she force-fed me cookies in handfuls, but also because she actually cared. She cared about Mae's cheerleading and her homework and eating dinner together as a family as often as possible and making

DIY videos, among others, to share with the world. She was all about family and keeping a family running smoothly.

I wondered what she'd think if she knew I slept in my car last night.

"You kids excited about graduation?" Yoko asked.

"I'm sure Jackson is," Mae said, shoving my shoulder. "He's going to be valedictorian."

Yoko's eyes crinkled again. It was hard to remember her family had come from Japan. She'd been immersed in American culture so long, she barely had an accent. She even used Mae's teenager slang sometimes, *whatevs* and *totes adorbs*, which embarrassed Mae and entertained the rest of us.

I wouldn't have minded a mom to be embarrassed about.

"Valedictorian?" she asked. "Really?"

I shrugged. I knew I was, though. I didn't have much of a choice if I wanted my scholarships to go through. I had to be on top of my game at school, at work, in my lies…but I'd be eighteen this summer, and things would be easier—even *if* I had to work my ass off to make extra money.

"Don't be modest," Robert said. "He's taking every AP and honors class he can, and working, too."

"Where are you working?" Yoko asked.

"I'm in between jobs right now," I said smoothly. Which was true. I tutored a few kids during the school year and then helped paint a house last fall. I was stalling on getting something new, maybe because I was still waiting for that magic number to make it all easier. Eighteen. But I really needed to do something soon.

"What about tutoring?" Mae asked. She'd only eaten half of her cookie and the rest sat on a decorative plate in front of her.

I tore my eyes away. "I'm always available if you know anyone who needs me."

And hopefully she did. Just one more job would finish up the community service hours I needed for college.

"You should tutor Zoe," Mae said, glancing at her mom.

I angled my head. "Zoe?"

Like I didn't know who she was. The idea of seeing Zoe again *and* a possible tutoring job had me smiling.

Yoko sighed, rearranging a trio of perfectly placed candles. "It's math mostly. And physics. But that's a lot of math, right?"

I nodded. Physics was my specialty. But calculus could put me in a good mood, too. Kind of like Horse on Chair. You got what you saw. It was definite.

Robert started talking basketball, and Yoko turned her attention to him while I pulled my phone out of my pocket. Rogue2015 had left me a message.

Say hello to my little friend.

I laughed when I saw she'd taken my knight with her bishop, and immediately I typed, **Don't get too cocky,** before I made my move on our virtual chessboard.

I snagged another cookie and followed Mae and the group into the living room for the movie, discreetly keeping up my conversation with Rogue2015 the entire time. I didn't have many days where the world seemed to work out just how I wanted it to, so I planned on enjoying it.

10.

Rogue2015: If Wolverine and the Hulk were friends, would they play chess?

BlackKNIGHT: Depends. Is the Hulk angry?

Rogue2015: Why does that matter?

BlackKNIGHT: If the Hulk is angry, he has smash hands. They're too big to move pawns.

Rogue2015: Good point. Then no, he's not angry.

BlackKNIGHT: Yeah.

Rogue2015: Yeah, what?

BlackKNIGHT: Yeah, they'd probably play chess. And yeah, you're probably ono of the most interesting people I've met.

Rogue2015: Online?

BlackKNIGHT: Anywhere. Online and in real life. Though, I've probably never been there.

Rogue2015: Where?

BlackKNIGHT: Wherever you're from.

Rogue2015: Maybe it's not so interesting here and that's why I play online. You ever think of that?

BlackKNIGHT: No, I didn't. I hear you, though. It wasn't too interesting where I was from, either.

Rogue2015: Was?

BlackKNIGHT: Am. Was. I don't know. I don't really…

Rogue2015: You don't really what?

BlackKNIGHT: My home life was complicated. So I decided to move out.

Rogue2015: Where do you live now?

BlackKNIGHT: Not at home.

Rogue2015: What does that mean?

BlackKNIGHT: It means I live here and there. It's a long story.

Rogue2015: I'll let it go for now. But this sounds like a story that needs to be told.

BlackKNIGHT: Maybe. So, what's it like there? All corn and livestock? Big city? Eiffel Tower? Stonehenge?

Rogue2015: It's probably not too different from where you live. Although…sometimes it feels like a whole other planet.

BlackKNIGHT: I know exactly what you mean.

11.

ZOE

By the time Mae returned from school, I'd completed forty-nine circuits, half of Cassiopeia, and reviewed my mom's YouTube video, *Distressing a Dresser*. And now I had to find somewhere to hide because Mae dragged Jackson home with her and I couldn't be out there with him.

I couldn't talk to him. What was I supposed to say? I'd babble about chess and paper, and he'd look at me like he used to. Like he wanted to know more. But I couldn't even say a whole sentence without stumbling over my words.

I wished I could talk to BlackKNIGHT. *He'd* know what to do. What to say when you wanted to talk to someone so badly but you feared the worst.

I ran out of my mom's studio even as she yelled at me, "Wait, it's not finished!"

"Go make some cookies," I shouted back.

Mom had tens of thousands of subscribers waiting to see how to distress a dresser, but that wasn't as important as hiding. Jackson was here, and he couldn't see me like this: sans contacts and in my geeky glasses—or sans anything halfway cute. Not that he'd say anything.

Jackson always seemed to be nice to everyone, and that was part of what made him so wonderful. One time he'd sat on the bleachers with me and listened to me blabber on about chess. I didn't want to subject him to that again.

Although I did kind of want to show him my paper wall— just because he was obsessed with astronomy. Mae said he was going to college to study that.

I heard voices as I ducked into my paper haven. I recognized those voices because I listened to them all the time. Mae was only a year older than me, and even my parents couldn't tell our voices apart. Her best friend, Kelly, was also a cheerleader, and she sounded like she'd just inhaled helium. Mae's boyfriend was captain of the basketball team and joked a lot with Mae, which made her happy and made me gag. And then there was Jackson.

No gag factor there. Just a smooth, musical voice that was constantly upbeat and inquisitive. I could hear his smile every time he talked. I was pretty sure I'd never met anyone who smiled as much as Jackson.

Sometimes as they watched TV in the living room, I stood at the end of the hallway, just out of sight, and laughed at their jokes.

I paused at the desk and decided to work on Neptune. I had a pile of blue and green sheets of paper that needed to be folded into 3-D shapes. I wished I could take an art class, but that would mean leaving the house. That would mean going to school and facing hundreds of students. Teachers who would expect me to speak up in class even if it felt like all the oxygen had been sucked from the room.

Dr. Edwards said lots of people had anxiety, and it didn't have to come from some big, traumatic event.

Being in my dad's commercials *felt* traumatic, though. People watching you, telling you where to stand and how to act. I wasn't a natural like Mae, and I always seemed to do it wrong. I'd completely missed the last one because of the fear. Because that was the day everything else had come crashing down on me, too.

After that, I wasn't just scared of commercials and public speaking and every single new social situation. I was terrified.

My computer *ding*ed.

BlackKNIGHT had made a move.

I leaned in and studied the chessboard onscreen. I was white, like always, and my opponent was black.

"Crap," I whispered. Smart move.

Tapping my finger against my bottom lip, I debated. BlackKNIGHT wasn't an idiot. He'd know what I was doing if I moved my rook. And he'd take it with his knight in a few moves if I wasn't careful. Then again…

Don't go easy on me, BlackKNIGHT wrote.

I smiled. In my fantasy, I was playing some genius college kid with nerdy glasses like me. One day he'd win a Nobel Prize or, even better, be signing autographs at Comic-Con for something geeky and awesome and he'd say how he owed his creative genius to Rogue2015 and all her hours chatting over magnificent chess games in the wee hours of the night.

But most likely, he was a middle-aged man who lived in his parents' basement and couldn't play much during the day because he worked a nine-to-five job creating dull software programs or fixing broken iPhones.

My fictional life was so much more exciting than the real thing.

Either way, BlackKNIGHT was the closest thing to a best friend I had. He was also the only one who never tried to change me. Who accepted me like I was—even after I'd told him my fears about not being as much as I should be. And about not living up to my promise to Mae.

I typed a message to BlackKNIGHT. You're getting awful cocky. Then I smiled at his king sitting right there in the third row. I went for the intimidation move just to show him what he was dealing with—a play called the Absolute Skewer, forcing his king to move aside and let me take his knight.

Then I asked him about the Hulk to take away the sting, and laughed at our exchange.

After a short conversation, I snagged another piece of paper for the planet and frowned. Paper. Wasn't Mom going to the store this afternoon? What if she left before I could remind her again?

I reached automatically for my phone to text her and then frowned. My gaze swept the room and my desk again in case I missed it. Where was my phone? It had to be here somewhere. I closed my eyes with a sigh. Crap. I left it in the kitchen. Out *there*.

I bit my lip and pressed my ear to the door. Nothing. No voices, no sounds of running water or dishes in the kitchen. Maybe they were in Mae's room or out on the balcony. Kelly and Mae liked to practice their BE AGGRESSIVE, B-E AGGRESSIVE cheers in the sunshine on days like today.

But where was Jackson? Outside, too?

I *needed* that paper. I heard Mom's voice, saying something about heading out. Paper, paper, paper.

I could go fast. Run straight to the kitchen and back without anyone but Mom seeing me.

With a deep breath, I opened the door. As I rounded the corner, I ran into someone so hard we both stumbled. Hands gripped my arms to help steady me. I winced at the pain in my shoulder even as my cheeks heated.

"There goes my spleen," Jackson said.

Oh my God, oh my God, I broke his spleen. Was a spleen

even something we needed? "I'm sorry—I didn't mean to—"

"Are you okay?"

His hands were warm and solid on my arms. My neck was on fire, flames licking up the sides of my face. Like I was paper. I was paper, and I was about to become ash.

"Um," I said. "I'm—I'm okay. My spleen is intact."

His laughter made me blush harder, and I couldn't meet his gaze. He wore Converse. I spent a lot of time staring at shoes. He had big feet.

Why couldn't I talk to him like a normal person?

It was so easy online. I could give advice to BK like I knew what I was talking about. But in real life, it wasn't ever the same. The real world was like paper, and one screw up, one spark, and the whole thing would go up in flames.

His silence lasted long enough to make me glance up. He stared into the study, gaze captured by the Milky Way.

"Did you do all this?" he asked, taking an automatic step toward the door.

I tried to block his path without touching him, embarrassed like I'd been caught playing Barbies. "Yes, but—"

"Is that Venus?" He stood a whole head taller than me, but he still lifted on his toes to peer farther into the room. "And a meteor? Zoe…wow."

He'd never said my name before. A shiver rained down my body. "It's just a—just a—"

He stopped looking in the room in order to smile at me, eyes full on my face. He wore geeky glasses, too, but they made him look older. Smarter. Cooler. Confident. Everything that I wasn't.

He should have been labeled a nerd or a dork because he was so smart, but his rating on a scale of coolness was at least 150.

-400 for being in the chess club at school. (Yes, it got points with me because chess ruled and it's something we both loved, but at school, chess = dork)

+575 for being on the basketball team

-100 for being on the Honor Roll (although again, in my book, this was a +)

+75 for actually looking cute in his thick-rimmed hipster glasses that weren't just for show but for actual vision problems because, according to Mae, he was so blind he had to take his driving test three times.

In my fantasy world, I took his hand and led him inside, saying, "Come and see," in a voice equal parts sexy and mysterious. I was that perfect piece of paper. No creases, a color that was hard to find, the perfect shade to make something awesome—like a star cluster.

"There's supposed to be a meteor shower soon," Jackson said. "Two nights in a row."

All sixty-two inches of me, foot to head, flushed. Small talk. I was terrible at small talk. Small talk was the bane of my existence. "That's cool," I said.

He tried to peer into the room again, his hand propped on the door. His fingers were long and slender, but they looked strong. Capable. What would it feel like to have him hold my hand? For him to brush those long fingers on my cheek as we sat in my galaxy.

I could show him. I *should* show him because he looked interested, but what if he got inside and hated it?

He smiled and glanced into my study. "I guess you probably already knew that."

I should have. But in all honesty, my Milky Way masterpiece was entirely because of Jackson. I hadn't had much of an interest in astronomy before him. Paper, yes. Planets, no.

"Did you know that there's a Super Massive Black Hole

at the center of the Milky Way?" he asked.

I opened my mouth. Nothing came out. I tried again. "You learn something new every day."

His eyes lit, crinkling as he smiled. "You do."

He remembered. He remembered our conversation on the bleachers. My heart ached. I wanted so badly to show him the stars and planets. To talk like normal people did. But all I could manage to do was stare at his shoes.

"Oh-kayy," he said, the word long and drawn out, and I knew I'd let him down somehow. "I should let you get back to it."

"See ya," I mumbled.

I ran to the kitchen, snagged my phone, and then whipped back around to head to my study. When I peered down the hallway and saw that Jackson had vanished, I darted to my room and then shut the door quickly behind me.

I sagged against the surface, cheeks still warm and heart thumping hard.

My phone *ding*ed with a text. Mom.

Did you need something at the store?

Nervous laughter bubbled up. I texted back Paper!

12.

JACKSON

Keeping to his agreement, my dad had left my mail in the mailbox for me to pick up. I swung by after leaving the King household. From top-of-the-city living to a dingy white house on a cul-de-sac that I wished my father would just sell already.

Every shutter, every warped piece of wood on the porch, every crack in the driveway was there when Mom was alive, but none of it had seemed out of place then. *Then*, I would have said it had character. Now I just thought it was trashy—probably an embarrassment to the rest of the neighborhood.

Sure, it wasn't a rich area, but people kept their property orderly. Clean. Cheerful, even. Like how our house used to be when my mom was alive. Dad had never cared about the place, always wanted to use extra money for his music or other hobbies (I hadn't known then that drinking and drugs were a hobby).

Here, in the sunlight of mid-spring, the house looked as sad as it had when I'd left two winters ago. There wasn't any trash on the lawn this time, though, so that was an improvement. I wouldn't have been surprised if the neighbors had cleaned it up so it would feel more like the neighborhood they once had.

Since my dad's car wasn't in the driveway where he usually parked it, I figured it was safe to assume he was out. I didn't hesitate to sit in my car and look through the envelopes without worrying Dad might see me. He was probably somewhere trying to score his next hit. Drugs and alcohol were his life. Even when Mom was sick, getting high had still been his priority.

Bastard.

The first envelope had the name of my car insurance company on the front, and I set it on the bottom of the pile. Bills. Of course. If I didn't need my car to sleep in at night, I wouldn't have one at all—it was just an extra expense that I didn't need.

Everything at this point felt like an extra expense I didn't need. Even college. I knew going was the right thing. I'd promised my mom I would—and not just for her, but for myself. Our love for astronomy was something we shared since my first memory. I would never forget it.

But the stress over saving enough money was killing me. I understood enough about debt to know it was something I never wanted to experience. It could rip a family apart.

I glanced at the house again, this time with regret. College was the only thing life hadn't taken from me. Deciding not to go would be like...giving in.

And I knew Mom would hate it. This was the one thing she wanted for me, the one thing I could give her even though she wasn't here anymore.

You can do this Jackson, she'd say. *I'm right here with you.*

I'd figure out this tutoring thing, that's all. I'd gather my letters of recommendation, put a notice on the school board and a few places online and see what came of it. I'd even add my name to the board at the library. There was bound to be someone who needed a little extra help. And maybe, just maybe, I'd get lucky and be able to tutor Zoe. Then she'd let me see her galaxy.

It reminded me of what Rogue had said about where she lived. *Sometimes it feels like a whole other planet.* That's what Zoe's paper room felt like. A whole other planet. An escape.

The next envelope was from the cell phone company, addressed to my father. I was still on his account because I was underage, but he had no problem letting me pay my part of the bill—and sometimes his part, too.

When I flipped it over and saw the envelope was already open, I frowned. I pulled out the bill and spotted a haphazard note scribbled on the total.

Already paid. I paid for car insurance, too.

Dumbfounded, I flipped the bill over, like there might be some sort of explanation on the back. Dad didn't pay my bills. That was fact. So, what was this?

And insurance? He hadn't paid my car insurance since I was sixteen. Even that was sporadic at best. Besides the fact he couldn't seem to keep a job, all the money he'd gotten from my mother's life insurance had been used for drugs or alcohol, as far as I knew.

I read the brief note again, searching for insight. Nothing hit me. It didn't make sense.

I'd check the account later. Both accounts, because this was probably a joke. Dad might have been a drug addict, but he still had a sense of humor. Maybe this was his sense of humor on drugs.

When I looked at the house again, I straightened.

What the…?

Dad walked out the front door and paused on the porch when he spotted my car on the other side of the street. After a long moment, he lifted his hand in a wave.

I put the car in gear, pulled away from the curb, and flipped around so I could exit the cul-de-sac.

My stomach growled. Partly out of hunger and partly out of anger. What was he doing? Waving? Writing me notes? We had an agreement. He stayed out of my life and I stayed out of his. The only reason I'd stopped by before the sun had set was because I was in the neighborhood and didn't want to waste gas.

When I almost zoomed through a stop sign, I gritted my teeth and forced myself to breathe. He wasn't worth getting worked up over. I swung into the nearest Starbucks parking lot, grabbed my laptop and charger, and wandered inside, searching for an empty table.

A small one sat unoccupied in the corner, right next to a table with two teenagers making small talk over a book they both had. I forced a smile as I passed, claimed the table, and plugged in my laptop.

I pulled off my glasses and rubbed my hands over my face as the computer booted. When the main screen came up, I held my hands over the keyboard. They hovered there, a small tremor running through them.

To prove to myself I wasn't affected by my dad, I went to the *Chess Challenge* website first.

I finally found myself able to relax when I saw Rogue2015 had made another move.

13.

BlackKNIGHT: How old are you?

Rogue2015: Old enough to know your queen is in trouble.

BlackKNIGHT: She's making friends with your castle guy.

Rogue2015: Don't pretend you don't know what it's called. Stalling is the most obvious sign you're not confident of your next move.

BlackKNIGHT: Checkmate.

Rogue2015: Wait. What?

BlackKNIGHT: That's got to hurt.

Rogue2015: You've been practicing.

BlackKNIGHT: Not much else to do in the evenings. Just stalk you on *Chess Challenge* and try to learn your moves so I can dominate.

Rogue2015: What about family? Don't you spend time with them?

BlackKNIGHT: Not really.

Rogue2015: I'm sorry. I forgot. You said you had a complicated home life.

BlackKNIGHT: No problem. That's life, right? What about your family?

Rogue2015: My family is...close. But I don't really fit.

BlackKNIGHT: Why do you say that?

Rogue2015: Because they all want me to be someone I'm not.

BlackKNIGHT: Isn't that the way of the world? Trying to change you so you can fit? I like you just the way you are.

Rogue2015: You might not say that if you really knew me, but thanks.

BlackKNIGHT: I do feel like I really know you. Even though you won't tell me your name. ☺

Rogue2015: I tell you other things, though. Do you have a job?

BlackKNIGHT: Here and there.

Rogue2015: What's that supposed to mean? Wait, I know. You're independently wealthy. You have a trust fund.

BlackKNIGHT: Ha. I wish. You have a job?

Rogue2015: This is pretty much it. Too bad we don't get

paid for being chess masters.

BlackKNIGHT: You're right. That's too bad. Otherwise, we could team up and beat everyone, amass a fortune, and spend all our days traveling.

Rogue2015: Where would you go?

BlackKNIGHT: It doesn't matter. Anywhere. Where would you go?

Rogue2015: Everywhere.

14.

ZOE

I was starting to forget what our apartment building looked like from the outside. Even the last time I'd come inside, knowing I never wanted to leave again, I didn't pay attention to anything. As we'd walked into the lobby, then to the elevator, and then rode thirty stories up to our penthouse, I'd been paying more attention to my shoes—the bright comics I'd drawn on them. And I hadn't left since.

In my fantasy world, I rode the elevator to the lobby every morning. I greeted the doorman and set off for a three-mile walk along the downtown streets. I strolled the 16th Street Mall and bought hot dogs from the vendors there. In my fantasy, I was a part of the city as much as it was a part of me.

Tonight, Dad arrived home from work at 6:15, the elevator opening to reveal him carrying his briefcase in one hand and his striped tie in the other. He entered the kitchen where Mom and I had prepared five pounds of meatloaf, some for tonight, and some to freeze for later. Mom froze everything she could get her hands on—and called it being time and money conscious.

She was remarkably frugal for a woman who lived in a penthouse.

Dad kissed Mom on the lips long enough to make me cringe, and then he kissed me on the head.

"Dinner's almost ready," Mom said. "How was work?"

As the Car King, Dad worked day in and day out, running three dealerships. He was a businessman through and through. Last week, he starred in his first Car King commercial since I'd refused to do the last one. It made me uncomfortable to even watch. How had he stood up in front of the camera like he was best friends with the world? I probably would have thrown up on his selection of new Toyotas. Or had another panic attack. Just like the last time.

"Our new lot is almost open," Dad said, draping his tie over the back of a chair. "How was your day?"

Mom smiled. "I made a YouTube video on how to fêng shui your house."

Dad looked around the kitchen at the same time I did, trying to find what she might have moved.

"Balance," Mom continued, holding her hands out and moving them up and down like scales. "Yin and yang."

He pointed to the living room. "That's why the couch has to face the other way now?"

"Exactly." She bobbed her head emphatically. "You want good flow, right?"

Dad's lips twitched. "Flow?"

"Energy flow."

"I want good energy flow in the house because…?"

Oh no. Now he'd gotten her started.

Mom waved her hand from the living room to Dad and back. "Good energy flow in the house means good energy flow in the personal life. You want that. Good energy flow, good success in your personal and professional life. You want good success in your professional life, right?"

Dad nodded seriously. "Absolutely. You think I should

fêng shui the lot at work?"

"Couldn't hurt," I told him. "Hire Mom for the day. Get your flow right."

He grinned at me and then asked, "Where's Mae?"

"Her room," I said.

Dad nodded and filled a glass of water. He and Mae were close, probably because Mae was basically a female clone of the Car King. She got people excited and on their feet through cheering. Dad did it with his charm and his commercials. Come to think of it, Mom did it by decoupaging things.

I was pretty sure I was adopted.

When Mae joined us, Mom said, "Let's eat."

Mae came to the dining room table, still in her cheerleading uniform from practice. Dad wore a suit. Mom had on a skirt and bright shirt with a bulky necklace she'd probably made herself. I was in yoga pants. Black. Which of these things did not belong?

Dad asked Mae about cheerleading, and while we passed the meatloaf, Mae filled us in with a deluge of "OMGs" and "likes" and "BFFs" and "proms." If I could monologue like that, I'd have a thousand friends and I'd talk to Jackson. Flirt with him a little. In my fantasy, words were like paper, and there was always plenty to go around.

"How was your session with Dr. Edwards today?" Dad asked me. Dad and Dr. Edwards were old friends from college. Words were easy for them, too.

"It was Dr. Price this time," I mumbled.

"About that," Mom said.

I wasn't truly worried until she set down her fork. Mae lifted her eyebrows at me. She got to deal with my parents' serious conversation faces when they were talking about colleges. I got it when they were talking about my therapy.

Mom sipped her water before meeting my eyes. "Dr.

Edwards mentioned that, as one of your goals toward stepping out of your comfort zone, we should think about sending you back to school."

Mae choked on her iced tea. Dad patted her back absently, but he nodded like one of those bobble heads, moving his head up and down as though Mom's words were completely reasonable. Usually he found something else to do, like build a castle out of his mashed potatoes or talk to Mae about taking business classes in college. According to him "business classes will help you a lot more than Chaucer or Shakespeare."

"I go to school," I said. They all stared at me in the silence that followed. I ducked my chin. "Sort of."

"And you have a D in Physics," Mom said. "It's almost the end of the semester."

Mae's eyes rounded at me as she realized how serious Mom was. But what was I supposed to do? Physics was a concept made up by Martians. I bet even Dad didn't understand it.

"I'll get more help. Mae can help me," I said, smiling at her hopefully.

"I had a tutor, remember? Physics is evil."

Dad grunted his agreement.

See? I wanted to tell Mom. *Physics isn't going to get me anywhere!*

"And it's not just Physics. It's Algebra II, also."

That was because, if physics was evil, algebra was the devil itself. I couldn't believe she thought the solution was going to school. Actually stepping foot inside a physical building made for teaching.

I pulled a piece of paper from my pocket and started folding it in my lap. Both Mae and Dad were building shapes in their food. If I ate another pea, I'd vomit.

"I have a goal. I talked with Dr. Price about it," I said.

"What goal?" Dad asked.

"Going to Mae's graduation, remember? She said she could help, and we're—I'm taking steps."

"Going to school would be a good one," Dad said.

He stopped playing with his food. His eyes held compassion, but he didn't relent, either. "You could finish out the rest of your junior year. You have prom this year." I was really going to vomit now. "Pep rallies," he continued. I was getting dizzy. "College applications and—"

"Dad," Mae said, coming to my defense. "One thing at a time."

Mom nodded. "Mae's right. One thing at a time. I think preparing for school will help prepare for graduation, too."

"I…" There weren't words. School? *School.* I pleaded with Mae with my eyes. *Help!*

"Maybe you could work on getting your grades up some first," she said, shrugging, "if you had a tutor."

The blood drained from my face. "A tutor?"

"Someone who can come here. Yes, that's good," Mom said, smiling at me like that would make it better. She nodded, already on board with the plan. "That will help you take those steps, right? Like you and Dr. Price discussed. I'll check with her, but I think it'll be a good start."

What's next? *More* torture? I silently folded the piece of paper into a crane. I didn't have to see, only feel. It was keeping me grounded right now. Paper was the only thing that didn't seem to change, to let me down.

"A tutor," Dad said, bobble-heading again. "Good idea. Maybe someone from school."

"And we already know who the smartest kid in school is," Mom told Mae with a smile. Had they *talked* about this? "Someone who's really good at math and physics."

Mae grinned. Speaking of evil. "Jackson," she said.

"Smartest kid I know."

"Great!" Mom clasped her hands together while I died in my seat. "Let's see if Jackson will do it."

Mae walked into my room just after ten that same evening as I put up the last of my sticky notes. The lamp on my end table lit the dim room, but light from the moon filtered in through the blinds. I kept them open as much as possible, to see the world I was so far away from.

"Don't be mad at me." Mae looked at the second row of my sticky notes. Two yellow ones had her name on them. She plucked one from the door and read it aloud. "Replace sugar with salt in Mae's coffee."

I sat on my bed and folded my arms. Of course I was mad at her. She knew how hard this was for me—she could have helped me out. Just a little.

"There's more where that came from," I told her.

She set the note on my desk. Just to prove how angry I was, I didn't put the note back, even though it stared at me from the surface.

"You know Mom and Dad just want you to get out. Do all the things they think a kid our age should do."

I leaned back on my pillows and rubbed my hand over a spot above my heart that tended to ache a little whenever I talked about all the things Mom and Dad wanted. What everyone wanted from me. I wanted those things, too. I didn't want to be afraid of everything, but that's just who I was.

"Mom and Dad have pretty grand ideas of what a kid our age should do. I mean, come on. Mom likes having hundreds of thousands of people watch her on camera. Dad is pretty much the same. He actually likes talking to people he doesn't know. And you…"

She smirked. "What?"

"You're Miss Popular. Not all of us like to be the center of attention. How do you get up in front of stands full of people all the time?"

She gathered her dark hair into a ponytail. It was the exact same shade as mine, but while hers was long and straight, mine stopped just above my shoulders and fringed my eyes with bangs I couldn't seem to find the courage to grow out. Even our haircuts were as different as they could be.

"It's not a big deal. Everyone's cheering and worked up. I just go for it. It's fun."

Even the idea made my stomach hurt. "What if you mess up?" All those eyes staring at you, voices whispering about you. Nightmare.

She shrugged. "Who cares? You think they're perfect? You just shake it off and move on."

"I'm not quite that Taylor Swift," I mumbled. "That's the difference between you and me."

"Most everyone is too wrapped up in themselves to care about what you're doing. And even if they do, it's their problem, not yours."

I pulled a pillow into my lap and squeezed it tight. My arms throbbed. "It's not that simple."

"Isn't that what Dr. Edwards and Gina are trying to help you with?"

"Yes." But it was hard. Things always came easier to Mae.

Mae shifted on the bed. "I think a tutor is a good idea."

"Thanks, *Dad*." But she was right in a way. A tutor was better than going to school. It was an easier step, so I wasn't completely overwhelmed.

"No, really. Jackson is nice, and he's really good at physics."

"Seems like he's really good at everything," I said, my

attempt to make it sound like a joke not going over well.

She smiled slowly. My cheeks caught on fire. Mae already knew I liked him. She had to, because every time I was around him, I couldn't speak. Worse than usual.

"You should show him your paper room. He's totally into all that stuff," Mae said.

"P-paper?"

She threw a pillow at me. "Stars and planets. Astronomy."

Like I didn't know this. I'd listened to him enough and asked Mae enough questions to discover a lot of things he liked. "He probably won't have time to tutor me. He's probably busy."

"He does it all the time." Mae grinned. "And I'm sure he'd be extra happy to work with you."

My heart lurched into my throat. "What's that supposed to mean?"

She jumped up from the bed and snatched my glasses off my end table. She put them on and said, "He asks about you sometimes. He's like"—she switched to a low voice—"'So how's Zoe? Should we see if she wants to come out with us?'" Mae took off the glasses and switched back to her voice. "And I'm like, 'No, she probably won't want to.'"

Which made me sad, because that wasn't the entire truth. I wanted to, it was just…too scary.

Mae returned the glasses to her face. "And he's like, 'Are you sure? It's nice out.'"

The words touched something in me. The part that longed to be close to someone else. "You're just saying that."

She removed the glasses and set them next to the yellow sticky note. "Why would I do that? You know, the whole world *isn't* out to get you."

I squeezed the pillow tight, swallowing hurt.

Mae sighed. "Don't look like that. I'm sorry. I agree with

Mom and Dad, okay? So, I'm a traitor. I think you're missing out on a lot, and you don't even know it."

I knew it. I knew it so well my soul ached.

"Fine." Mae walked to the door, making bunny slippers and messy hair look fashionable. "But one day, you'll know what I'm talking about."

"In your dreams," I mumbled.

She flashed a smile at me. "I'm going to be checking my coffee tomorrow, just in case."

"I'll do it when you're least expecting it."

I threw the pillow at her, but she blocked it, and then she let out a squeal of laughter when I pretended to chase after her. Once she vanished down the hall, I closed my door, threw away the yellow sticky note, and sat at my computer.

The chess match BlackKNIGHT and I had been playing for a week popped up. He was getting better. Probably because he'd copied my moves from our last game. He learned fast.

I was wrong before. Mae understood me, but not better than BlackKNIGHT. Sometimes our conversations made me feel whole.

And not alone.

I wondered if BlackKNIGHT was good at physics.

15.

JACKSON

The city dissolved outside the window. Rain had been pouring down on Horse on Chair the entire time I worked in the library, and my mood lifted despite the fact I hadn't slept well the night before.

I didn't mind the back seat of the car, but I was short on places to park and I hadn't chosen wisely last night. A police officer had tapped on the window at two a.m., jerking me out of a dream about climbing Mt. Everest and asking questions I couldn't give the answers to.

It took ten minutes to convince him I'd gotten locked out of my house and my cell phone battery was dead so I'd hopped in the back of my car to wait for my dad to get home and had fallen asleep.

A lie, sure, but enough to make him let me go. And encourage me to get home.

So I'd had to find a new "home" in the middle of the night, awake enough I couldn't go back to sleep. Not when my mail was still in my backpack with my dad's note confusing the hell out of me.

He'd paid my phone bill. *And* my car insurance.

It should have relieved me to find myself richer than I'd expected to be, but instead it threw off my rhythm. We had rules. We had an agreement. And he was ruining it. The least he could do was stick to something—especially this something—that made our lives so much easier. I couldn't stand to live at home with him, and if he'd just let me have my space, maybe I'd be able to forget how badly he'd fallen apart after Mom's death, when I'd needed him the most.

Or how he hadn't shown up for her last hours in the hospital.

In the middle of my rare brood, Mae had called me with a request to tutor Zoe. Mom had always offered those cheesy one-liners, like, "When one door closes, another opens." And this time she was right.

I needed a job. I got one. I wanted to see Zoe, and now she was my pupil.

See? I heard my mom's voice in my head. *Things always work out in the end.*

"It's just a job," I answered under my breath.

Just what you needed.

She was right. Even though she'd been gone for a long time, I could still feel her optimism.

You're going to help that girl, and everyone will be better for it.

She was right about that, too. Except for one thing. "Hopefully she won't be too scared of me to learn something."

Opening my laptop, I remembered the look in Zoe's eyes when she ran into me at her house. Panic, pure and simple. That was pretty much the last thing a guy wanted to see when a girl who intrigued him met him head-on. Then she'd spent the rest of the time staring at my shoes.

They were boring shoes. But I'd resort to putting math and physics equations on them if I had to. Or I'd talk to her about the paper Milky Way she'd strewn up around her study. How the hell had she done that? It wasn't just planets and stars; I swear she had a wormhole in there.

How did a perfectly normal teenager go from reading on the bleachers in high school to hiding in her house and creating galaxies of paper?

I planned on finding out.

The slow slide and *thud* behind me caught my attention. Dale rolled his cart, loaded with books, as he stocked the shelves.

I opened my mouth to say hi. To say *anything*, because we'd never once uttered a word to each other except for my thank-yous when he gave me another offering. But what was I supposed to say to a man four times my age who knew nothing about me? Who I knew nothing about?

He didn't even glance my way, so I let him do his job and focused on my computer. Rogue2015 had made another move. I sighed. I was a seventeen-year-old senior, not a chess master. I should have been playing basketball or video games. Or working. Instead, I was hooked on a girl I hardly knew, studying her chess moves so she'd keep initiating matches with me, and intrigued by another girl who was even more of a mystery.

Chess girl and paper girl.

Definitely a sculpture someone should make.

But Rogue…she wasn't like Zoe. She told me things straight. She kept me motivated even when I wanted to give in. I was hooked on her because she was the best friend I'd ever had. The one person I could tell anything to—except that I was homeless. But I'd almost told her. When we'd been talking about secrets, I'd almost put it out there. Just to get it off my chest. And because I knew nothing could happen from it. I couldn't get in trouble because I had no idea who

Rogue was and she had no idea who BK was.

Zoe, on the other hand—she couldn't even look me in the eye. Maybe that's why I was so intrigued. She'd seemed so confident on the bleachers that day, and this time…so scared. Even so, I wanted more. I wanted to know her and uncover all her layers.

I pulled up some basic notes for algebra and physics, but I'd have to see what Zoe was working on to be useful. There wasn't much time until the semester ended, which meant she needed help fast to get through her classes. We'd have to skip some of the basics and work hard to get her on track. *Then*, if we had time, we could start at the beginning and make sure she had the foundational tools for both her classes.

If I even tutored her that long.

Maybe she'd need help over the summer, too. To make sure she was caught up.

Two books slid onto the edge of the table next to me. I glanced up, but Dale was already walking away, pushing his cart to another grouping of shelves.

I slid the books closer. The one on top was a book on chess. I glanced again to Dale with a grin. What? Had he been watching me? Watching me lose, probably.

The book underneath was about black holes and "other cool cosmic things"—at least, according to the title. It also had sections devoted to constellations. I wondered how many of those were on Zoe's ceiling.

Maybe I could suggest we work in her study so we'd have a distraction topic in case she didn't want to talk to me. Or maybe…just because I really wanted to see her art.

I clicked over to the University of Colorado website and looked at the page for Astrophysical and Planetary Sciences. Part of me was afraid to look into it more. I still had a few months left of school, three months until I turned eighteen, and a whole summer to get through. Not to mention I had to save my ass off to even make it through the first semester. But here it was. The dream. Not just mine—my mom's.

I only let myself look for one more moment before pulling up the site for my phone bill. My stomach clenched.

The screen read, *Thank you for your payment!* and showed a balance of $0.00.

He really did pay it. My dad had paid my phone bill. And my part of the car insurance as well.

Shit. What was he doing? How had he even had the presence of mind to remember there were bills to pay, let alone pay them?

Someone had said something. Social services had come by or—

I shut my laptop. For my dad to act like he was a real father, there had to be a problem. That was the only thing I could think of.

After all, he hadn't said more than ten words to me in the last year and a half. He had no idea what it meant to be a parent, and he had no reason to start being one now.

Something was wrong. It had to be.

With a heavy sigh, I gathered my items. I couldn't focus now. I shoved my books in my backpack and rode the escalator to the first floor. I waved to Diane, who spent most of her mornings listening to books on tape in her headphones while she dusted every wooden surface in the large library. I took a left into the children's section, passed two kids playing checkers on a large felt checkerboard, and walked to the pavilion.

Story time was over for the day, so I sat in the middle of the floor and gazed up at the room. It looked almost like a tree house from outside, and even though the inside wasn't as exciting, it still gave me good memories.

My mom used to volunteer to read here. All the kids would circle around her while she rhymed Dr. Seuss or said good night to everything around the room and then pretended to sleep.

She had been fascinated with the stars, with everything "out there" that kept us asking questions. So many things in my life kept me questioning right now, it was nice to have a constant. The library. The memory of my mom. Even *Chess Challenge*.

Rogue was always there, always making life seem a little easier. Too bad I had no idea who she really was.

16.

BlackKNIGHT: Are you ever going to tell me how old you are?

Rogue2015: I'm 16. Doesn't it say that on my profile?

BlackKNIGHT: Just wanted to hear it from you. See? That wasn't so hard.

Rogue2015: How do you know I'm not lying?

BlackKNIGHT: I didn't consider it until you said that. But…I don't think you're lying.

Rogue2015: Why not? You barely know me.

BlackKNIGHT: I know more than you think. You're short. You're 16. You're a girl.

Rogue2015: How do you know I'm short?

BlackKNIGHT: You said once that short people are discriminated against.

Rogue2015: I was joking.

BlackKNIGHT: There's always some truth behind humor.

Rogue2015: I never said I was a girl.

BlackKNIGHT: Your screen name is Rogue. Easy.

Rogue2015: We should play the game.

BlackKNIGHT: ☺ One more thing. You're shy.

Rogue2015: How do you know that?

BlackKNIGHT: Every time I compliment you or try to talk about you, you steer us back to the game.

Rogue2015: I do not. But really, this game is taking forever. We should play.

BlackKNIGHT: ☺ I have a question, though.

Rogue2015: Is it about chess?

BlackKNIGHT: It's about a girl.

Rogue2015: Ah.

BlackKNIGHT: What's that supposed to mean?

Rogue2015: Nothing. I don't know how much help I'm going to be with girl issues.

BlackKNIGHT: We just established you're a girl, right? You're already way ahead of me. I don't know how to get her to open up to me.

Rogue2015: You could play chess with her.

BlackKNIGHT: Well, sure, that's a good fallback, but I want her to talk to me, too.

Rogue2015: I'm definitely not going to be any help with that. Why do you think I'm on *Chess Challenge*? No face-to-face. Then I can be who I really am.

BlackKNIGHT: And you can't do that in person?

Rogue2015: Not as easily. It's hard to talk to people in person. So much pressure. What about you?

BlackKNIGHT: Can I be me? In person? I think I can. You think that's what I should do?

Rogue2015: Absolutely. But first, you should prepare yourself. I'm about to take your king.

BlackKNIGHT: #@!$

17.

ZOE

Gina was here again, in my paper room. She wore another fluffy scarf that looked like it had horses or dogs on it. She was trying to get me to open up, like always.

In my fantasy world, I told Gina I knew she was analyzing me, and the only thing she really needed to know was that people—especially the analytical ones—were what scared me. In real life, I walked to the window in my study and stared at the tops of buildings. There was a rooftop garden on the next building over, and I spotted little specks of blue and red, people sitting at a table. Maybe drinking coffee. Things I felt like I might never do.

Outside, a blackbird fluttered by the window and swooped to perch on top of the greenhouse. I'd watched a lot of things from this window. Garden parties, planes, fireworks on the 16th Street Mall on New Year's Eve. The sun falling in rays that couldn't quite seem to reach where I was standing.

I might not be able to tell Gina how I really felt, but I was definitely better at the Quiet Game. She spoke first.

"I'm really encouraged you're going to go through with this tutor thing. Going to school is a huge step, so I think this is a more reasonable start. It'll also be less stressful while you work toward attending Mae's graduation."

"It wasn't really my choice."

"You always have a choice. And what about socializing? It might help that, too. Another small step."

Having Jackson help me with math homework probably wasn't fit to be called socializing. Staring at people's shoes was more like…creepy. He'd be teaching; I'd be shoe watching.

"Zoe," Gina said, coming to stand beside me. She kept her distance, but it still felt too close. I stepped a foot to my right. "I know it's hard."

How did she know? Was she a former recluse? Probably not. She didn't dress like a therapist, she didn't act like a therapist, so how would she know?

But on the other hand, she treated me like a regular person. Maybe she was just a regular person, too, and she knew *exactly* how hard it was to live in the real world.

"But staying inside here all the time isn't living your life. Real life, *your* life, has to be outside of this house eventually."

I gritted my teeth, surprisingly hurt by her words. "I—I know what real life is."

"How do you know?"

"Because I'm not living it."

Gina turned to me. She smiled, which seemed like the most inappropriate response she could have given. I met her eyes long enough to see they were green with yellow flecks. Then I stared at her shoes. Black flats with bows on the tips. No, not at all like any therapist I was used to.

"This is good." When I didn't answer, she continued in a voice that very much made her sound like a therapist. "This is a step in the right direction. It means you're longing for something more. You're ready to move on."

"Wanting it and being ready for it are…*very* different

things." But I applauded myself for being able to express this to her without stuttering. Or vomiting. Progress.

She nodded. Out of the corner of my eye, I saw her fiddle with the scarf around her neck, fanning it out as though she was hot. "That's true. But wanting it is the first step. And I think you're brave enough to give it a try."

"Give what a try?"

I remembered that Jackson was coming by later. I had to talk to him. He was going to be my tutor. Nerves rattled my insides.

"Your goal."

I swallowed. "My goal is to go to Mae's graduation. I promised her. I just need to…" I blew out a breath. "I need to be able to do that."

"Are you ready for that?"

My stomach clenched hard. "No."

"Then let's work on getting there by starting with some-thing that isn't so intimidating," Gina said. "A smaller goal. You set one, and I can help walk you through steps to get there."

The word "goal" sounded ominous when she said it now. Taboo.

"I *do* have another goal. I do. Bring up my math grade. Physics, too."

"I mean one that directly correlates to your social anxiety."

I checked the pedometer app on my phone. I could have been walking more right now. Or making more of Neptune. But instead, I had to make a goal. I had to correlate things. This blew. A goal correlating to my anxiety meant doing something this house couldn't keep me safe from.

But wasn't that the point? How was I ever going to make it to my sister's graduation if I couldn't even do something smaller?

"What about one of Mae's cheerleading meets?" Gina asked. "I know she and your mom really want you to go. You'd be with your family, but out of the house."

Mae had meets in big convention centers sometimes. She had a *huge* competition coming up, but there were going to be hundreds of people there. Maybe thousands.

Panic flickered through me.

"Or even a school function where she's cheering," Gina pressed. "Kind of like a mini-graduation trial run."

I immediately thought of basketball—Robert and Jackson playing for the school team, and Mae cheering on the sidelines. Then I'd have two people to watch, both Mae and Jackson.

"I think you could do it," Gina said gently. "I'll help."

"How?"

"We'll work up to it. Some test runs. And you can use Dr. Edwards's coping techniques. You can do this."

Outside, the blackbird flew away. I wished I could, too.

"Zoe," Gina coaxed.

"I don't know."

"Yes, you do."

She was right. I knew what I wanted. To live my life outside of this apartment. But…

"Zoe," Gina said again. "Come on."

I frowned at her. "Peer pressure. This is peer pressure, right? I think Dr. Edwards would like to hear about this."

She laughed. Squinting eyes. Damn. That was pretty convincing.

"Fine," I mumbled. "Where do we start?"

"You're doing it this afternoon. Your first meeting with your tutor. *Talk* to him. Try to make eye contact."

But it was Jackson. Eye contact? It was hard enough making eye contact with regular people. With Jackson, it was so much harder. Especially when he was that close. My body and his sharing a space. I shivered.

"You can do it," she said. "I know you can."

I was glad she was so confident in me. All I knew was that I felt like I was going to throw up. I was sure I could figure out the velocity with some sort of physics equation, however, and then it'd be educational, too.

Paper. That's all. I had to look at it like a blank piece of paper. No expectations, just ready for whatever I wanted to create out of it. I was in control here.

"I expect a full report the next time I see you," Gina said.

My stomach felt like something from the Cretaceous period was swimming inside, trying to get out. Since Gina left, it had seen fit to remind me nonstop that I had to sit in the same room as Jackson the whole afternoon and do my best rendition of "normal" as possible. I already knew I was going to fail.

I always did.

This wasn't like paper at all. Paper was fragile. And so was I.

In my study, knowing Jackson was going to be here any minute, I prepared. I took out two mechanical pencils, one notebook, Mae's old Physics book, and went through the stack two more times to make sure I had everything. I didn't want Jackson thinking I was unprepared. Or that I didn't appreciate him helping me, though I wished we could do it online somehow, so I didn't have to be in the same room as him.

I was actually pretty composed when all I had to do was type to someone. My brain functioned in coherent patterns, focused on topics. And you couldn't stutter when you were typing.

When I heard the *ding* of the elevator and my mom's cheerful voice welcoming Jackson into the apartment, my hands shook on my notebook, and the pencils I'd gathered scattered onto the floor.

Mom knocked on my door. "Zoe? You coming? Jackson's here."

I'd put in my contacts, brushed my hair, worn pants that didn't have an elastic waistband, and yet I still felt woefully unprepared to face Jackson. Or even to stare at his shoes.

There were so many things that could go wrong, and I was the root of all of them. The more I thought about it, the larger the disaster grew until my embarrassment at facing Jackson became the equivalent of the naked dream.

You know, the one where you walk into some big event completely naked and everyone stares at you. Except in mine I was walking into the prom wearing an embarrassing Hello Kitty hat like that was going to cover me somehow. I said "checkmate," and everyone started laughing.

My life was that dream. Every. Single. Day.

"Zoe?" Mom said again.

I gathered my pencils off the floor. "I'm coming."

With my books and pencils clutched against my chest, I walked down the hallway one, two, three…twelve more steps to add to my daily goal. They were in the kitchen. An audience. Mae, Jackson, and Mom, all looking at me. The freak who didn't leave the house.

I wondered how surprised they'd all be when I actually *did* show up at the graduation ceremony. If I actually walked confidently to my seat and pulled out my phone to take pictures of Mae. It would almost be worth it just to see the shock on their faces. Almost.

Jackson wore his beat-up Converse. I didn't think I'd ever seen him in something different. He probably went everywhere in them because, for him, the world was a big place full of possibilities. I wore socks because leaving our shoes by the door (or the elevator, in our case) was pretty much the only tradition Mom had brought with her from Japan. But these socks had walked dozens of miles in this apartment, and they still looked brand new.

"I made lemonade," Mom said, gesturing to the center of the table. Mae made a face behind her, and it only heightened my nerves. "And cookies."

They were oatmeal cookies. The kind that crumbled all over the place when you took your first bite. Normally my favorite, but not when someone was watching me make a mess of myself.

What did she think this was? Afternoon tea? A date?

Oh God, I couldn't even think the word "date" without blushing.

Jackson smiled at me. I tried to return it, but it came off feeling more like a grimace. I stared at his shoes again while my whole face lit on fire.

Mae plucked a cookie from the pile and said, "I don't envy you guys."

"Come on," Mom said. "Math can be fun. Right, Jackson?"

Mae almost choked on her cookie when she laughed.

I could tell Jackson was trying to hold in a smile. "It can," he said. "You just have to understand the basics."

Mom nodded like she was ready for her lesson, too. Mae poked her arm. "Don't you have a closet to macro-organize or something?"

My mom smoothed her hair. "I should probably work on my video. I'm doing a segment on homemade and all-natural cleaners."

Mae mimed falling asleep before she poked Mom's arm again. "Let's go."

Jackson reached for a cookie. "Thanks for the cookies, Mrs. King."

Mom beamed. This was probably the first time she'd seen me in a room this long with other people my age. And standing next to Jackson...Oh my God, to her this probably *was* a date. She looked happy enough to reupholster a chair. "I'll let you get to it, then."

I used my eyes to plead with Mae as she walked toward the living room with her cookie and a water bottle, but she just smiled and waved.

Gina would be saying, *This is good, Zoe. Step out of your comfort zone. The more you do it, the easier it'll get.*

And then I was alone in the cavernous kitchen with Jackson and oatmeal crumble cookies.

Here goes nothing...

18.

JACKSON

"**Y**our mom's funny," I said, trying to ease the tension.

Zoe made a noise of agreement but stared at my shoes. She looked different today—and that in itself wasn't a bad thing. But she was wearing her contacts, which made me jealous because I really wanted something besides my two-year-old glasses. Her hair billowed around her shoulders, and she had the same fringe of bangs in her eyes that I wanted to reach out and brush aside. And she wore blue-and-white striped socks instead of her Manga-covered sneakers. It struck me how much you could learn about someone by visiting them in their home.

"Should we work at the table here?" I asked. "Or—"

"No— Yes. I mean, this is good. Right here." Her cheeks burned a bright red as she sat at the table.

I pretended not to notice and instead slipped my backpack onto one chair and sat next to her. My elbow brushed hers. She jerked her arm away and tucked her hands under the table. I pretended not to notice that, either, even though her skin was so smooth and warm I wanted to touch it again.

She played with a strand of her hair, wrapping it around

and around her fingers. I imagined those fingers working quickly and deftly on paper, making the stars and planets in her secret room.

"How do you feel about physics?" I asked.

She glanced up then dropped her eyes to her notebook. "It's evil."

I laughed. I used to think so, too. "You either love it or you hate it. But it's pretty simple, really."

"So, you love it," she mumbled.

"What was that?"

"You love it? Physics?"

"I do. Everything has an answer. It's explainable."

"Like numbers." She brushed her hair from her eyes.

"You like math?"

"No. But it's—it's definite, like you said. Everything has an answer. There's c-comfort in that."

She stared at her notebook again, even as I nodded. "I agree. Numbers are comforting."

"So, uh—uh—" She almost knocked the plate of cookies off the table when she slid her notebook closer.

I caught it smoothly and pushed the plate to the center of the table. Never mind shy—she was nervous. That's what it was. People tended to feel that way when they had to learn something new.

"You only have a few months left of school," I said. "What can we do?"

"Wh—what?"

"What would help you bring your grade up the most?"

"Passing my tests."

"Good. Let's aim for that. What are you working on right now?"

"Right now?" Her gaze flashed around the room. "Like my assignment?"

I nodded. "Can I see? So I know where to start, or what you'll be tested on? I mean, we'll go over basics, too, but let's at least get you past your test."

"I don't—I mean, it's on my computer. I could—I didn't—" She stood, knocking the notebook off the table. "I can go print it out."

I stooped at the same time she did to retrieve the notebook.

She paused and murmured something under her breath. It sounded like "eye contact." Then she looked me straight in the eyes. "Thank you."

"I'm sorry," I blurted out.

"Wh—what?"

"I'm sorry if I make you uncomfortable."

"It's not—I mean—" She took two long breaths in and out. "It's not you. It's everyone."

Everyone? Everyone made her uncomfortable? I opened my mouth to ask, to understand, but she stood abruptly.

"I'll get my homework," she said.

"I can just look at it from your computer."

Panic flickered in her eyes.

"Is that where you do all those paper designs?" I asked, longing to get a peek at her galaxy again.

She nodded.

"I'd like to see," I said.

"It's not—I mean, if you want to."

I stepped back with a smile. That was easier than I thought it would be. "I really would."

"Okay," she whispered, already walking to the hallway. "Come on."

When we reached the door, she stopped with her hand on the knob. "It's sort of messy," she warned.

"I doubt it," I answered with a laugh. She didn't seem like the type to leave anything unorganized. "Open up."

She opened the door and stepped inside, brushing past me close enough I could smell her hair. Something floral on her skin. I swallowed. Then I moved into the room, already searching for her art.

The Milky Way spilled from the walls and the ceiling, shooting stars and planets everywhere. My vision was dazzled by colors and shapes, by Zoe's creativity.

I didn't think I'd ever met someone who could say so much by saying so little.

"This is amazing," I said, trying to take it all in.

Her eyes widened.

"Really. How long did it take?"

"Months. Lots of m-months," she stuttered, and then she blushed again.

There was no way in hell I was going to tell her it was actually cute when she stammered like that. I was starting to think her social ineptitude was the whole reason she wasn't in school anymore. That seemed to be the likeliest explanation. And she'd told me everyone made her uncomfortable. Everyone, as in, *everyone*? The whole world?

I kept my focus on the wall. "It looks like it's to scale."

"I had to—to use some program online. You know, to calculate it—and—and then I measured it out." She waved a hand above her head. "The meteors were just for…fun."

I walked closer to her, peering up at one of the meteors. I didn't miss her sharp intake of breath, or the floral scent again. Jasmine, maybe.

A scent my mom might have worn.

Mom's words came back to me, something she'd said at the hospital, holding my hand tightly and trying to impart years of experience to me in a short amount of time. Like she'd known she wasn't going to make it.

Sometimes what you're looking for finds you first.

Maybe she was talking about a career passion, or that one friend that felt more like family. But in this moment, it felt like she was talking about Zoe.

"The meteors *are* fun," I said to the ceiling. "How many are you going to make?"

"A lot more."

I smiled, keeping my gaze focused on the meteor. Rogue told me to be myself, so that's what I was going to do. And right now, I was interested in Zoe's paper wall.

"Is that what you're working on right now?" I asked. "Meteors?"

"I'm working on Neptune. And—and Saturn's moons, too."

I glanced around, eager to see her progress.

"It's—I just started it," she said, edging toward her desk like she was ready to hide whatever I wanted to find. "I had to get more paper for the outside parts. So the color kind of fades as it gets bigger."

I nodded and faced the wall again. "You know what would be cool?" I asked her without turning around.

It took her a minute to answer. "What?"

"A giant chessboard." I glanced back and smiled when her eyes widened. Maybe she thought I'd forgotten about her love for chess. "You could do all the pieces, make them 3-D like this."

When I turned around, her eyes were still locked on me. Okay, maybe she didn't love chess anymore. Maybe paper was her thing now, and she didn't care about the game at all.

Then she nodded. "I hadn't thought of that."

"What did you learn today?" I asked, grasping for anything that might link us and get her to open up.

Her chin lifted. Something sparked in her eyes. "I don't know," she mumbled.

"You have to have learned something new today."

She looked away. I kicked myself for not asking something simpler. But finally, she said quietly, "The day's only halfway through."

My hand twitched, wanting to reach out and brush the bangs from her eyes. "True."

"I guess I figured maybe—maybe your math lesson would be my new thing for today."

I smiled. "You're probably right."

With those words, she lifted her eyes to mine again, just briefly. They melted like dark chocolate. *Sometimes what you're looking for finds you first.*

I seriously needed to get my mom's words out of my head. This was Zoe—a girl I barely knew.

"What's your—what new thing did you learn?" she asked.

"Oh, that's easy. I learned that Dale is a stalker."

She gurgled out a startled laugh that made me laugh as well. She did my job and brushed her hair out of her eyes, leaving me useless.

"I know, it doesn't make any sense. Just a guy from the library," I said.

She opened her mouth, but nothing came out. Part of me wanted to wait for her response, for her to ask more, but the other part of me knew it wouldn't come.

"Your math assignment," I suggested.

That made her jump into action. "Oh, sorry. I'm sorry—of course—"

She hurried to her desk and opened her laptop. I spotted what looked like a chess game, but she was quick to minimize the screen—so fast I wondered if I'd imagined it.

But if I hadn't? My fingers itched to grab the mouse and find the game. Maybe she was on the same chess website where I'd met Rogue2015. I just needed a quick peek…

"It's right here." She pulled up a math assignment, and

then one for Physics, both easy concepts for me.

"Let's start with math."

When she heard my voice so close, she edged away, leaving the screen in wide view. It took everything I had not to minimize the page and check the one that looked like *Chess Challenge*. Then I'd know.

I glanced to the ceiling. Paper. That seemed to be the way to her heart.

My cell phone buzzed in my pocket. I pulled it out...and froze. My dad. His name appeared on the screen, **Austin**, followed by his number.

Zoe blinked, waiting for me to answer the call. I only smiled at her and shoved my phone back in my pocket, pretending nothing happened.

"Zoe," I said, her name rolling off my tongue. I liked it. And right now, she was the key to distracting me from my dad.

"Wh—what?"

"By the time school ends, you're going to be a master at algebra and physics."

Her breath released slowly. She didn't answer right away. I got the feeling she was counting something in her head.

After another long moment where I half expected her to kick me out of her room, she said calmly, "Then I guess we'd better get started."

19.

Rogue2015: I'm tired of people always thinking they know what's best for me.

BlackKNIGHT: I know. Do they forget what it's like to be 17?

Rogue2015: I know! 16 here, but still. Do you really think I'm going to use the Pythagorean Theorem or need to know how to carbon date something in the real world?

BlackKNIGHT: Depends.

Rogue2015: On what?

BlackKNIGHT: Are you going to be a chemist? An astrophysicist? Are you going to discover the cure for something deadly like a flesh-eating bacteria that turns half the population into zombies?

Rogue2015: Good question. NO!!!

BlackKNIGHT: So what *are* you going to do?

Rogue2015: Beat you at chess. Your knight is in serious trouble, and your queen's crying because he won't protect her.

BlackKNIGHT: Maybe you should tell stories for a living. You'd be really good at that.

Rogue2015: You're just trying to distract me.

BlackKNIGHT: No, I'm just curious about you.

Rogue2015: Not much to tell. I'm kind of a boring person.

BlackKNIGHT: I really don't believe that.

Rogue2015: It's true.

BlackKNIGHT: You can't just say that. I need proof. Why do you think you're boring?

Rogue2015: Because I never do anything or go anywhere.

BlackKNIGHT: Well, if you live in a cornfield, like I'm starting to believe, then that makes sense. Do you go on field trips to see cows?

Rogue2015: Ha ha. I've never seen a cow close up in my life. But I haven't seen a lot of things.

BlackKNIGHT: Why not?

Rogue2015: The world is a scary place. I can't stop thinking of all the things that could go wrong if I went somewhere. Anywhere.

BlackKNIGHT: That's interesting.

Rogue2015: Why's that?

BlackKNIGHT: Because all I want is to be out in the world. All the time. Away from home, on my own.

Rogue2015: I guess that makes sense since you said you moved out. You said you stay here and there. What does that mean?

BlackKNIGHT: Nowhere, really. I stay in my car or at a friend's house. I visit my favorite places during the day. But I don't really have a home.

Rogue2015: Wait. You're homeless?

BlackKNIGHT: I don't really call it that.

Rogue2015: That's terrible. I'm sorry.

BlackKNIGHT: Don't be. It's better this way. Maybe we should talk about something less heavy?

Rogue2015: What about that girl you were telling me about? How are things going with her?

BlackKNIGHT: I'm still working on it.

Rogue2015: You'll figure it out. If you can figure out real life—way better than I can, apparently—you'll figure this out.

BlackKNIGHT: Kind of the same thing, right? Chess and real life. It's all strategy.

Rogue2015: I guess you could put it that way. Zugzwang.

BlackKNIGHT: What?

Rogue2015: You know, that chess term. Zugzwang. That point in a chess game where you're forced to make moves that might cost you pieces. But you have to do it. Kind of like in real life. You just get to a point you have to make those moves.

BlackKNIGHT: Yes, I've heard that term before. That makes sense.

Rogue2015: All right, so make your move.

BlackKNIGHT: In the game or in real life?

Rogue2015: Both ☺

20.

ZOE

I stared at the elevator doors. Soon, Gina would be here and Mae would go off to practice and Mom would run her errands, and life would continue outside this apartment whether I saw it or not. And BlackKNIGHT—who knew what he was up to?

I couldn't believe he'd told me he was homeless and that he slept in his car. My heart ached for him. If I knew who he was, if he lived close by, I'd make him a paper house with everything he could ever want inside. Food, friendship, a million chessboards. Whatever made him feel like he had a place.

After all, I knew what it was like to feel lost. I had a place to live, but even then, it didn't feel like I belonged. BK didn't judge me when I told him I don't ever go anywhere or do anything, but I felt judged at home.

I should probably take my own advice. Make my move. I choked on a nervous laugh. No way. Too scary. It was safer up here in my apartment and safer if I kept my mouth shut.

Besides, I still had a life in here. Maybe it wasn't the life I wanted, but it was still a life.

Our penthouse meant the top floor, elevator access to only those with a key card, or special visitors on the list at the security desk downstairs. Jackson was a special visitor.

He was my special visitor. One I couldn't seem to get out of my mind. BlackKNIGHT was the one I could talk to, the one who I felt comfortable with, but Jackson was the one that made me want to be more, to do things, to live a life—one that might have him in it.

If I closed my eyes, I could hear every breath he took and the smile in his words. If I closed my eyes, I could see his inquisitive gaze, peering through his dark-rimmed glasses as if saying, *Zoe, why won't you just talk to me?*

He wanted to know me. Not Mae's sister. Not the Car King's daughter. Just Zoe. The irreversibly quirky, dorky, and socially inept girl who had been crushing on him for two years. Just thinking about it made my whole body buzz.

"Did you just go into a coma?"

I yelped and jerked my gaze away from the elevator. Mae stood there, arms folded and a sly smile on her face.

"You look like you're in love with that elevator." She walked to the elevator, pressed a hand flat against the surface, and fluttered her eyelashes. "Oh, Elevator, you sure are handsome. So tall and—and strong. You take me to new heights—"

"Mae!"

Her laughter rolled out, effectively popping my dreamy bubble. Jackson didn't like me. He wasn't curious about me. He was just being polite. After all, Mom was paying him to tutor me.

"You're a jerk." I reached in my pocket and pulled out my phone to check my steps.

My phone was a fairly new model despite the fact that my social circle encompassed my closest family, a faceless seventeen-year-old chess boy, and Therapist #5 (and #6) in case I had a panic attack. Most of my friends from before I shut myself in this apartment had slowly lost touch once I started homeschooling.

But Mom was a big fan of "one day's."

One day you'll be back in school and need a phone.

One day you'll have a boyfriend and want to text him all the time.

One day you'll stop making faces about YouTube and subscribe to my channel.

Yeah, Mom was a shameless self-promoter.

But one day hadn't come yet.

"You look different today," Mae said, crossing her arms again. "Happy."

"Huh?"

She narrowed her eyes at me and then flashed a grin. "Come to practice with me!"

My heart jolted.

"Like you used to. You'd sit on the bleachers and draw in your notebook and totally ignore me unless I was at the top of the pyramid."

I made a face. "You want me to come with you and ignore you?"

"*Yes*. Just like before. You'd draw fancy numbers on your notebook and hold them up for me to see when I was at the top of the pyramid. Remember you even gave me a ten once? Sure, it was probably just to humor me or because you were in a good mood that day, but it was nice."

Conflicting emotions slithered through me. Mae wanted me to go. I had no idea she even cared that I used to go to her practices. But that was outside. *Outside*. There were people there.

This could be a pre-graduation trial run, I told myself. Just like Gina had suggested.

"One practice," she said. "You don't even have to talk to anyone. I'll drive us there, I'll practice. You can bring your notebook. And we'll drive back. Less than two hours."

My mouth hung open, but nothing came out. I wanted to. I really, really wanted to. And when she made it sound simple and straightforward like that, my brain responded with, *She's right, just two hours. No big deal.*

My chest squeezed.

"Never mind," Mae said when she saw my expression.

"I want to," I whispered.

She'd already turned to grab her bag off the table in the foyer. "Sure."

"Mae, really. I'm—I'm sorry. I'm scared. I don't—"

"Then stop being scared."

I swallowed a lump of heartache. We used to be close. We used to do everything together. And I'd ruined it.

"I'm sorry, Mae."

She straightened her ponytail and lifted her chin, her expression blank. "Whatever. Mom, I'm going!"

Mom called back from the kitchen, "Wait! I made muffins for you and the girls!"

"Not this time," Mae said, her voice hard. She pressed the elevator button and stepped inside when it opened. She wouldn't even look at me before the doors closed.

Mom hurried out with a container of muffins, her cheeks flushed. "Her muffins," Mom said, looking lost.

"She was late," I lied. "She had to go. Freeze them. You can use them later."

"I already froze four bags. These are warm. Jackson's coming later, right? I bet he'll want some muffins. He always eats whatever I bake."

Mom's mention of Jackson sobered me even further.

Jackson was one of *them*. The outsiders. The people who lived beyond the walls of my apartment and managed to survive the world.

And I was just Zoe. Paper girl. I belonged on my study wall, not out there. With them. Where the world was waiting.

I kept my back pressed to the brick just outside the glass door of our balcony. It was really more like a terrace, with room enough for a table and chairs, for the plants and decorations my mom always had out. It was lined with a ledge tall enough that I wouldn't accidentally fall off.

But still, it was outside. *I* was outside.

I wanted to look at it as a step in the right direction, but I had to admit, it didn't take much bravado to stand outside when I was technically still in my own apartment.

When the door opened next to me, I expected Dr. Price, but it was Dad. He held a door sign, one that said *Welcome* on planks of wood that looked like they used to belong to a fence.

"Hi," he said.

My mouth opened and closed in surprise. "Did you...are you sick?"

He angled his head. "No. Just came home from work early."

I blinked. *Why?*

He read the question in my eyes and stepped outside. "Mom thought it might be good to be here more often. You know, so I could...we could talk. Or spend more family time together."

"Gina's coming soon."

He nodded. "Your mom said. I just thought I'd check to make sure you're okay." He glanced around the terrace. "Are you okay?"

"I'm…" I swallowed, trying to see this as a good thing. Dad was here. That was nice of him to check on me. But did I look like I was okay, plastered to the side of the building? I redirected my focus. "I thought Mom mailed that sign."

Last week she'd had a giveaway on her blog and thousands of people had entered to win. She'd been thrilled. I'd made faces the whole time the entries were piling in until she let me use the random number generator to pick a winner.

Dad grinned. "She made another because she thought we needed one, too."

"Where's she going to put it?" I asked.

He shrugged. "Inside the elevator above the button for the top floor?"

I laughed, and the motion relaxed me some. "That would work."

"So…you're okay?"

"I'm okay," I said in agreement. At least, that was what I was working toward.

"Good." He nodded and held up the sign. "Back to work."

He vanished inside, leaving me alone again.

When Gina appeared, I was still glued to the side of the building.

She wore a red jacket. I considered it progress that I noticed her jacket before her shoes. Dr. Edwards was hard to relate to in his stuffy sports coats and tasseled loafers. Who still wore tassels on their shoes?

"Would you like to talk out here today?" she asked.

"If that's what you want."

She walked straight to the round table and pulled out a chair. I didn't know how she wasn't dying of heat stroke with her jacket and canary yellow scarf on. "It's a nice day. We should sit."

"Or…" I inched farther down the wall. Progress.

"Would you like to sit?" She continued to stand by the chair. "Your study," she said when I didn't answer. "Let's go inside. You seem more comfortable in there, and then we can talk."

I didn't respond, and I hated that it relieved me to be heading back inside to where I was most comfortable. I led her to the study, padding down the hall in colorful striped socks and black leggings under a billowy dress.

Inside the study, there were two chairs at the desk now, so Jackson could sit when he came to tutor me. But Gina didn't sit. Instead, she removed her jacket and set it over the back of the chair.

"Are you okay?" Gina asked, just like my dad had.

Not really. I couldn't even sit outside and talk to her. She knew I'd be more comfortable in here, just like Mae knew I wouldn't come to her cheerleading practice. After dealing with that, I was beginning to think I was failing pretty miserably at stepping out of my comfort zone.

"I'm fine."

She pulled the chair around to sit directly across from me, making me nervous. I wished she'd pace like she did last time. Or look out the window. Or, at the very least, not make eye contact.

"Are you really?" she asked.

"Yes."

"Really?"

I stared at her hands. They rested on top of the desk, almost like she was about to type something on a keyboard. Maybe notes about me and my issues. That was what she was missing. A notebook. Dr. Edwards always had a notebook. Some way to write down what I said or what he was thinking. Or maybe he was just doodling.

Gina folded her arms. "I think you're upset. I don't know

why, but I can tell. And I'm telling you, you're allowed to be upset—about anything. *And* you're allowed to tell me. That's what I'm here for."

"Is Dr. Edwards coming anymore?"

She nodded. "He'll come and check in here and there. But he and your mom agreed it might be good for me to come alone for a while. A new perspective. Is that okay?"

Was that okay? Dr. Edwards never asked me if anything was okay. He just gave me ideas and assumed I'd follow through. Gina was…trying to relate to me.

I wish I felt comfortable enough to talk to her. I wanted to. How come BlackKNIGHT was so easy to talk to? Because I didn't have to see him face to face? Because he was like my paper habit. Reliable. Comfortable. He never let me down. He was always there.

Gina still waited for an answer. I nodded. I'd pretend she was BlackKNIGHT if I had to. I thought of how disappointed Mae seemed and realized I had to do something to change it. "That's fine."

She smiled. "Okay. What do you want to talk about?"

"Well…" I pressed my lips together tight.

She kept smiling. She was making me talk. Dr. Edwards usually directed the conversation. He asked me questions, and I answered. Usually.

"Nothing, really," I lied.

"Maybe about why you were outside on the balcony?"

I dropped my chin. I discreetly pulled a piece of paper from my pocket and started folding it. "It's a nice day."

"On nice days, people take walks. Go to the park. Have a picnic."

I bit my lip hard. "A picnic sounds scary."

"Do you want to go on a picnic?"

Yes. But she already knew this. I wanted to go on a picnic,

I wanted to go to Mae's graduation. I even wanted to go to the stupid prom. I wanted the world, and today I had to start making changes or it was never going to happen.

"How about yesterday?" Gina prompted. "Your tutoring session?"

"Oh."

"It's for Physics, right?"

"And Algebra."

"Who's your tutor?"

"Someone from Mae's school."

"A friend of hers, right? That's what your mom said."

I gripped my hands together tight in my lap, crushing the paper, and then purposefully relaxed them. "I tried to do the eye contact thing."

"How'd that work out for you?"

"Okay."

"If you can't look in the eyes, look at the forehead."

I lifted my eyebrows at her. "What?"

She smiled. It was an easy smile, kind of like Jackson's. Like both of them had no cares in the world. "When I was in school, I had to give a lot of speeches in front of the class. And during my internship, I had to talk to a lot of people who were pretty intimidating. When I got nervous, I'd stare right here." She pointed to the center of her forehead.

I stared at it.

"See? It makes it seem like you're making eye contact, but you aren't really," she said. "Good trick. I have others, too. Tricks to make social situations easier."

"Really?"

She relaxed in her seat. "What are you making there?"

I set the paper on top of the desk. "Nothing."

"You want to tell me why you were outside on the balcony?"

God, she was persistent.

"Zoe?"

"It was Mae."

I glanced at her face. She was good at keeping her reactions under control. She didn't raise her eyebrows or blink or even angle her head. She just nodded for me to continue. "You were outside because of Mae."

"Yes."

She waited. We battled it out in the silence of the room, each of us unwilling to say the next word. But this time, she won.

"She wanted me to go to practice with her, and I said it was too scary, and she acted like she missed me coming—"

"Do you think she was acting, or do you think she really does miss you being there?"

My mouth dried. I didn't answer.

And, though it seemed entirely inappropriate, Gina smiled. "I know what's going on here."

My pulse picked up. Oh no, it was like she could see straight to my soul. Read my mind. It was embarrassing feeling like she knew everything about me when I'd hardly said a word.

"I have an idea," Gina said.

"Oh, crap," I blurted, then pressed my hands to my cheeks.

She only laughed. "Yeah, it's going to feel like that a lot. I swear I have at least a dozen 'oh, crap' moments a week. But, it's a good thing. Keeps me on my toes. And it helps me grow as a person. You're going to have to trust me, though."

No, thanks.

"Zoe?"

I looked up.

"Do you trust me?"

I swallowed, shaking my head even as I said, "Yes."

21.

JACKSON

After school, it took two buses and a mile walk to get to the cemetery. Since I couldn't afford flowers, I'd plucked some pretty weeds from next to the fence at the last bus stop. If I was Zoe, I probably could have made a bouquet of paper flowers, but since I wasn't, this would have to do.

I walked several rows east, and then turned south. One, two, three headstones later, and I was at my mom's. Cecilia Ann Knight.

There were already flowers. Daisies—her favorite. One of her friends probably brought them. Everyone liked Mom. She had a lot of friends.

I put my offering next to the white daisies, and then sat on the grass by her headstone. A wave of clouds rolled over the sun. I wiped a drop of sweat from my neck and sighed.

"I know it's been a while," I said, like she'd made a comment about me finally visiting her.

But I could hear her answer as though she were right here with me.

You're busy, Jackson. You don't have to visit me all the time.

"I want to." I smiled. "You're good company."

What about Dad?

I sighed again. I was having a good week, and thinking about him threatened to take that away. I didn't want to contemplate what was going on with my dad, but everything else that had fallen into my lap this week made me believe in the kind of optimism my mom always used to have.

Before the brain tumor came, she was an optimist. During her treatment, she was an optimist. In her final days, she was even more cheerful (when she wasn't sleeping or so loopy from the medication she hardly recognized me).

It was the kind of optimism that infected people, that made my occasionally melancholy dad believe today could be just as good as any other day. It was the kind of optimism that made me give school another chance instead of ditching every day like I wanted to.

The kind of optimism that had made me want to talk to that quirky girl on the bleachers because, in my mom's words, *There's a whole world out there, and you'll never experience it fully if you keep your head down and your mouth shut.*

Maybe not the best motto to live by, but certainly not the worst.

I couldn't keep my mouth shut around Zoe. I wanted to know what was behind her paper art and why she'd left school. I wanted to know what secrets she held on her computer and why she couldn't ever seem to look me in the eye.

I also kind of wanted to know why I was drawn to her in the same way I was drawn to Rogue. Zugzwang. She'd said that to me just like Zoe had. After I'd told her about being homeless. I couldn't believe I'd actually told her. But Rogue was being open with me, and it was so nice to finally, finally get it out in the open. To finally tell someone my secret.

You're smiling.

I glanced at the headstone with a chuckle. "It's a girl. Does that make you happy?"

And it was like I could hear her laugh along with me. My mom had never pushed me to date—I didn't care about it much at that age. But I know she would have liked to see who I might have been interested in.

"She reminds me of you." I plucked at the emerald blades of grass. "We're just friends."

I don't know why I said it. Maybe because I was reminding myself that's where I stood. I was intrigued by Zoe, but I wasn't sure how far that would get me.

And college?

I was glad she changed the subject. "I'm making sure I've got everything together. I still need to do more tutoring for this one scholarship. It'll help a lot." I needed it desperately, but I'd make it work. It wasn't something I'd want my mom to worry about even if she were here. "I'm working on it."

Good.

We sat in silence for another ten minutes, watching the clouds dance across the sky. And when the world felt at peace again, I stood.

"I have to go," I said.

To see the girl.

I laughed. "And work. Gotta make a living."

I adjusted her flowers before turning away, and it was probably just me, but I could hear the words *I'm proud of you* floating along the wind as I left the cemetery.

When I arrived at the King household, the elevator doors opened directly into their foyer. The air smelled like a bakery. Two steps inside, on the shiny tiled floor, I stopped and stood still.

My family had never been rich, but Mom had made being poor seem like an adventure. We had taco night, where we'd get three tacos for a dollar over on the corner. We made spaghetti in large potfuls, and Mom would always encourage me to throw the noodles against the wall to test them. And then we'd eat leftover spaghetti for a week because it was inexpensive. It could have been miserable, or at least frustrating, not having new Nikes like the other kids in school or the newest iPhone. But it wasn't. It was *our* life, and sometimes the smallest reminder that it was missing hit me so hard in the chest I could barely breathe.

It was a shock to me to find that same kind of optimism and family togetherness here in the King household, thirty stories above the downtown streets of Denver, where brand new tennis shoes weren't hard to come by, and gas money was pocket change.

"Jackson?"

I smiled at Mrs. King when she came around the corner. "Hi."

"I thought I heard the elevator, and Brett called up from the desk. You look like you could use a muffin."

I wasn't sure what one looked like when they could use a muffin, but she was right. She didn't give me just one muffin; she gave me a whole plate of them.

"I really shouldn't," I started, even though I wanted the muffins.

"I made too many," she said almost apologetically. And that was just another one of her quirks—being overly generous to her guests. I followed her to the kitchen. "You're welcome to take some home for your family."

I opened my mouth to argue, but she made a waving motion with her hand indicating I should keep them.

Mae wandered into the kitchen with her hair in braids,

and she eyed the plate of muffins. "You really think he's going to eat all that?"

Mrs. King's eyes went wide, like she hadn't even considered I might not want a whole plate of muffins. And again, she was right. I would have taken two—but only because she insisted.

"They're not good?" she asked.

"You should really be nicer to your mom," I chided Mae jokingly. "Trying to feed people isn't a crime."

Giving a satisfied smile, Mrs. King answered the phone when it rang. "Hello? *Genki?*" She paused. "*Genki desu.*"

Chattering in Japanese, she walked out of the room, leaving me and Mae standing at the island.

She looked tired and irritated. I should have kept my mouth shut, but thanks to my mom, I couldn't do that.

"Are you okay?"

She yanked on one of her braids. "Zoe and I had a fight."

"I'm sorry."

Another shrug. "It's the same thing we always fight about."

"Probably not muffins," I ventured.

Her eyes lit with amusement. They looked almost identical to Zoe's. Bright. Expressive. But unlike Zoe, Mae could meet my eyes. She could engage.

"No, not muffins."

"Anything I can help with?"

Mae's chin dropped this time, reminding me again of Zoe. "Not unless you can get her out of the house."

I started to answer, but she straightened and shook her head. "She's in her study. I'm sure it's fine if you go on back."

Get her out of the house? What was that supposed to mean?

Yeah, I got that Zoe probably didn't leave much because she was homeschooled, but that didn't mean she didn't do her own thing here and there, right?

I'd probably just gotten myself into the middle of a fight I didn't belong in.

I walked down the hallway to the study. There was a new addition to the door: a paper design in 3-D that said Zoe's name. I touched the corner of the *Z*, the paper drifting out to form a butterfly. How the hell did she do that? And with such precision?

I knocked. There was shuffling before the handle twisted and Zoe appeared, her hair twirled up with a pencil.

Her smile faltered. "Hi."

"Hey." I shifted my backpack on my shoulder. "Ready for more math?"

"No." She sighed, stepping back. "But I have to. I'll grab my notebook."

"We could work in here," I suggested, already trying to peer inside the room to see if she'd added anything else to the ceiling or walls.

Her eyes flicked to my face, then to my shoes. I should have remembered to take them off at the elevator like the rest of her family did.

"Or…outside?" I amended. "It's nice."

Her cheeks reddened. "I already tried that today. It—it didn't work so well."

I blinked and raised an eyebrow. "That was cryptic. You should tell me what that means."

"I…" Her eyes came up again, looking unsure.

"We could take a walk." I was inspired by what Mae had said. "You can tell me about it."

"Oh…" She backed up, leaving the door open for me to step through. "I—I can't."

Why? The word was on my lips, but it was one of those times when keeping my mouth shut was probably a good idea.

It didn't stop me from wanting to get her to open up,

though. To solve the riddle of Zoe. It was that same feeling I always got around my mom. I just wanted to help—wanted her to want my help. It was hard being the one on the other end, knowing something was wrong and not being able to do anything to fix it.

Or maybe I was thinking that because I'd just visited my mom. Because we'd talked about Zoe.

She bit her lip. "I mean, I should, but I can't. I—I—"

"It's fine. We can study."

Her head jerked in a nod. "Yes. I have to. I have to pass my test."

"Okay." I kept my voice easy. "That's what I'm here for. To help you pass."

"I'm sorry." She grabbed a piece of paper off her desk and folded it into a triangle so small it disappeared in her tiny hand.

I wanted to pry her fingers loose and hold her hand in mine. To run my finger along her palm and see how soft her skin really was. But I kept my distance.

"You don't have to be sorry about anything." When she didn't seem convinced, I took off my backpack. I couldn't stop myself from glancing up into her conflicted eyes. Or stop my gaze from dropping to her lips. "Can we work in here?"

She nodded. I had to bite my tongue to keep from asking her about *Chess Challenge*. Probably not a good idea to make her even more uncomfortable right now.

"I brought worksheets for practice," I said. "That's exciting, right?"

She gave a short laugh, and then she stared at her feet this time. "Exciting."

"Zoe…"

The word lingered in the air, touching every surface, every floating piece of paper, and evaporating into nothing. I could feel her trepidation, the nerves thrumming off her. It baffled me, but I couldn't bring myself to question it. Not right now.

So I said, "Let's start with math."

She nodded. Her shoulders sagged with relief. "Math. Good."

Right there, I made it my personal mission to get Zoe King so comfortable being around me, she'd not only talk to me in full sentences, but she'd do it while meeting my eyes.

22.

BlackKNIGHT: I have a dilemma.

Rogue2015: Your castle is trapped and your queen feels exposed?

BlackKNIGHT: Not that kind of dilemma.

Rogue2015: Have you noticed the rankings?

BlackKNIGHT: What?

Rogue2015: You've dropped to 5th place. The only dilemma you should be focusing on is how to free your castle and save your queen.

BlackKNIGHT: Are you mad at me?

Rogue2015: What? This is a game. There is no mad. There's win or there's lose.

BlackKNIGHT: What a wonderful life motto.

BlackKNIGHT: Rogue, you still there?

Rogue2015: Okay, what's your dilemma?

BlackKNIGHT: It's not working.

Rogue2015: What isn't working?

BlackKNIGHT: This girl...she still won't open up to me.

Rogue2015: Keep trying. You got me to open up.

BlackKNIGHT: True. Any suggestions?

Rogue2015: Try a new defense. A sly one. One that comes out of nowhere. One that dazzles.

BlackKNIGHT: ?

Rogue2015: Don't give this person a chance to be nervous around you. Show her you want to know her. Believe in her.

BlackKNIGHT: Are you sure you're 16?

Rogue2015: Absolutely. Now, your queen needs your help. Play the game!

BlackKNIGHT: Yes, ma'am.

23.

ZOE

The numbers blurred on the worksheet Jackson gave me. I had no idea if the answers were right. I felt like they were. Well, maybe half of them. Or a few...

How was I supposed to know if I was on the right track? It wasn't like I could get Jackson to check, because then I'd have to call him. *Talk* to him on the phone like we were friends or something.

I turned down the volume of my music and then got up from the desk in my study and admired Calisto. It was one of Jupiter's sixty-three moons, and it was perfect. Except for...

I caught myself before adjusting it. No, I was supposed to be working on homework. It would be so much easier if Jackson were here. Then he could give me his take on Ganymede, too, another of Jupiter's moons. I wasn't sure on the color and—*no!* Homework.

I grabbed my worksheet and then left the study and wandered to the kitchen. Mom stood at the counter, frowning over a pile of papers. She looked up when I walked in.

"Zoe. Good. I need your help."

"I don't know how to make homemade soap."

She smiled.

"Or reupholster a chair." Though, I'd watched her do it once, and I was pretty sure I could handle a staple gun.

Her smile grew wider. "It's a paper project."

"Oh. Lay it on me."

"I thought I might do a segment on card making. Maybe do a mock-up of three or four different types of homemade cards so I can do segments for each of the holidays." That was Mom. Making her cards months before actual holidays so she was prepared. So she could share them with her fans. "I thought maybe you had some ideas."

My cheeks warmed. She usually only asked for my help to pick contest winners or to follow her around with the camera if she needed to move a lot for one of her videos. "I have lots of ideas."

She smiled again. "Good. Dr. Edwards said it might be good to get you involved more."

I deflated. "Oh."

"That's not—I mean—" Mom walked around the counter to me. She usually never got flustered, and she shook her head. "That's not what I meant. I asked you because I thought you could do this. It just popped into my head that this might be one of those things we could do together. Dr. Edwards said maybe I needed to take more of an active part in your life."

I swallowed painful emotions. Sure, I wanted my mom to be more involved in my life. But not because Dr. Edwards assigned her to.

"I need a..." She waved her hand, like swirling the air would make the word come to her. "A do-over. I need a do-over."

That made me smile a little. "Why?"

"I didn't say that right. Sometimes I wonder if..." She sighed. "Sometimes I wonder if you're—you're afraid to go out and be part of the world because I kept you too close when you were younger. Mae was always out doing cheerleading and being social, and you were always here with me, even once school started. I don't…" She touched my shoulder. "I don't want you to miss out on things because you're afraid."

Longing churned inside of me, reminders of missed moments and moments I might never have. Reminders that Mae's graduation was less than two months away and I'd made a promise. I hated breaking promises.

Mom stepped back with a nod. "Let's talk about it later. And if you still want to help me, I'd appreciate it." She eyed my worksheet. "Did you need something?"

"Help with my math."

She wrinkled her nose and looked at the sheet. "I think…" I could see the strain on her face. Yeah, Mom hadn't done algebra in years. I wouldn't, either, if I had a choice. "I think it looks right. You could ask your dad."

I wandered to the living room, following the trail of low light right up to the wide bank of windows that looked out over the glittering city. Dad spent a lot of time staring out of those windows, thinking. I was pretty sure the Car King came up with all his good ideas with a good view.

"Hey, Zoe." He scrubbed a hand over his face. "What's up?"

I fumbled over my words, already sensing he was tired and ready to call it a night. He usually got up before any of us and was out the door before I'd even gotten out of bed. "I—uh…can you help me with my math?"

His eyebrows scrunched together. I could hear the words he wasn't saying out loud. *Isn't that why we got you a tutor?*

Or maybe Dr. Edwards was right and he wasn't thinking anything like that at all. But still…I was bothering him…

"It's just a sheet I got today. I just—I wanted to see if

someone would check my answers."

His face mirrored my mother's when he said, "Maybe you could…ask your sister?"

I held in a grumble. That's exactly what I was trying to avoid. Mae was still mad at me, and she'd made her point by staying in her room all night. Mom forced her to come out for quiche, and then she'd vanished again, saying she had a book she wanted to finish.

When my phone *ding*ed in my pocket, both Dad and I looked in that direction like we'd just seen a mouse.

"Was that your phone?" he asked.

My mind drew a blank. It was my phone, but that was the sound of a text message, and the only one who'd message me was Mae. Or Mom. Dad might have messaged me once, but that went something like **Your mom's not answering the phone. Can you get her for me?** My old friends messaged me before, but the more afraid I became of going anywhere or doing anything, the more our relationships dropped away.

I pulled the phone out of my pocket. The screen blurred before me because I didn't have my glasses on, but I squinted and spotted an unfamiliar number.

My heart shot out of my chest when I read the message. **Hey, Zoe, it's Jackson.** He was texting me? And why did he always have to say my name? Like it was his new favorite word or something. Still, it made my stomach flutter. **How's the math coming?**

I blinked, and then held the phone away from me like it was contaminated.

"What?" Dad asked. "Wrong number?"

I shook my head.

"Mae, probably." He sighed. "Can't she just come out of her room to talk to you?"

I mumbled something about homework and walked away,

confusion sweeping my mind before it dawned on me. Mae had given my number to Jackson. It had to be her.

Why would she do that?

It's okay to tell people how you feel. It's okay to express yourself, Gina had told me earlier today.

Fine. I'd express myself to Mae and see how she liked it.

I knocked on her door, barely waiting for her response before marching inside. I lost a little of my nerve when she glared, and dropped my gaze to the floor. "Did you give Jackson my phone number?"

The bed squeaked as she shuffled forward. I glanced up, frowning when I saw her smile.

"Why? Did he call you?"

"He texted me. Why are you smiling like that?"

She pulled her hair over her shoulder to braid it. "Feisty."

"Mae," I whined.

"He asked, and I gave it to him."

"He asked for my number?" The anger faded, and I sat right there, in the middle of her fluffy, powder-blue rug.

"Zoe." Mae sighed. She pulled a hair tie off her wrist and secured her braid. "Don't be dense."

"Don't be mean."

Her mouth opened, in surprise, I think. But when she spoke again, her voice was gentler. "He likes you. And he's invested."

"Invested in what?"

"You. Making sure you pass your tests."

"Mom and Dad are paying him." No way was I going to believe it was anything more than that.

Mae pulled her knees up and rested her chin on them. "They're paying him to tutor you, not to text you. Not to care about your paper room and some weird chess defense."

Something sparked in my chest. "Chess? What?"

"I saw him reading this book on chess. One you used to read."

Jackson liked chess? I mean, *really* liked it?

"He asked me about your paper art when he left, too," Mae continued. "Then he asked for your number. He actually asks about you a lot. I can guarantee Mom and Dad are *not* paying him to do that."

My stomach jumped. "No."

She laughed. "No, what? Are you saying 'no' you don't believe me? Or 'no' he doesn't like you? I'm pretty sure I have more experience than you in this department."

The words hung in the air for a long moment before falling to the ground and shattering. I stood up. "Okay."

"No, wait." Mae stood, too, her toenails painted a shade of pink so bright they looked like candy. "I'm sorry."

"Okay."

"Say something besides 'okay.' You came in here ready to yell at me. Now you're going to leave?"

I stared at her, verging on crying. There was a little hope inside of me that Jackson liking me was true, and it scared me all over again.

"You're still mad at me," I said quietly.

"I'm not mad at you!" She tossed her hands into the air. "I was upset. I was—okay, yeah, I was mad because you didn't want to go to practice with me. And we don't do anything together anymore."

"I'm not—I'm not like you, Mae. Everyone likes you, and you aren't scared of anything. I—I'm scared of everything."

"Well." She sighed. "You're just going to have to get over it."

Her words jolted me, but I blurted, "That's what Gina said."

It was true. Gina didn't sugarcoat things like Dr. Edwards.

She told me things even though they hurt. But, surprisingly, they made me want to try harder.

"New therapist lady?" Mae smiled. "What else did she say?"

"She said I need to take steps. She said…" I sat on her bed. "I have to step out of my comfort zone."

"Good."

"Bad."

"Why?"

"I can't."

"The more you do it, the easier it gets," she said.

"That's what Dr. Edwards said."

Mae grinned. "It sounds like I should be a psychologist. I'll help you."

"What?"

"Step out of your comfort zone. Take those steps Gina told you to take."

"She…gave me an assignment." I looked down at my worksheet, my actual assignment. The one I was supposed to be focusing on.

"This?" she asked, pointing to my sheet.

"No, this is Jackson's assignment."

Mae sat next to me. "Okay, one at a time. Jackson's assignment."

"Math homework. Could you check my answers?"

Mae looked over the sheet, biting her lip. "It looks right… You could always ask Jackson. He texted you, right?"

"Yes."

"Well? What did he say?"

"He asked how my math was going."

"And what did you say?"

"Nothing yet."

Mae rubbed her hands over her face. "You have to answer

him. If you don't like him, be normal. Say 'Math is good. Thanks for your help.'"

"Like a robot?"

She laughed. "Yep. But if you *do* like him…"

I held my breath. Then what?

"You *do* like him, don't you?"

Staring at my feet, I mumbled, "Yes."

"What was that? You think he's hot and you want to kiss him?"

I jumped up from the bed. "Mae."

Laughing, she lay on her back and folded her hands on her stomach. "Tell me the truth."

Crossing my arms, I said, "I think so."

"Think or know?"

"Know."

"Good. Answer him. Flirt with him a little."

"I don't know how to flirt."

She rolled her eyes. "Of course you do. You flirted with that one kid—what was his name?" She snapped her fingers rcpeatedly. "The one with the hat? The—the kid who played the trumpet—"

"Brian?"

"Yeah, you flirted with him all the time your freshman year."

"That was…." I dropped my chin. "Before."

"And this is after. New comfort zone. Text him back."

I pulled my phone out of my pocket and stared at Jackson's text. "What do I say?"

Mae snatched the phone from my hand and typed in a message faster than I could blink. **Math is good. I might need extra help with this worksheet.**

She sent the message before I could say anything, and then she passed the phone back.

"That wasn't flirty at all," I told her.

"Which is exactly why it'll work."

I cocked my head at her.

"It invites a response," she said. "That's a good thing. He has to say something back, and it shows you want his help. Easy and to the point."

Another message from Jackson came through. I can come over tomorrow if you'd like. I'll bring more worksheets.

Mae peered at the screen. "Good. Tell him that's great. Show him you want him here. And then KISS HIM!"

She fell on the bed in a fit of laughter. I didn't know why that was so amusing to her. She kissed Robert all the time, and even though I made faces, she seemed to like it.

And I seemed to be jealous.

Jackson's kisses were probably like his smiles. Overwhelming. Brilliant. Like the shooting star I'd just made with bright yellow paper and sparkles.

"Oh my God." Mae stared up at me with wide eyes. "You're imagining kissing him right now."

"Shut up." My cheeks flamed, and I turned toward the door.

When Mae hopped up and followed me, I changed course, stalking through the dim living room and to my study. I tried to get in and shut her out, but she slapped a hand on the door and forced her way inside.

And then stopped. Her eyes drifted to the ceiling, taking it all in. It had been weeks since she'd been in here. "What's this?"

"It's called a study."

I set my worksheet on the desk and turned my music up. One of my sticky notes had fallen off the board by the door, and I stooped to pick it up.

I'd almost told Mae about my assignment from Gina, and now I was grateful I hadn't. She'd probably laugh at me like she laughed at everything else. She had no *clue* what my life was like—and I had no clue what hers was like, either.

We didn't know each other anymore.

"This is really cool. No wonder Jackson likes to come in here."

I turned and stared at her.

"Really. He likes to come in here. Sure, he's an astronomy geek, but even for those of us who don't live with our heads in the stars, this is pretty cool." She sighed. "Okay, tell me."

"What?"

"What your assignment from Gina is. I want to help."

"No, you don't." My voice came out in a pout, but Mae deserved it.

"Are you finished?" she asked, sounding just like Mom.

My lips twitched, but I wouldn't give her the satisfaction of smiling.

"Good," she said. "Now tell me."

"Just to give you fair warning, it's absolutely horrible."

She walked to the desk and plopped in a chair. "Then I guess I'd better sit down."

24.

JACKSON

I learned to appreciate showers. When you had to work to hunt one down—especially on the weekends—it was the best thing in the world.

But I still felt guilty about taking up the hot water at Robert's house. I used to hang at his house all the time before the mess with my dad, but now that circumstances were different, it wasn't the same. It wasn't the same because Robert's parents didn't know about my situation. It felt like I was taking advantage of them every time I used something of theirs when they weren't home to know about it.

Even with the guilt, after I got out, I wished I had stayed in longer. Towel wrapped around my waist, I checked my phone, hopeful for a text from Zoe. What I found instead was a voice message from my father.

My focus cracked. Didn't he understand what an agreement was? You gave your word, you stuck to it. He should have been living every day in a perpetual state of bliss. No responsibilities, no teenager running around demanding food and shelter. His life was cake.

In fact, his life had been cake when Mom was alive, too.

He'd barely had anything to do with us, and went out all the time with his friends at the bar. After Mom had gotten sick, he'd spent more time being angry with her than sympathizing— even blaming her at some points.

Once she'd died, he made it very clear being a parent wasn't a priority. He wanted his own life. And now I was letting him have it.

So why the hell did he keep bothering me?

Especially at…I checked my watch and frowned. Eight thirty in the morning. Austin didn't typically start the party until two a.m. First, a few beers, then tequila, and if that didn't get him where he wanted, he'd hit the heroin. He should still be asleep right now.

I used to feel bad for him. He obviously needed that escape from losing my mother, and I half envied him for being able to find it. But I didn't envy what it was costing him. I didn't envy him being so cavalier with his life and what he had left. Mom had fought as hard as she could to keep us together, even when she was sick.

And in six short months, Dad burned it to the ground.

I dried off, dressed, and tried not to think about what possible reason Dad could have for calling. Repeatedly. My usual guess would have been money. But since he'd paid my bills this month, he'd found cash somewhere.

I wandered into the living room and saw Robert sprawled on the couch asleep. I grabbed the controller that was about to fall off the cushion and returned it to the game console.

"Why?" he mumbled, shifting onto his side.

"Why what?"

"Why do you always get up so early?"

Habit. When you slept in your car like I did, it was best to move on before sunup.

"To see your ugly face," I retorted, smacking a pillow

against his head.

"Ugh!" Robert threw the pillow back. "I need breakfast."

He looked hungover. But, as I'd spent the night at his house, I knew it was a combination of Twinkies, Mountain Dew, and playing *Fallout* until his eyes were so dry they almost dropped out of his head.

"Cereal?" I asked, already heading for the kitchen.

"Nah." Robert shifted, snagging the box of Twinkies off the coffee table and opening one with his teeth.

I grimaced. But it was better than eating Robert's cereal. If I did, then I'd feel guilty about sponging off Robert's parents even more. Since I'd bought the Twinkies, my guilt lessened some. I caught the box when Robert tossed it at me.

"Mom and Dad are gonna have a barbecue for all the basketball parents," Robert mumbled around puffy Twinkie crème.

The Twinkie lost some of its flavor. "Yeah?"

"Yeah. An end of the year kind of thing. You think your dad would come?"

I shrugged, swallowing hard to get the bite down. I set the box aside. "Doubt it."

Robert sat up, hair sticking out in all directions. "You could ask him."

"Pass."

"Why?"

I shoved my hands in my pockets, trying to think of an excuse to leave without treating Robert like shit. It wasn't his fault he was curious, especially not since he let me stay here under the guise of "getting some space from my dad."

"He doesn't do that kind of stuff," I said. "You know how he is."

Robert unwrapped another Twinkie like he hadn't heard me. He glanced down the hall, as if checking to see if anyone else was coming. His brother had stayed at a friend's house, so it was just me and Robert. His parents weren't going to be home until the afternoon.

"So." Robert cleared his throat. "My mom was grocery shopping the other day and she saw your dad. In the cereal aisle, she said, 'cause, you know, moms notice that stuff."

I tensed, my hands clenching in my pockets. How did she even remember him? Yeah, Robert and I had spent a lot of time at each other's houses, but that was back in the day. Before my mom died. I'd barely recognized my father in the last few months before I left; I had no idea how in the world Robert's mom had.

Robert wouldn't look at me, like he felt guilty bringing it up. "She asked him how you were—like she doesn't see you every week."

I gritted my teeth, stopping myself from saying anything. The less I said, the better. Mom used to be a big fan of letting people get it all out before you responded. She said sometimes people worked through an entire week of problems without you having to say a word. Kind of contradicted what she was telling me the rest of the time—to say how you felt—but it seemed to suit this scenario.

"And you know what he said?" Robert asked.

"He doesn't care?" I couldn't hold in the nasty comment.

Robert wadded the transparent Twinkie wrapper in one hand and then passed it to the other, going back and forth a few times before he answered. "My mom said he told her he wouldn't know because he can't get a hold of you. He asked if she'd pass along the message to call him if she saw you."

The Twinkie churned in my stomach. For some reason, at that moment, I thought about Zoe and her paper room. Of her hiding inside, safe from the world while she made her own small, beautiful world around her.

And I wanted to be there.

"How long has it been?" Robert asked. "Since you saw him?"

I willed myself to stay calm. "You know my relationship with my dad is complicated."

Robert nodded. "And has been since your mom died."

Since before my mom died. "Right."

He tried unsuccessfully to pat his hair into some semblance of order. "So you finally did it?"

My mind drew a blank at his words. "Did what?"

"Left home. Ran away like you used to say you were going to." Robert frowned at the box of Twinkies then reached to draw another one out. He looked up at me. "Right?"

I stared at my shoes. A Zoe move. I wanted my own paper room, sans Twinkies. Anything but to have to face this.

"I get it," Robert said. "If that's what you did. But, man… this isn't…"

"It's not your problem." I shook my head when he lifted his eyebrows. "I didn't mean that the way it came out."

"The way that makes you sound like an ass?"

I blew out a breath of laughter. "Yeah. That way. I meant it in the way that doesn't want you to have to deal with it, to be involved in something you shouldn't have to be involved in."

"And you should?"

"It's my life."

Robert finished the other half of his Twinkie in one bite and stood, stretching his long legs. Then he scratched his chin. "You can stay again tonight if you want. Mom and Dad won't care."

I shook my head. "No, I'm good."

"Jackson."

Giving him an easy smile, I repeated, "It's my life."

He snagged the box of Twinkies and tossed them at me.

"Better take nourishment, then."

With a laugh, I tucked the box under my arm while I grabbed my backpack. Even though the idea of Twinkies still made me queasy. "I've gotta get going."

"I'd ask you where you're going, but I doubt you'll tell me."

"To the library."

"Serious?"

With another laugh, I headed to the door. "Serious. I have work to do."

"You work at the library?"

I chucked the box of Twinkies back at him. "I think you need nourishment more than I do. No, I don't work at the library. I study there. Maybe you should go back to bed."

Robert looked longingly at the couch. "Yeah, maybe."

"Do it. I'll see you at school on Monday."

I let myself out and walked to my car. I opened the trunk and transferred my bag of toiletries to the duffel, tucking it next to the clothes I'd washed at the laundromat yesterday, and stuffing books and notes in my backpack instead.

When I shut the trunk and glanced at the house, I saw Robert watching me from the window.

It killed me that I couldn't tell anyone about my situation, but it was better this way.

Shooting Robert a wave, I climbed in the driver's seat and checked my gas. I could drive to the library this once, since I didn't feel like walking, and do some homework before I went to Zoe's. Maybe apply for more scholarships. And then I'd figure out what to do about Dad.

Tomorrow.

25.

BlackKNIGHT: My king is tired.

Rogue2015: He hasn't done much work.

BlackKNIGHT: Sometimes it's exhausting waiting for the next shoe to drop.

Rogue2015: He just needs a pep talk. Get your queen to cheer him up. Tell him all is not lost.

BlackKNIGHT: All is not lost.

Rogue2015: That's right. Sometimes when you think you see the end, another beginning happens and you're back in the game, so to speak.

BlackKNIGHT: So we're not talking about the game?

Rogue2015: Sure we are. That's what I meant.

BlackKNIGHT: That felt like a pep talk.

Rogue2015: Still waters run deep and all that.

BlackKNIGHT: I'll say. Tell me more.

Rogue2015: About what?

BlackKNIGHT: I need more. More pep talk.

Rogue2015: Uh…

BlackKNIGHT: More, please.

Rogue2015: What's your bright side?

BlackKNIGHT: Excuse me?

Rogue2015: You know how people are always telling you to look on the bright side?

BlackKNIGHT: Yeah, people say that. I guess.

Rogue2015: Yes, people say that all the time. My mom does.

BlackKNIGHT: Your mom? Tell me about her.

Rogue2015: Okay, erase that last line. Yes, *people* say that. So, what's your bright side?

BlackKNIGHT: Right now? Don't have one.

Rogue2015: You have to. Otherwise you might as well forfeit. Come on. What's your bright side?

BlackKNIGHT: Home.

Rogue2015: Home?

BlackKNIGHT: Never mind. Erase that last line. I should go.

Rogue2015: BK…?

(BlackKNIGHT has logged off.)

26.

ZOE

Gina was evil.

She had this plan to torture me. A way to help me get over my anxiety and join the real world again. But who *really* wanted to be part of the real world anyway? I mean, people were jerks. They drove badly and littered. There was pollution. Snow turned black with car exhaust and made you dirty. Everything cost too much.

But no, she still had a plan because she said I needed to take steps if I was going to make it to graduation—and prom. Her words, not mine. So I had to wait all day long, through torturous hours of anxiety, for Mae to get home from school and help me, because she promised she would.

Mae didn't like breaking her promises, either.

"This is just the first step," Mae said as we stood together and stared at the elevator. She was evil, too, because she was making me do this.

Not only that, she'd made me wear something other than my billowy dresses or leggings.

We both wore skinny jeans and tank tops from her closet. I'd slipped on sandals with jewels decorating the straps. I *looked* like I could go out of the house, but I didn't feel like it.

Never mind the shoes. I couldn't live in a sparkly world. That was looking at the bright side.

My thoughts shifted to BlackKNIGHT and our strange conversation last night—how he'd vanished. I wanted to think we were two robots, emotionless shells just playing a game, but we were real people.

If I expected him to look at the bright side, I should, too.

"It's just mail," I whispered. "She just wants me to go downstairs and check the mail."

Mae nodded. "That's right. Mail. Maybe that catalog you like is in there. Or the paper you ordered last week. Mail is fun."

A laugh bubbled out. "This doesn't feel fun."

"That's because you're not used to it."

"Gina should have given me an easier task," I mumbled. I could joke—on the outside—but my hands still shook. And on the inside, it was even worse. I felt like a fragile single sheet of paper, ready to tear.

"If it were easy, it wouldn't do any good."

Mom joined us at the elevator. "Are we waiting for something?"

"Yes."

"Zoe's first step," Mae said.

"Ooooh." Mom's voice turned hushed. "What does that mean?"

"It means she needs space," Mae said.

Mom blinked. "Space?"

"Yes. Space."

"I only get one buddy." I couldn't take my eyes off the elevator doors. Gina had told me I could bring someone with me, but not to make it a big deal. To try to make it seem like this was something I do every day.

My guess was so that she could make me do it every day. But who knew? This was only the first of Gina's tasks for me. And if the first one was this traumatic, I was *not* in any way excited to hear about the rest.

"I'm not your buddy?" Mom asked.

Mae smiled at her. "Not today. Besides, you're making a casserole."

Mom glanced back to the kitchen. "The oven is preheating."

"Mom," Mae said.

Mom lifted her hands. "Fine. Casserole. But *I* don't get a casserole buddy."

She walked off, barefoot and mumbling about buddies, as Mae stepped to the elevator doors. "Let's go."

"Right now?"

"We've been standing here for ten minutes."

"I'm preparing. Mentally."

"You can't prepare for everything. Life is going to throw curveballs at you all the time. You have to learn how to deal in the moment."

I nodded. What was my bright side? I stepped up to the elevator. After this, Jackson was coming. He was coming early, in fact. So I'd focus on the fact that I'd get to see him.

Jackson was my bright side.

"Press the button," Mae said.

I obeyed, my mouth going dry. I prayed for the elevator to break. To get stuck. Not my fault if it didn't work.

But after a short moment, it *ding*ed, and the doors opened.

"You have your key card?" I asked her.

"Yes."

"And the mail key?"

"Yes. Stop stalling. Get in."

One step. Two. Three. Four. Turn and face the doors. Four more steps for my total count. I could do this. It was exercise.

I clasped my hands together tightly when Mae pressed the button for the lobby. My stomach lurched when the doors closed and the elevator started moving.

Nausea crept up. *Oh, no...* "Mae, I don't think I can—"

"We'll check the mail," she said, smiling and pretending like everything was fine. "I'll show you the doorman if he's there. He always says, 'Good morning, Miss King,' when I go to school or practice, and when I come back, he says—"

"'Good afternoon, Miss King'?" I asked, though my voice was barely above a whisper.

Mae grinned. "He says 'Welcome back' like he's spent the whole time I was away pining for my return." She fluttered her lashes. "And I smile at him like this. And he fumbles for the door handle to let me in."

The elevator continued to descend. I was pretty sure she was telling me this story to prove that I wasn't the only one who got flustered, but all I could see were the numbers above the doors going down, down, down...

Ding!

Hands glued together, feet fused to the floor, all I could do was stare at the yawning lobby. It stretched long and wide with shiny tiles and contemporary furniture, metal, white, and clean.

"We're here," Mae said, touching my arm.

I forced myself to step out of the elevator before people walked up, wanting to get on. *This is a bad idea, a* terrible *idea...*

The air was different down here. More constricting. It felt like I was a breath away from my lungs shutting off, my throat clogging, me passing out.

"See?" Mae said. "It's nice. You've got your odd grouping over here of chairs that look comfortable, but no one ever sits in. They're right in the middle, and it's awkward. Everyone would be looking at you."

"Everyone *is* looking at me," I whispered, chest tightening.

Mae laughed. "Really? That guy over there with the toupee? Nope, he's watching that blonde with the generous... assets."

The pressure in my chest eased slightly. Mae led me a few steps to the right, toward the wide bank of windows that showcased a small courtyard.

"And that lady? Nah, she's focused on her kid. He just dropped his sucker on the ground, picked it back up, and stuck it in his mouth."

I followed her gaze and saw a sticky little kid and his mother's horror as he dropped the sucker again. He bent to retrieve it, and she swooped in before he could.

"That's disgusting."

"Welcome to the real world." Mae pointed. "The mailboxes are over there."

My sandals tap, tap, tapped on the tile as we walked across the entire lobby, fifty shiny tiles, to a small alcove off the main desk. There was only one other person inside, checking her mail—an old lady wearing a hot-pink visor.

I focused on her. Focusing meant shutting out the rest of the world. It was the only way I could do this.

"Hello," Mae said, nudging my arm.

I forced my gaze up, met her eyes briefly, and mumbled, "Good morning."

The lady smiled, wrinkles lining the corners of her eyes. "Beautiful day out there."

"It is," Mae answered, pulling her key out. "Great day for a walk."

"Absolutely."

Mae nudged me again, but I couldn't force out anything else before the lady walked off. Her sneakers matched her visor.

"Not bad." Mae took out a pile of envelopes and passed them to me. "Now you should say hi to one more person. Without them talking to you first."

My heartbeat picked up. I looked through the lobby at the dozen or so people who were busy doing their own thing and didn't need to be bothered by someone like me. *They're all looking at you.*

"Brett. The guy at the desk," Mae decided. "He's nice."

Clutching the letters close to my chest, I walked from the alcove and promptly bumped into someone. My breath caught as the envelopes scattered across the tiles.

"Oh God, I'm sorry—" My gaze flashed up, and I got another jolt when I saw Jackson staring back. Then I promptly dropped to my knees to pick up the mail, my world tilting. "I'm sorry, I didn't see you—"

Mae crouched next to me, and Jackson followed.

"I keep bumping into you," Jackson said, the usual smile in his voice. One of his sneakers was untied. "Sorry."

My cheeks lit on fire even as my panic made me speechless. *This can't be happening, this can't be happening…*

"It's just mail," Mae said calmly, grabbing the last piece. "It's fine."

No, it's not. It's not fine, everything is falling apart. My first venture out of the apartment, and it was all going wrong.

When Jackson gripped my elbow to help me up, the air vanished from my lungs. I pressed a hand to my chest, the muscles constricting like a vise. I turned stricken eyes to Mae as the pain traveled to my shoulder.

A heart attack. This was it. My body was finally shutting down.

Breathe. Gina's voice popped in my head. Yes, breathe. I wasn't dying, I was panicking.

"I…need to go upstairs." The words were near impossible

to get out. The elevators looked miles away.

Jackson wouldn't release my arm. "Are you okay?"

When I couldn't answer, Mae shook her head. "She's fine. It's—"

Don't say it, I silently pleaded with her. It was too embarrassing. But I couldn't say anything because I couldn't draw any air into my lungs.

"She's not feeling well," Mae said.

Jackson's hand was warm when he slid it down to my forearm. "Upstairs then?"

I gave a tight nod.

My shoes sparkled with every step to the elevator, like Dorothy's ruby slippers on the yellow brick road. We both just wanted to get home.

And clearly, BlackKNIGHT wanted that, too. Whoever and wherever he was right now, I hoped he was finding a way.

We reached the elevator after a million years, and Mae quickly pushed the button, her mouth pressed into a serious line.

Jackson squeezed my arm, and even through the pain in my chest, I could feel the strength and certainty in his grip. "What did you learn today?"

My mind whirled with possibilities. And then choked on reality. "It's seventy-six steps from…from the mailboxes to the elevator."

The doors popped open, and he guided me inside. Mae used her key card and pressed the button for the top floor. When the doors closed, the rest of the air vanished with it. My fingers clawed at Jackson's arm, squeezing tight.

"Zoe?" Mae asked, her arm brushing mine. "Just breathe."

I could push air out, but not much would come back in. Panic gripped me, making me look at Mae.

"Remember what Dr. Edwards said? It's not going to kill

you. You're in control of this."

She was right. I knew deep down that a panic attack wouldn't kill me. It was a matter of making it through the worst part and believing that I wasn't going to die, even though it felt like it. The calmer I was, the faster it would pass.

But instead of Dr. Edwards's voice in my head, I heard Gina's. *These are steps, Zoe. Even if they're hard, they matter. They're progress.*

"Almost there," Mae said.

Jackson's thumb rubbed my arm. "Did you know that you can get kidnapping and ransom insurance?"

I took a short breath and ventured a glance up. "In case... you think you might get kidnapped and ransomed?"

A smile in his eyes, he said, "Absolutely. You can't be too careful."

The pressure in my chest eased some. "Can you get it on your pets?"

"Hmm, not sure on that one."

The elevator reached our floor. Mae was out fast, looking toward the kitchen for Mom. I shook my head.

"I'll go distract her," Mae said, kicking off her shoes and dashing away.

I made it out of the elevator but stopped there, waiting for the worst to pass and grateful Mae was distracting Mom.

"I'm sorry," I whispered.

Jackson didn't answer. He just held on. I tried to toe off my sandals, but the right one kept catching.

"Here," he said, crouching down.

"You don't have to..." Oh my God, his hand was on my foot, warm fingers that tickled the side. "Jackson."

He looked up. "Yes?"

All the words trickled back down my throat. His eyes were hazel, flecked with yellow around the irises. And all this time,

I'd been staring at his shoes.

His finger hooked in the strap of my sandal. He pulled it off smoothly and tickled my foot again. He grabbed both sandals and set them near the elevator with the other shoes all lined up and waiting. He removed his sneakers and smiled at me.

Well, he wasn't wearing shoes now. And socks were definitely less interesting to stare at. Might have to do the eye contact thing more often.

I thought Gina was weird—after all, none of her ideas were anything like Dr. Edwards's. But maybe...maybe there was something to Gina's assignment after all.

27.

JACKSON

As usual, the King household smelled like a restaurant. This time, the air was filled with spices and promised everything a Twinkie never could.

I was also close enough to Zoe to smell jasmine, the same scent she'd had on the last time I'd been near enough to brush her hair from her eyes.

"What do you need?" I asked her, having trouble keeping my hands to myself. Her feet had been soft. They made me want to touch her again.

"I'm just…" She stared at her bare feet. "I need to stand here for a minute."

She did. Like a statue. And, helpless to do anything more, I said, "I'll get some water."

Her shoulders relaxed. I didn't want to leave her, but I didn't want to stand there staring at her while she collected herself. She was clearly embarrassed about what had happened.

A panic attack. That's what it looked like. My mom had one two weeks after she found out about her illness. Suddenly she wasn't just planning dinner or which bills to pay next; she was planning for her death. I'd come home from school to find her sitting motionless at the kitchen table, staring at a centerpiece of daisies.

"Just give me a minute," she'd whispered, as though it hurt to push the words out. "Wait until it passes."

And so I had, doing chores around the kitchen and fetching her a glass of lemonade, unable to stay as calm as she was. I didn't want my mom to panic. That was my job. She'd always been the calm one, and all of a sudden, the roles were reversed. I hadn't been able to help her, and now I couldn't help Zoe, either.

Mrs. King beamed when she saw me. Probably because she was making food and she figured she could foist it off on me. I didn't mind being foisted on, but the guilt flickered anyway.

"Try this," she said, handing me an entire plate of mini quiches.

I glanced at Mae, who met my eyes with a smile that didn't stretch as wide as normal.

"All of it?" I asked.

"Mom." Mae took the plate from me and set it on the counter. "You can't make him eat all of this."

"Not *making*," Yoko insisted. "Asking. Encouraging. Growing boys need nutrition, and I made too much."

"What's all this for?"

"I'm putting together a Fourth of July party menu."

"For your blog?" Mae asked.

Yoko nodded, nudging the plate on the counter until it almost reached me. I gave in and lifted one of the quiches to my lips.

Zoe walked into the kitchen at the same time. Her eyes met mine as I sampled the food, but she dropped them before I could smile. She still clutched a few envelopes in her hand, and she set them on the counter.

Yoko blinked. "You got the mail?"

Zoe glanced at Mae and shrugged. "Sort of."

"Yes." Mae nodded. "She got the mail. And we saw Mrs. Webber, who had a hot-pink visor on today, which means she has a visor in every single color of the rainbow."

"And every one in between." Yoko smiled at Zoe. "You need food, then."

Which must have been her way of showing how proud she was. She frequently offered Mae food when she got her report card or mentioned a cheerleading meet their team had won.

"I'm not hungry." Zoe ventured another glance at me. "I have homework."

I nodded. "Right. I said I'd help you with the worksheet."

It felt strange to walk through their apartment only wearing socks, but I realized I should have been more respectful long ago. Even Mr. King took off his shoes when he arrived home in the evening, and something about the gesture made me feel more like a part of their family.

At the door to Zoe's study, she stopped and turned, lifting her chin to look me straight in the eyes. "Thanks for...you know, not saying anything to my mom."

"Sure."

She fumbled for the doorknob, and I reached past her to grab it with a steady hand. Her breath rushed out, fluttering her bangs, and it was all I could do to stand there and let her walk past.

I wanted to pull her against me and say ridiculous things like how it would be all right, and that she could talk to me, and that I understood—even if I didn't. It felt right to want to comfort her.

Even if I was in my socks.

But then I stepped inside the study, and the computer was on. My eyes went straight to it because it was the first source of light I saw. Since I was wearing my glasses, I could actually see what was on the screen halfway across the room. *Chess Challenge*. Just like I thought.

Zoe didn't notice. She walked straight to her desk and grabbed a pile of papers off the surface. I followed her, almost holding my breath. As though she could feel my eyes on the screen, Zoe shut the lid of the computer with a swift gesture, and then she turned with her worksheets.

"I finished the sheet." Her cheeks flushed, and she bit her lip. "What's wrong?"

"It's…nothing." I smiled at her. It was crazy. There was no way Zoe was Rogue. There were thousands of people on *Chess Challenge*, and for me to be playing the same person I knew in real life? The odds were completely against that. Then I also remembered… I'd told Rogue I was homeless. That was huge. A huge secret. "I want to help."

She looked at the papers in her hands, and then up at me.

"Not with your math." I adjusted my glasses. "I mean, not only with your math. With…everything. You can talk to me."

Her mouth opened, just a hint of rose on her lips, and the room seemed to shrink around us.

"Why did you stop going to school?" I asked.

Her eyes glittered with moisture. Shit. I'd been tactless. She needed a little more build-up, not an outright question like that.

"I couldn't be there anymore," she whispered, dropping her gaze again.

"I understand." When she looked like she didn't believe me, I continued. "I mean, I understand about not being able to be somewhere anymore. Not that you don't want to be there, or that you were forced to leave or anything. Just that you can't."

The papers in her hand shook. "The same thing happened at school."

"What same thing?"

"The same thing as downstairs." Her words were heavy, laced with defeat.

"A panic attack?"

She nodded, chin still angled downward. "It makes me nervous to leave the house. To go to school. To…talk to you."

I reached out, closing my hand around hers to still the papers. She froze as if a bee had landed on her.

"I'm not going to judge you, Zoe. We're all screwed up in so many ways. I'm screwed up, too."

"But…"

Her hand shook underneath mine. I wished I could send her some of my calm. I understood nerves. But not to the point where I couldn't even leave my house. So what had she been doing downstairs? Just checking the mail?

"Would it help if we did some math?" I asked.

Her nervous laughter bubbled out, making me smile. "I didn't think I'd ever say this." She glanced up, eyes still moist. "Yes, I think math would help. On the bright side, at least I'm learning something new for the day."

On the bright side…

I forced myself to release her, but stayed close as we sat at the desk, going over her worksheet from yesterday. Just because Zoe and Rogue said the same things didn't make them the same person. And the sooner I got that through my head, the sooner I'd stop driving myself crazy.

28.

BlackKNIGHT: I'm sorry.

Rogue2015: Okay. Why?

BlackKNIGHT: For leaving yesterday.

Rogue2015: You're allowed to have a personal life. Whatever that is. It's your turn.

BlackKNIGHT: I have a personal life. Sure. But I didn't have to be rude.

Rogue2015: You weren't rude. You know we get more points toward our total score if you play faster.

BlackKNIGHT: Or in my case, I lose points. Right?

Rogue2015: You have a point there.

BlackKNIGHT: Terrible pun.

Rogue2015: Yeah, I know. I'm tired. Okay, take your time.

BlackKNIGHT: Why are you tired?

Rogue2015: It's almost midnight.

BlackKNIGHT: Really? It's almost midnight here, too. I think…

Rogue2015: What?

BlackKNIGHT: Maybe we live closer than we think.

Rogue2015: You live near a cornfield?

BlackKNIGHT: Ha ha. We're in the same time zone.

Rogue2015: That's…a strange coincidence.

BlackKNIGHT: Yeah. Strange. You still okay to play?

Rogue2015: Of course.

BlackKNIGHT: Why are you so tired? What did you do today?

Rogue2015: Is this a new chess strategy? Distracting me? Because it's not earning you any points, either.

BlackKNIGHT: I feel like talking instead. We're still anonymous, so you could tell me all your wildest secrets and no one would ever know.

Rogue2015: No one but you.

BlackKNIGHT: That's right. No one but me. Tell me something you've never told anyone else.

Rogue2015: Or else?

BlackKNIGHT: Or else I'll…take your queen and steal

this match point from you.

Rogue2015: Ha! So much confidence. Or is that... bluffing?

BlackKNIGHT: Talk, or I'll do it.

Rogue2015: *sigh*

BlackKNIGHT: Is that the sound of you giving in?

Rogue2015: I'm too tired to argue. Okay. One thing. I have a stack of DC comic books hiding under my bed.

BlackKNIGHT: That's your wildest secret?

Rogue2015: No, that's *a* secret. I'm too tired for wild ones right now.

BlackKNIGHT: Who's that a secret from?

Rogue2015: The stack of Marvel comic books hiding under my desk. You have to swear you won't tell either of them. They get jealous so easily...

BlackKNIGHT: *groan*

Rogue2015: What? Not a big enough secret for you?

BlackKNIGHT: It's not that.

Rogue2015: Then what is it, BK? You seem to have something in mind.

BlackKNIGHT: You're very careful what you say to me.

Rogue2015: It's a gift.

BlackKNIGHT: I don't disagree. But I want...

Rogue2015: What?

BlackKNIGHT: I want to know you. Does that make sense?

Rogue2015: I'm not used to talking about these kinds of things.

BlackKNIGHT: What kinds of things?

Rogue2015: Things that matter.

BlackKNIGHT: I'm not trying to pressure you. Much.

Rogue2015: Ha ha. You *do* make it hard to say no.

BlackKNIGHT: Then tell me something else.

Rogue2015: Well, you *did* tell me about a girl you like. So I guess I could tell you about a boy.

BlackKNIGHT: Yes, tell me.

Rogue2015: Not much to tell, really. I like him. A lot. But I'm super nervous around him. Like, throw up on his shoes nervous. You know that feeling?

BlackKNIGHT: Sure. I've felt it once or twice.

Rogue2015: I'm pretty sure if he knew how much I want to talk to him, he'd laugh at me. Plus, I know way more about him than I should.

BlackKNIGHT: So that's your secret? You're a stalker?

Rogue2015: :-P No. I'm not a stalker. I learned about him from other people. But I'm like those hopeless little girls who write their first names with the last name of the boy they like. You know, like we're married.

BlackKNIGHT: Ah, I see. Does this boy know how you feel? Maybe he'd like your stalkerish tendencies.

Rogue2015: No way! Pathetic, right? I'm pretty sure if I told him, he'd never want to see me again.

BlackKNIGHT: You never know.

Rogue2015: No, I *know*. In case you've forgotten, we're teenagers. These things are fragile.

BlackKNIGHT: You're right, they are. But that means he's a teenager, too, right? He probably has the same kinds of thoughts. He probably wants to know about you just as much as I do.

Rogue2015: I wish you were right.

29.

ZOE

I did wish BK was right. Even though it scared me to death, I wanted Jackson to know me. Whenever he turned those quizzical hazel eyes on me behind his thick glasses, I wanted nothing more than to cuddle up next to him and spill out my heart and soul. In an elegant way, of course.

In my fantasy, we'd walk hand in hand down the Denver streets while the sun warmed my cheeks and everything I said would impress him. And then we'd stop, and he'd kiss me, right in the middle of the sidewalk. He'd slide his hand down to the hem of my shirt, where a sliver of bare skin was exposed and—

"Zoe?"

I jerked in my seat, almost tumbling out of my chair. I reached up and adjusted my glasses, irritated I'd lost track of time and hadn't put in my contacts before Gina got here.

My fantasy bubble popped. I didn't want Jackson to be anything like BlackKNIGHT, or Rogue to be anything like me. I liked being Rogue because she reflected a side of me I didn't—no, couldn't—show anyone else. But in real life, I wasn't there yet. I was just...

Zoe.

I touched the sleeve of my sweater to the corner of my mouth, sure I'd drooled during my reverie. If Gina noticed, she didn't say a word.

She only walked inside my study and asked, "Do you want to talk in here today?"

"Sure."

Her eyes met mine. Her scarf looked like it had lily pads on it, and it matched her eyes. "Good."

I'd done something right. Probably my optimism.

"You usually say 'If that's what you want,' or 'Whatever you want,' when what I really want is for you to just tell me how you feel," she said as if reading my mind.

She sounded just like Jackson. Straightforward. To the point. He told me how he felt. Come to think of it, BlackKNIGHT did, too. I was the only one who couldn't ever seem to say how I was feeling.

Instead of sitting, Gina walked to the Milky Way wall and examined the sun, which was only halfway finished. "It's big."

"One hundred and forty-three sheets of paper so far. But I'm not finished."

She looked closer. "That's a lot of paper. How do you fold those pieces at the center so small?"

"I have small fingers." And patience. There was nothing more soothing than focusing on one sheet at a time, hour after hour, folding it into tiny triangles to make one larger piece.

She chuckled, and a wave of warmth washed over me. So far so good. I wasn't embarrassing her or myself.

"I like how it's tinier at the middle and gets bigger as it expands." She turned to face me. "I heard they're doing a paper art exhibit at the museum."

Delight hit first, then dread. Yes, I'd love to go. No, I couldn't go.

"It starts next week," Gina said. "A good amount of time."

I ducked my chin. "For what?"

"To work up to it. How did your assignment go?"

"Project: Mailbox," I mumbled.

Her shoes moved into my vision. All I could think about were Jackson's socks. Jackson's warm hand on mine. Jackson saying he wanted to help, and me wishing desperately for the courage to let him.

"How did it go?"

"Mae went with me."

"That's all right. Sometimes we all need a little help getting from point A to point B."

"We took the elevator, and I walked to the mailboxes."

"Good."

"And then I couldn't breathe."

Gina didn't speak for a minute. I glanced up into kind eyes.

"Let's back up," she said. "What happened before you couldn't breathe?"

"I was nervous, anyway," I said with a shrug. "It was inevitable."

"No, it wasn't. It wasn't, Zoe." She gestured to the desk. "Why don't we sit?"

I took the chair opposite her and stared at the grains of wood on the table. Marker and pencil marks marred the surface. Mom had built this desk for me—one of her YouTube projects. Perfect height, perfect width. Perfect for me to spend hours and hours at while the world went on all around me.

"This is what we're working on," Gina said. "Retraining your mind not to think the worst. Why don't you tell me what happened?"

"I got the mail, and I said hi to this lady with a visor."

"And what did she do?"

"She smiled and talked with Mae."

"Pretty smooth so far, right?"

"Right."

"And then?"

"And then I turned around and ran into Jackson, and the mail fell on the floor."

"Jackson is your tutor, right?"

"Yes. He was coming to help me with my math worksheet."

"What did he do?"

My mouth opened. Nothing out of the ordinary, I realized. "He apologized, then helped pick up the mail."

"He felt bad."

"It looked like it."

Gina leaned back in her seat. "But you were embarrassed you dropped the mail?"

I nodded.

"And that you ran into Jackson?"

"Yes."

"But Jackson wasn't embarrassed, was he?"

I frowned, and that seemed to amuse Gina.

"He was probably just sorry he ran into you and wanted to help by picking up the mail," Gina said. "Sometimes what you see really is what you get."

My frown deepened. It looked different in hindsight, of course. But I couldn't help those internal feelings, the ones that said I was making a fool of myself. That everyone saw just how awkward I was. Including Jackson.

Gina snagged a pen from the holder on my desk and tapped it against her hand. "When I was in my second year of college, I used to go to this coffee shop up on the hill—one with these really uncomfortable metal chairs. We'd study there on Friday nights. Yeah, I was a dork and studied on Friday nights."

My frown relaxed some.

"There was this really cute waiter who'd bring us coffee. He always smelled like scones. Blueberry ones, which, in case you're wondering, are my favorite."

"I'll be sure to tell my mom. She'll stock you up for a year."

She smiled, still tapping the pen. "Great. So, one day, the waiter came by to pick up empty cups. And I thought I'd help him out, hand him a few, you know? Give him a cute smile to see if he'd notice me. But I bumped my elbow on the back of the chair when I turned, and dropped three mugs. Two still had coffee in them. They all shattered right at his feet and coffee splashed all over his legs."

I pressed my hand over my mouth.

"Yeah. I just stared at his feet, and he stared at his feet, and everyone started clapping. It was...not my best moment. But I helped him clean up and said I'd replace his shoes, which maybe wasn't my best line. Anyway, I offered to take him out that weekend, and though he didn't want new shoes, he still went out with me. And we dated for a year."

"That's a nice story."

"It has two things you can take away from it, too, so bonus, right?" She grinned. "One: we all make mistakes. We all do stupid things. We all break the mugs or drop the mail. It happens. Two: it is what you make of it. If you chide yourself over it and make it a big deal, something that isn't a big deal is elevated to disaster status. But if you just apologize or shrug it off and move on, it'll only take up as much of your time and angst as you let it."

When I didn't respond, Gina set the pen down. "I know. It's easier said than done. But it's part of training your mind to understand you're not so different from anyone else."

"I can try."

She nodded. "Good. When something like that happens, take a breath and think 'It was an accident—the same thing happens to everyone else.' And you should go get the mail again tomorrow."

"That's my assignment?"

"That's one of your assignments."

My stomach dropped. "What's the other one?"

She grinned. "A social experiment."

The rules were more complicated this time. They stated that I had to do this on my own. If I'd had Mae's help, it would have been done in ten seconds. But me? I was working on three hours so far.

Jackson arrived early today. He'd texted me to make sure it was okay, and I'd blushed, and my heart raced, and I'd formulated three different sample texts before I returned one to him that said, Sure.

But now he sat next to me, close enough that I felt the need to lean a few inches away. I was sure he had no idea he was in my space bubble. Every bit of bare skin on my arm could feel the warmth from his a few inches away.

I'd expected him to ask more questions, like he did yesterday, but he was ready to get right to work, and that slowed my momentum.

Gina wanted me to ask him to stay for our Friday night movie. Sure, Mae had already invited him, and she already said he'd agreed, but Gina wanted me to do it again, so he knew I wanted him to stay. It was the perfect opportunity for my social experiment, but I couldn't seem to unglue my mouth to say anything more than "x equals four."

It was painful really, knowing I should say more, *do* more, and words just wouldn't come.

"Does it make you nervous when I watch you do your

problems?" Jackson asked.

I scooted my arm closer to my body. "I'm sorry. Yes."

"You don't have to apologize." He turned in his chair to face the other way. There was a smile in his voice when he said, "Is this better?"

I blew out a laugh. "Yes."

Then I hurried to finish two more problems so they'd be done before he turned around again.

"Finished?" he asked.

"It's…I'm supposed to…" Damn. What was I supposed to say? *My therapist wants me to ask you to hang out with me?* That was a major loser line if I'd ever heard one. "It's Friday."

The smile still sounded in his voice. "It is Friday."

"So…it's movie night."

"That's right."

I couldn't force more words from my mouth, and Jackson swiveled in his chair again. His knees bumped mine and then rested there so we were touching.

"Is that all?" he asked.

His knees were warm—electric against mine. I dropped my chin. He had a hole in the toe of his sock. He reached out and touched my leg, making my breath catch.

"I wish you'd talk to me," Jackson said, voice low.

My heart beat so hard and fast I was sure he could hear it. There wasn't even a coffee mug to shatter to distract him. It was just me and Jackson in the Milky Way, our knees touching, and my mind whirling because his gaze wouldn't stop dipping to my lips.

"About what?" I asked.

"Anything. Everything. Zoe," he said when I continued to stare at his feet. "What were you going to say? About tonight?"

"We're watching a movie. Mae has—got one—you know, from that box. She, uh, it's a thriller or horror or something, and we're going to watch it tonight."

He smiled. "She told me."

"So, I know she already invited you, but I just…wanted to see if you'd come—I mean, if you're coming."

"You want me to stay?"

My breath rushed out, and I nodded.

Jackson smiled. "Good. I want to stay."

His fingers squeezed my leg. "Let's go over this one more time so we can finish and not have to think about homework the entire weekend."

"Good idea."

He stretched his legs under the desk, his foot nudging my stack of comics. I really needed a better filing system, but I liked to keep them handy so I could snatch one up and read it whenever my paper-folding muse vanished.

"Sorry," Jackson said, stooping to fix the pile. He stopped, staring at the comics.

Crap. Now he was *really* going to think I was a geek.

"You like comics?"

I swallowed. "Y—yes. Sometimes."

He glanced up with a slight smile. "You mind if I read one while you're doing your problems?"

"Uh…no. I mean, sure. Go ahead."

Then he was back to sitting too close and pretending not to watch me as I tried to figure out the value for *y* this time.

30.

JACKSON

Rogue was Zoe. Zoe was Rogue. They *had* to be the same person. The chess, the paper planets, the Marvel comics under her desk.

What was I supposed to do? Should I say something? No way. She had no idea who I was, so she didn't know about all the secrets. She didn't know I—Jackson, not BlackKNIGHT—was homeless, and right now I had to keep it that way. It was my only choice if I didn't want to get in trouble for running away from home. No one could know, because then it would mess up everything.

I'd just do one more test. Just to see for sure. And if Zoe was Rogue…I'd keep it a secret, which was probably better for both of us. Just keep my mouth shut, and she'd never know.

I told myself it was better this way. I couldn't take such a huge risk right now.

Mrs. King had ordered enough pizza to cover the entire surface of their large island, though she insisted she could have made it just as well as Giuseppe's. I was pretty sure she almost had a coronary when Mae used the paper plates that were delivered with the pizza instead of something more civilized.

But she took it in stride and reminded us there were brownies for after dinner. And that she made some flavored popcorn for the movie. She also had ice cream and a myriad of other snacks she'd just "whipped up" that afternoon.

I knew better. I'd been at her house all afternoon, and she'd been baking nonstop, singing along to music Mae had turned on to pass the time.

Unfortunately, once Kelly and Robert arrived, Zoe had hardly said two words. More than once, I saw her glance longingly to her study.

"Let's eat outside," Kelly suggested, grabbing her plate and heading for the balcony.

Beside me, Zoe's entire body tensed.

"I'll sit next to you," I offered, giving her arm a nudge. Trying to relax as hard as I was trying to get her to relax. She had no idea I was BlackKNIGHT. No reason to worry. "I'll distract you."

Her eyes widened, making me grin. The others had already walked outside to a warm evening and the sun close to the horizon.

"I…" Her mouth opened and closed.

"Please?"

Her gaze dropped to the single slice of pizza on her plate. "Okay."

We walked together to the back door.

"Why don't you ever wear your glasses?" I asked as we stepped outside.

"Uh…" Her plate wobbled and she laughed. "It's—I—I don't like them. And…they always fall off when I wear them and do my paper stuff. I need new ones, but…"

"That would mean leaving the house."

She stopped walking, blinking up at me with a pained expression.

"I'm sorry," I said. "I just…want to know." Did she *ever* leave the house? She had to, right? Life still went on regardless of our situations.

But judging by what Rogue had told me, things were more serious than I would have guessed. It almost wasn't fair that I knew things about her that I shouldn't, but it wasn't my fault. She gripped her plate with her other hand to stop the shaking, but it didn't help. She looked away, and I barely heard her say, "I want you to know."

I almost grabbed her hand right there to tell her we could talk inside. In her safe room. But that probably would have embarrassed her even more, so we both sat at the table as the last of the sun's warm rays dashed across our faces.

Kelly started talking about colleges right away, dominating the conversation with her enthusiasm over the dance program at the university she'd chosen. It was easy for me to lean toward Zoe and lower my voice to have our own conversation.

"Are you okay?" I whispered.

She picked at her pizza, glancing up in surprise when she heard my voice. Her dark brown eyes held an ocean of emotions.

Her head bobbed in a short nod.

"You should try to eat." I didn't know what else to say, except that eating seemed like a good idea. She rarely seemed to eat anything, now that I thought about it.

"I'm trying." She put a bite of pizza into her mouth.

"So that meteor shower…it's next week. I want to watch it."

She glanced over at me. "You should."

I smiled. "There's a proper way to watch a meteor shower."

Another bite. Good. Progress.

"How's that?" she asked.

"One, you have to have company. Or else it's like the whole tree falling in the woods thing. It's like it never really happened." She angled her head at me so I continued. "Then you have to have a place to watch. A rooftop or wide field. Somewhere dark, open, and preferably where you can put a blanket."

She smiled.

"And finally, you have to have drinks and snacks because you have to be able to endure several hours of this. Meteor showers aren't a short undertaking. Or an early one."

By now, she'd finished half her pizza as the rest of the group argued over colleges.

"When does it start?" she asked.

"Probably the earliest you even want to consider going out is midnight. I think this one will peak at two or three."

Her eyes widened. "That's late."

"That's early." I reached out, touching her arm just briefly. "So, I think we should do it. Watch the meteor shower."

I didn't miss the shift in her position. The way her entire back went straight and how she dropped her pizza back on her plate.

"Jackson," she whispered.

Before I could argue my point, Robert interrupted.

"Jackson! Hey."

I glanced over at him. "What?"

"College. You're all set, right?"

I abandoned my pizza as well, brushing my hands together and telling him the truth, though it still felt like a lie. "I'm all set. I need more scholarships, but otherwise, I'm good to go."

Mostly. I didn't have as much as I wished I did, which meant financial aid. And financial aid made things more complicated. But what choice did I have?

"Must be nice," Kelly said.

"I'm working on it." I shrugged. "Working to save up money."

It wasn't just classes. I had to pay for housing and books and food. Transportation if necessary. My mom had been helping me save for it, but my dad had spent it all in one evening.

Robert snorted. "That's what loans are for."

"For debt?" I asked, forcing a grin at him. "Good luck with that."

But I knew he wouldn't be in debt. His parents could afford to send him to college. And the same with Kelly's parents. Mae's, too. They were probably smart enough to have been saving for years.

Even my mom, who'd barely made enough money to keep our household running, had planned for me to go to college. *I'll work two jobs if I have to*, she'd said. *I'll rent an apartment close to campus so we can all live together and save on the dorms. Whatever it takes.*

It was her dream. And my dad had ruined it. Now…I couldn't imagine going into debt for school. Or for anything. But what choice did I have? I couldn't do what my mom wanted for me and manage to pay for it all. I couldn't balance so much, and it killed me to admit that to myself, but it was there. Always in the back of my mind.

I shrugged again. There weren't words.

To my surprise, Zoe touched my hand under the table. "I could help you apply for more scholarships."

I looked at her. "Meteor shower."

She narrowed her eyes at me, but I saw the amusement there.

"What's the movie?" I asked, buying her time to answer. Buying myself time to get my shit together.

Distracted, Mae leaned in close to the lantern on the table and said, "It's a slasher film. One that takes place on prom night."

Robert groaned. "I didn't bring any Twizzlers."

Zoe gave him a blank look.

"I didn't bring Twinkies, either," I said.

Mae shook her head. "Doesn't matter. This time, the loser can clean up our mess. And I plan on being messy."

"This is going to take more pizza," Kelly said.

Mae decided we should start the movie right away. I wasn't sure if it was because she saw how uncomfortable Zoe was, or if she was just excited to watch.

Slasher movies were the best. It gave everyone license to yell and throw popcorn at the screen and groan at the bad special effects, and no one judged you. It also gave Zoe a reason to have to sit on the couch, next to someone (who I was going to make sure was me) she could hold on to during the scary parts.

We all brought our food inside, and when Zoe wandered to the kitchen, either to refill her glass or take a breath, I followed along.

"Have you done this before?" I asked her as she rounded the counter.

She glanced back, surprised to find me there. "What?"

"Slasher movie night. Where we guess how many people get slashed."

"No. Mom doesn't like horror movies."

I smiled. "Then this is a very special occasion."

"With rules, apparently."

I set my cup next to hers, grabbed the Pepsi, and filled both cups almost to the rim. "Yes, there are rules, which I'm sure Mae will go over. She always does. Sit next to me."

She blinked. "That's a rule?"

I walked around the counter, stepping close enough without standing on her feet, which were covered in striped socks. "I should have asked. I'm sorry."

"You…" She dipped her chin.

"Zoe?"

When she didn't answer, I brushed her bangs from her eyes. She jumped, and I froze. "Is this okay?"

Her breath caught, but she nodded.

"Please don't be nervous around me." I let my fingers linger on her cheek before dropping my hand to my side. "I'm just…a regular kid."

"Not regular."

I smiled. "No?"

"Smart," she mumbled. "Confident. Nice." She met my eyes. "Definite college material."

"I'm trying," I said, feeling the pressure all over again.

"I could…help you."

I took her hand, deciding to lighten the situation. "What does that entail? Because I'm pretty sure I'm in."

She laughed, fingers squeezing around mine. "I'll think about it."

"And I'll convince you to do the meteor shower. I already know how I'm going to do that."

"How?"

I leaned in, brushing my cheek against hers to whisper in her ear. "I'd better not tell you right now. It'll make you blush."

She choked on words and surprise, and blushed anyway. Her eyes strayed to the hallway where her study was.

"You can do this," I said. "The movie. Unless you don't want to."

"No. I mean, yes. I want to." But she glanced to her study again. "I'll be right back."

She vanished before I could say anything. But when I

heard a familiar beep from my phone, I pulled it out and saw a message from Rogue2015.

As we exchanged a brief conversation, my mind boggled. I couldn't believe it. Rogue really *was* Zoe. But still, I reminded myself, she had no idea who I really was. She didn't know I was homeless.

And I planned on keeping it that way.

31.

Rogue2015: Sorry, only one move tonight.

BlackKNIGHT: Hot date?

Rogue2015: Wow, you don't hold back, do you? I'm going to have to take your knight because of that.

BlackKNIGHT: You don't hold back either. I knew you were going to do that, though.

Rogue2015: Sure.

BlackKNIGHT: You know, you don't have to tell me if you have a date.

Rogue2015: I don't have a date.

BlackKNIGHT: I'm not sure I believe you.

Rogue2015: Try.

BlackKNIGHT: ☺ I'm working on it. I'll try not to be jealous.

Rogue2015: Funny. I can hear your sarcasm through the computer.

BlackKNIGHT: No sarcasm here. I can understand why someone might want you all to himself.

Rogue2015: You're delusional.

BlackKNIGHT: You're going to miss me.

Rogue2015: It's just a movie with some friends.

BlackKNIGHT: Wait. Is *he* going to be there? The boy?

Rogue2015: Yes.

BlackKNIGHT: See? I told you he wants to know you.

Rogue2015: It's just a movie.

BlackKNIGHT: What movie?

Rogue2015: A slasher film.

BlackKNIGHT: Scary. Have fun!

Rogue2015: I will. Good night.

BlackKNIGHT: You're missing me already.

Rogue2015: Good night!

32.

ZOE

The grin wouldn't leave my face. First, Jackson and his words, his steady gaze and his warm fingers. And then BlackKNIGHT. It was something I'd never had before. Someone who was interested in me romantically and as a friend.

Gina's social experiment was working out pretty well.

On my way to the living room, I ran into Dad in the hallway.

"Hey," he said, keeping his voice low. He glanced to the living room. "Sounds like you're having fun."

I nodded. "We are."

"So…everything okay?"

By everything, I knew he meant my anxiety. He'd never seemed to understand it before. But since Gina had started coming, my dad had been around more, too. It was kind of nice he was acknowledging how hard this was for me. How hard it had been.

"I think so," I said. He nodded, looking uncertain. "It's getting there."

"Best we can hope for sometimes, right?"

"Right."

We passed in the hallway, and I walked the rest of the way to the living room.

Mae stood in front of the large television, the remote in her hand. Robert occupied Dad's chair in the corner, and Kelly curled up on one end of the couch with Jackson on the opposite side.

Plenty of room for me directly in the middle. Embarrassment started to creep in again.

I thought I heard Jackson chuckle, but I didn't look at him.

"All right." Mae gestured to the screen. "What we have right here is prom night from hell. There will be blood, there will be cheesy lines, and there will be death. No candy bets this time. Loser, the one furthest from getting the right answer, cleans up the mess and that's it. Zoe, your job is to guess how many people get slashed—"

"Or killed in any way," Robert said.

Mae nodded. "Place your wager. How many people are going to die on prom night?"

"Six," Kelly said immediately.

Robert glanced at her with a laugh. "Seriously? You have far too much faith in the average American teen slasher film. There are typically at least two deaths due to stupidity."

"The hilarious sidekick friend with goofy glasses always dies, too." Mae smiled sweetly at Jackson. "No offense."

He laughed and shoved a hand through his already unruly hair. "No offense taken. Because you're right." When he lowered his hand, it rested between us on the crack of the cushions. "I'm going with ten."

My heartbeat picked up. I didn't miss Mae's secretive smile or the way my body responded to Jackson's hand just inches from mine.

Robert considered for another minute, then said, "A dozen. Seven girls and five guys. Maybe a cat."

"You're disgusting," Mae answered. "I'm saying nine. Right in the middle. Zoe?"

Everyone looked at me. My heart pounded. "Seventeen."

"Holy shit," Robert burst out, making me tense. "This isn't a shark movie."

Then everyone laughed, and my hands curled tightly at my sides. Every noise around me sounded louder. My cheeks burned hotter.

"I like the way you think," Robert continued.

For a moment, I still couldn't breathe. Then I realized none of them were laughing at me. They were just having fun. And who cared if I said a high number? That's what Gina would tell me.

I ventured a smile at Jackson.

He said, "Shark movies always have a higher body count."

I nodded like I was fully aware of this.

Mae walked to the same chair Robert sat in, plopped right in his lap, and started the movie. Her position made me overly aware of how close Jackson was to me. That I'd only have to scoot a foot to the left and our thighs would touch. I craved that contact so badly, but I was too afraid to do anything but watch the movie.

The opening credits already provided enough blood to make Robert cheer, and when a cat ran around the house in the first scene, he said, "That cat's a goner."

We all groaned. Kelly threw popcorn at him. I leaned forward to grab my drink off the coffee table and take a sip. When I leaned back, Jackson's arm was there, warm and solid behind me.

My throat dried. I wanted to reach for my drink again, but at the same time I didn't want to move. I was afraid he'd take his arm away.

As the movie continued, I relaxed, sinking into the

cushions. When the main character walked to her car alone after a school pep rally, Jackson booed her, and Mae threw popcorn at the screen.

"Next thing you know, she's going to trip," Mae said.

Sure enough, the main character glanced over her shoulder when she heard a noise, started running, and promptly tripped, twisting her ankle.

Kelly snickered. "Dumb move, Alisha."

"I don't think she's going to make it," Jackson said to me.

"Not at this rate," I answered, shooting him a grin.

He pulled his arm from behind me and clasped my hand in his, keeping his eyes on the screen. I held my breath, absorbing the strength of his fingers. And soon, it was normal again. Jackson next to me, with his hand around mine. I could almost picture going out with him at night to see the meteors. Lying on a blanket under the stars and being a regular teenager.

Halfway through the movie, Kelly was out of the game. Mae shot me a smile and gave me a goofy thumbs-up when she saw Jackson's hand linked with mine, making me roll my eyes.

Soon Mae and Jackson were out of the running as well, and we were rooting for people to die so I could win. It was horrible to cheer when someone died, but I wanted to win. This was one of the best nights of my life.

"If you get one more, you'll be closest," Jackson said when I leaned forward on the couch.

"Dude," Robert said with a laugh. "The chick is the only one left. They're not going to kill off the main character."

"There's still that geeky cop," Kelly reminded us.

Mae threw popcorn toward the couch. "Shh!"

The killer came around the corner with a knife. Jackson moved his hand to my knee, fingers warm when he squeezed.

The cop appeared out of nowhere and the killer knocked the gun out of his hand. We cheered when Alisha, our heroine, grabbed the gun.

"Shit. She's going to kill him," Robert said.

Mae smacked his arm, glancing to the hallway which led to my parents' bedroom. But they hadn't come out so far despite our ruckus. Either they were somehow sleeping through this, or they had their own television up loud enough to block out most of Robert's cursing and the general mayhem of homicide.

After a few cheesy last words, Alisha aimed the gun and fired. She got the killer in the arm, and he stumbled. She fired off another shot. The killer collapsed in a heap. Her shoulders drooped in relief, and she dropped to her knees, letting the gun clatter to the floor.

"He's not dead," Jackson and I said at the same time.

He grinned at me and proceeded to run his finger in slow circles on my knee. My heart hummed.

As expected, the killer wasn't dead. In a last burst of unnatural and bloody vengeance, the Prom Night Slasher jumped on Alisha, using his bare hands to strangle her. But the cop came to the rescue, saving Alisha and retrieving the gun to shoot the killer in the forehead.

"Nice," Kelly said.

Jackson and I cheered at the same time Robert cheered.

"Dude," Jackson said to him. "You didn't win. Why are you celebrating?"

He dislodged Mae from his lap and stood, shaking his head. "He was the killer. He doesn't count."

Kelly stood as well. "The rules say anyone who dies. We count every single dead body."

"No way! He's the one doing the killing."

Mae stood, raising the remote to get our attention. "Vote."

Robert groaned.

"Quiet," Mae demanded. "All those who think the killer dying counts as a dead body?"

Everyone but Robert raised their hands.

Mae grinned and looked at Robert. "All those opposed?"

With a growl, Robert scooped Mae up and threw her over his shoulder, declaring, "I need ice cream!"

Her laughter rang out as they raced to the kitchen.

Kelly sighed. "I bet six people. I lost. Bad."

She started collecting plates and then the popcorn on the floor. I stooped automatically to help her, and Jackson followed, getting to his knees on the carpet.

"You won. You don't have to clean," he said, stacking cups on the coffee table.

"I don't mind." When he snatched a plate before I could grab it, I smiled at him. "Does the winner get anything?"

"You get to pick the next movie," Kelly said, grabbing another handful of popcorn off the floor.

Jackson leaned back on his heels. "Mae's won the last three times in a row, so we're all secretly very happy right now."

He took off his glasses to clean them on the hem of his shirt, and I watched those long, deft fingers as they rubbed circles on the lenses. My throat dried. I had a mouthful of words for him, but I couldn't say any of them.

"I'm not that blind," he murmured. "I can see you staring at me."

I straightened, blushed, and then stood, mumbling, "Sorry," before grabbing a stack of plastic plates and turning toward the kitchen.

"Zoe, wait," Jackson said, hopping up and hurrying after me. "It was a joke."

Kelly plucked the plates from my hands, leaving me completely useless.

"Come outside with me," Jackson suggested. "Just to the balcony."

"Ice cream." Now I felt like an even *bigger* idiot. "I mean, Mae probably needs help."

"You can't help her."

"What? Why?"

"Those are the rules. If you win the body count game, you're not allowed to do any work. We just let you help clean up the popcorn and plates because this is your first time. You're not allowed to do any work for the rest of the night."

"But—"

"Yeah, you probably shouldn't argue. Rules are rules, right? And you don't want to break the rules."

When he smiled at me, I definitely *did* want to break the rules. He was making it sound so enticing. In fact, right now I wanted to do whatever Jackson said because I just wanted to be with him.

"Outside," Jackson said again, grabbing my hand. "Please."

I let him tug me to the back doors, out to the tepid night air with lights all around us. I could see the glow from Coors Field, where there was some kind of event tonight, and Pepsi Center, which was putting on a throwback concert. Farther in the distance, I spotted the lights from Elitch's, which used to be a Six Flags amusement park, and Invesco Field where the Broncos played.

I'd hardly been to any of these places. Until recently I hadn't minded. Now, with Jackson standing next to me, I felt like the world was beckoning. It was a huge, blank piece of paper, just waiting for me. The possibilities were endless, and I was stuck.

"You look sad," Jackson said.

I dug deep for courage and walked to the ledge of the balcony. The wind ruffled my hair as I stared across the city.

I still couldn't find words. Sometimes feelings were too big for words.

Jackson stood next to me. "You're a natural."

"At predicting the murderous tendencies of a homicidal maniac?"

He nodded. "Smart, too. I'm lucky."

I ducked my chin and tucked my fingers in the sleeves of my light T-shirt. "Why?"

"You haven't kicked me out yet, even though I keep torturing you with math."

"Well," I mumbled. "You *are* pretty good at it."

He laughed. "Torturing? Or math?"

"Math."

Jackson angled his head. "Are you cold?"

"No."

"You're shivering."

Nerves. Fear that I'd mess up the night somehow. Or fear that this whole day would crumble around me like it had never happened. Or fear that it all *had* happened and it never would again because I was too terrified to live my life.

Jackson shifted so his back was against the ledge. He reached for me. I almost tripped over his feet as he pulled me closer, but Jackson didn't seem to care. He just held on tighter, arms around my waist.

"Tell me," he whispered.

I couldn't stop shivering, but I laid my cheek against his chest, curled my hands up to rest on his soft shirt, and closed my eyes. "It sounds so stupid when I say it out loud."

"You want me to go first?" he asked.

Startled, I opened my eyes. Jackson's hand touched my hair, brushing his fingers down the length of it in the back, making me close my eyes again.

"I used to look for you," he said. "Whenever Mae would

invite me over, I'd look for you because I wanted to talk to you. I wanted to see you. So I'd make excuses to go to the bathroom or get more water from the kitchen, hoping I'd run into you."

"Really?"

His laughter rumbled in his chest. My heart danced in happy circles, even as my stomach churned with doubt.

"See?" he asked. "That sounds stupid saying it out loud, too, but it's a fact. I wanted to see you, and I guess that doesn't embarrass me because it's just feelings. It's…" I heard him swallow, felt the tension in his body when he continued. "My mom used to really live for the carpe diem mentality—she said life was too short to miss out on it."

"Jackson…" I whispered. I'd forgotten about his mom. No, I'd set it aside. I hadn't known Jackson well back then. I'd felt so bad for him, and then had to tell myself there was never anything I could do for him because I never saw him. Besides, I couldn't even help myself.

"Your turn."

I tipped my chin, looking up at his face. I wanted to know more about his mom. I didn't want to talk about me; I wanted to know Jackson. I wanted more. "I bet you miss her…"

"I can't talk about that right now," he said.

I dropped my chin again, my heart breaking for him. "I'm sorry."

"Don't apologize. Please. You're being yourself, and that's never something to apologize for."

I tucked my hands against my chest as Jackson squeezed his arms tighter around me, blocking the wind.

"I'm scared to go outside," I murmured. "I…okay, I'm scared of just about everything, but mostly social situations. Talking to people. Being around people. Going places that—that make me uncomfortable, which is basically everywhere.

I'm…I'm worried what I'm going to say is wrong—that everything I do is wrong."

His hand brushed my hair again. "How long has it been since you left your apartment?"

"I checked the mail," I said, trying at a joke. "You saw me. So, not too long."

I heard the smile in his voice when he said, "Before that."

"Over a year."

"You haven't gone out at all? Not for doctor's appointments or for a walk?"

Dread spiked through me. This was why I hadn't wanted to say anything. Now he knew what kind of person I was. How ridiculous it was that I was scared to even take a walk in my own city.

"It's stupid, I know." I eased back. "I can't help it."

"Zoe," Jackson said.

A thousand emotions traveled across his face.

Thankfully, Mae appeared at the door. "Plain ice cream?" she asked, holding up a plastic cup. "Or a root beer float?"

I shook my head, walking to her with a forced smile. "No, thanks." My stomach twisted into a hard knot of stress. "I don't feel very well."

Mae's eyes met mine, understanding in their depths. It wasn't the first time she'd heard those words. She usually questioned them or said something like, "It's all in your head."

In a way, it was. If I could just control my thoughts, my worries, the world, I wouldn't feel like this. But I was out of control, and there was nothing left but to shut myself in my room until it all went away.

Jackson followed us back inside, but I couldn't meet his eyes. I said good night to everyone and hid in my bedroom, sitting on the floor with my back against the door until I heard their voices fade and I was alone again.

Why couldn't I be more like Mae or Jackson, free to say whatever I was feeling?

Because I was just Zoe, and most of the time I didn't even know who *she* was.

33.

JACKSON

Curfew for minors in Denver was midnight on Fridays, so I didn't dawdle when I took the bus back to the light rail station where I'd parked my car. The police seemed to have better things to do with their time than fine a teenager minding his own business, but still. I didn't need any unwanted attention from the authorities. Which was also why I hadn't told anyone else about leaving my dad's house. Now, Robert knew—sort of—and I'd almost told Zoe tonight.

It was only fair, right? I knew her secret; I should tell her mine, too. Or that I knew she was Rogue2015. After all, she'd told me so much about herself online without knowing it was me. But then we'd both be exposed. She'd know I knew all about her little quirks and probably retreat back into her shell, and she'd know I was homeless. I could deal with the fallout of that if I had to. But hurting Zoe? That wasn't an option.

I chose a dark street to park on, knowing I needed to get to sleep soon if I was going to be up before sunrise to move my car. But my mind wouldn't slow down.

When I pulled out my phone, the message from my father

was still there. Unheard. It made me think about my mom and missed opportunities. It made me think about Zoe being too afraid to do anything outside her apartment.

But Dad had his chance and he blew it. I'd stayed even though he hadn't been there the night my mother died. I'd stayed the first time he'd gone to rehab. I'd stayed when he screamed about how he never should have had a kid. But after a while, it had been too much.

I squeezed the phone so tight it popped from my hand and tumbled to the floor at my feet.

Grumbling, I retrieved it and checked *Chess Challenge*. Nothing from Rogue. Zoe.

I missed them both.

With another heavy sigh, I climbed into the back seat, pulled on a sweatshirt, and stared at my phone. Then I pressed the button to listen to the message and turned the speaker on.

"Jackson, it's Dad. Austin. I, uh…" His sigh traveled through the phone, and it sounded weary. "I wanted to talk to you. To…see if you might want to come back home. I got in a little trouble." I almost hung up right there. Of course. He was in trouble. But then he continued in that same weary voice. "It was a while back and—and I had to do some rehab and now…well, now it's been six months. No, six and a half, which—well, that probably doesn't matter to you. It's—there are steps—and—"

He broke off again, sounding tired.

"Okay," Dad said. "Look. I messed up. Bad. And a lot. And your mom…" His voice lowered to almost a whisper. "She'd hate to have seen me the way I was. I don't want to disappoint her. I really loved her, even if it didn't seem like it. Give me a call if you want. Or stop by. I have a job, but I'm home in the mornings or afternoons. And I can make dinner or pick something up. Whatever. I fixed the washing machine."

I let out a reluctant laugh. It was so random, but it showed he was trying. Dammit. I didn't want him to try. Because then I'd feel like a dick for not trying, and I wasn't sure I was ready to go there yet. Or again. Or ever.

I lowered the phone to my lap when the message ended. Outside the window, headlights appeared down the street. I sank lower in the seat, trying to hide my shoulders under window level and keep my legs crunched up.

I saw the rack with lights on top and held my breath, waiting for them to start flashing red and blue. I was already coming up with an excuse in my mind, hoping it wasn't the same cop who'd caught me in my car last week.

After a moment, the cruiser drove away. I released my breath and stretched my legs as much as possible. I fit in this car just about as well as an elephant fit in an elevator. I'd had lots of sleepless nights in this back seat, but not as much once the weather started getting warmer. Then, I didn't need dozens of blankets. Then, I didn't see my breath fogging up the window. Sometimes I could even see the stars. I'd roll down the window and name the constellations like my mom used to, and things would be okay.

Lonely, but okay.

If she were here now, I know what she'd say. *Call your dad.*

"Nothing's changed," I mumbled.

He's trying.

"Because he fixed the washing machine?" My laugh was hollow.

That, and because he cared enough to call. Family is important.

I sighed. I knew family was important. But Mom had been the one holding our family together. She'd fallen in love with a different version of Dad, one I didn't know. One who had left when I'd been a little boy.

I didn't even know him anymore. Didn't know if I *wanted* to know him.

Even when things get hard, you still have to try.

I couldn't argue with that. Mom hadn't given up even when it was close to the end. If I gave up on school or Dad or anything, really, I knew I'd regret it. But that still didn't make things easier.

Easier would be standing with Zoe in her solar system right now, holding her hand and pretending the outside world didn't exist.

Phone still in hand, I pulled up her number. It was after midnight, but I hadn't left her house too long ago. Maybe she was still awake.

I texted her. Are you asleep?

Closing my eyes, I let the phone rest on my chest while I waited for her to get back to me. I'd started to doze when I felt my phone buzz. I jerked awake and read her message.

Not yet.

I could hear the soft sigh in her voice, picture her lying in bed with her bangs half eclipsing her eyes. I could feel the smoothness of her hand, how it fit so perfectly in mine, and smell the jasmine in her hair as she pressed close in a vulnerable hug, her nerves racking her body in shivers.

I typed a quick message. Are you okay?

When she answered back, her message was just as brief. I'm fine.

I could also hear the lie in the words. She was probably biting her lip or dipping her chin to stare at her hands. Probably wishing I'd just leave her alone. Maybe I should. But, God, it was like when my mom had died and I just had to sit there and take it. I didn't want to hang back and let this go. I wanted her to know how important life was.

There was a whole world out there. Mountains and trees

and meteor showers and Horse on Chair, and Zoe was in *there*, afraid to open up. It felt like my job to help her. To show her that she was bigger than all this. And that she meant enough to me I wanted to get her there.

Wherever "there" was.

So I tried again. Can I come by tomorrow?

It's the weekend. Do you have more homework for me?

I smiled. Work, yes. But not at home. I wanted to take her somewhere. I wanted to convince her to see the meteor shower. I wanted to bring her to the library.

I'd still like to see you, I texted.

I don't know. I have to help my mom with holiday cards.

Holiday cards? Of course, Mrs. King was always prepared for anything. She was living her life months in the future, prepped for the next holiday, the next big family gathering, the next seventeen meals, probably the apocalypse.

I tapped my finger on the knee of my jeans. Zoe was trying to avoid me. Because she was scared. Because she'd told me her secret.

I wrote another message but hesitated to send it. I didn't want to push her, so I was just going to have to be patient. I'd feel her out with a *Chess Challenge* conversation tomorrow morning, and maybe she'd feel better.

I'll talk to you soon. Good night, Zoe.

Good night.

I'd be patient, but I needed to help her. I needed to be there for her the way I hadn't been able to be there for Mom. Just another reason to keep my identities separate. It was better for everyone all around.

34.

BlackKNIGHT: I've got this.

Rogue2015: What have you got?

BlackKNIGHT: This game. I'm going to dominate.

Rogue2015: Sorry, *Chess Challenge* doesn't have an emoji of me laughing in your face, so this is the best I can do: ha ha!

BlackKNIGHT: Don't be so quick to dismiss my prowess.

Rogue2015: Well, it is true that you are currently ranked at number 4 on the leaderboard.

BlackKNIGHT: Yeah, ZeldaLegend lost to GryffindorChessMaster (which in my opinion is too much of a mouthful to even be able to focus on a chess match), so I moved up.

Rogue2015: We're chess nerds, BK. You can't expect overwhelming creativity in a handle. But then…

BlackKNIGHT: What?

Rogue2015: I'm beginning to suspect you're not a chess nerd.

BlackKNIGHT: Why do you say that?

Rogue2015: I have a theory. It's fairly extensive. I'd bore you.

BlackKNIGHT: I'm intrigued. Tell me. I have the whole day.

Rogue2015: I thought you were going to dominate.

BlackKNIGHT: I'm working on that multitasking thing. It's...coming along.

Rogue2015: Very convincing. But I don

BlackKNIGHT: Rogue?

BlackKNIGHT: Rogue?

Rogue2015: Sorry, I need to go.

BlackKNIGHT: Make one more move.

(Rogue2015 just took your rook)

BlackKNIGHT: Not that move.

Rogue2015: ;) Keep practicing.

35.

ZOE

Even card making couldn't cheer me up this morning, though I'd made a pretty cute 3-D one with a firework exploding on the front for the Fourth of July. I left Mom delighted with the idea and figured she wouldn't notice if I holed up in my study to play a match with BlackKNIGHT. I'd actually started to feel better when Mae knocked on my door, coming in before I could even grumble out a response that might make her leave me alone.

Her gaze swept the room before stopping on the computer. "More chess?"

I finished my chat with BlackKNIGHT and shut the computer. I grabbed a comic off my desk and flopped into a beanbag chair on the floor. I had stopped right when Silver Surfer was trying to cure Bruce Banner of being the Hulk.

"What's going on?" Mae asked, standing in front of me.

I looked up, enjoying the way Saturn's moons hovered over Mae's head like she had two bulbous growths. "I made a Fourth of July card." I held up my comic. "I learned more about Galactus. I almost won a chess match on my computer before you interrupted me. Seems about normal, right?"

"I mean after last night. You and Jackson seemed to be getting along until…ice cream."

I laughed, though my heart felt heavier in my chest. "Ice cream. Yeah. I sort of…told Jackson about my issue."

She sat in front of me and crossed her legs. "And?"

"And what? That's a big deal."

Mae scratched her arm. "He kind of already knew most of it. I mean, he has to come here to tutor you. He knows you don't go to school, and he knows you don't really leave the house."

"I *never* leave the house. That surprised him."

She leaned in closer, staring at Silver Surfer. "Is he an alien or something? That can't be a costume."

I frowned. "*Mae.*"

She tore her eyes away from the comic. "Jackson is independent. He never talks about his dad or doing stuff at home. I think he pretty much takes care of himself. So, yeah, he was probably surprised you never leave the house because he *always* leaves the house. He goes places and talks about things he's seen and…" She pressed her lips together when she saw my expression. "That's not helping, is it?"

"No. It doesn't help to know that he *loves* being out there. And I'm…always in here."

"You might love being out there, too."

"I didn't love checking the mail."

"You haven't been out of the house in over a year, Zoe. You have to expect a transition period. Check the mail again today, and do something else. Go outside and watch people walk around. Call Jackson on the phone. Do something more. One new thing every day."

I narrowed my eyes at her. "Gina? Is that you?"

"Funny. I want you to come to my graduation. I want you to come back to school. You're going to miss everything if you don't."

I forced a shrug like it didn't really matter, but it was a knife to the heart because I wanted all those things, too, and I wasn't getting there fast enough.

My mouth dropped open when she stood, pointing her finger at me. "We all have to deal with scary shit in life, and the only way we get past it is by being proactive."

"Mae," I whispered, surprised at the steel in her tone.

"Didn't we have fun last night?"

I swallowed and nodded. "Yes. But…I don't know if I like this new tough love approach."

She grinned. "Well, Mom and Dad aren't doing it, are they? Do you really want to be living here when you're thirty years old? Don't you *dare* say yes—I can see you considering it. My point is, you need to live your life. You can visit Mom and make freezer meals, but you're going to need your own place eventually. You're going to need a job. You're going to want a boyfriend—a *husband*—a vacation! That's going to scare the crap out of you if you don't start preparing for it now."

"Preparing—"

"Yes, preparing. Building up courage. Not stressing, *acting*. Dealing. And learning how to cope."

"Oh my God." I stood also, setting the comic on the desk. "You aren't Gina, you're Dr. Edwards. You could choose any superhero, and you chose to disguise yourself as Dr. Edwards?"

Mae rubbed her temples. "Okay, I realize there are actually people out there who think it's cool to like all this comic book stuff, but you know you're never going to meet them if you don't go outside."

"That's completely untrue. They're all holed up in their rooms reading comics, too."

"What about that big convention they have in San Diego or New York or wherever?"

"Comic-Con. They have one in Denver, too. So?"

"So you're never going to go to it. Thor could be there."

"Gross."

She angled her head. "Captain America?"

"Meh."

"Jackson dressed as Mr. Fantastic?"

My cheeks flamed.

"Oh, oh, sweet sister, you have it soooo bad for Jackson. Or Mr. Fantastic. Or both. In his tight superhero outfit with those sexy glasses—Mr. Fantastic *does* wear glasses, right?"

"When he's Reed—and how the hell do you know anything about Mr. Fantastic?"

Mae laughed. "Touchy. I know about Mr. Fantastic because I watched *Fantastic Four* with Robert. He wanted to see it and—hello, tight superhero outfits. Duh. Zoe, come on, we're not all that different." Her smile widened. "Jackson *does* kind of look like Mr. Fantastic or whatever his real name is."

I narrowed my eyes at her.

"If you don't like him, tell him."

"That's not—I mean, I don't—" I took a breath, dropping my chin. "I *do* like…Jackson."

"You're going to be seventeen in a few weeks. If Mom and Dad aren't going to make you live your life, I am."

I couldn't help the pout in my voice. "You're not the boss of me."

Mae laughed so hard I thought she was going to double over in the beanbag chair. "You think that crap is—is going to work with me?" She laughed harder.

I sat calmly at my desk, arms folded, and waited for her to collect herself. By the time she looked up, tears were streaming down her face.

"Are you finished?" I asked.

She wiped her cheeks, face going serious in an instant.

"You think I don't know what it's like to be scared?"

I blinked.

"I had to move away from my friends when I'd finally gotten used to where we were living so Dad could come here and be the Car King. I was *there* when you had your first panic attack, and you think I knew what to do? I'm going to *college* this fall and I'm trying to figure it all out on my own. Dad is so busy with work, and Mom is so busy putting glitter on everything, she forgets sometimes that I even exist. And you're always in here, or with your therapists, or freaking out, and I don't know what to do!"

The blood drained from my face. I'd never heard Mae this upset before.

She crossed her arms, posture mirroring mine. "And guess what, Zoe? I'm not *allowed* to be scared because *you've* got a monopoly on that emotion. So, when I freaked out because Robert asked me to prom last year and I'd never had a boyfriend before, Mom was like, 'Well, at least you can leave the house. Zoe's too scared to go anywhere.' So..." She sighed, her voice going soft. "Yeah, it's like I wasn't allowed to be scared. It's stupid, I know, but small things happen like that all the time."

"You could talk to me," I whispered.

"Maybe if I learned to play chess, then you'd want me around. Or if I was a piece of paper."

Throat dry, I could only stare at her. She was right. I wasn't there for her. And Mom and Dad hadn't been there for her because they were always there for me.

"It's selfish, I know," Mae said. This time she was unable to meet my eyes. "But I don't want you to do this anymore. I want to go places with you, and I want you to be able to be there for me. I want it to be like it used to be."

She walked out of the room, leaving me alone with Silver

Surfer and guilt so heavy I couldn't even stand.

My phone rang. I looked at the screen through blurry eyes. I took off my glasses, wiped my tears, and put my glasses on in time for my phone to stop ringing.

Jackson.

My stomach clenched. Why was he calling? Now he was going to think I didn't want to talk to him because I hadn't answered and—

Taking a sharp breath, I forced myself to grab the phone. I called back Jackson's number, almost hoping he didn't answer.

"Zoe?"

I gurgled out a greeting he probably didn't understand, and then tried again with a calmer voice. "Hi. I'm sorry I didn't get your call in time."

"It's okay. How's card making going?"

"It's—fine. We're done. I'm…"

"What's wrong?"

My throat clogged. "I got in a fight with Mae."

"You want me to come over?"

"I…" Yes. Or I wanted to meet him somewhere. "You don't have to."

"That's not what I asked. I'm close. Can I come up?"

It felt like the world shrank around me, bubble-wrapping me in my paper room. After what I'd told him last night, I wasn't sure Jackson would want to see me anymore. Finally, I said, "Yes."

"Good. I'll see you in a few minutes."

I stood, shoving my phone in my pocket, and reached up to touch my glasses. Great, I'd forgotten my contacts again. Nothing I could do about that now.

Before I could change my mind, I walked to the elevator. Dad was at work even though it was a Saturday. Mom was still in her office working on Santas, and Mae was probably in her room—and I didn't blame her.

I slid on her Toms and got into the elevator. Step one: Press the button. Step two: Watch the numbers to keep my breathing even. Step three: Don't expect *anything*. Just breathe.

When the elevator released me to the lobby, I stood there for a long moment, searching for Jackson. I didn't see him yet, and someone bumped into my arm.

"Excuse me," she said.

"Sorry, sorry," I mumbled, clasping my hands together. I stepped out of the way, my back pressing against the cold wall. My lungs tightened.

Two deep breaths. It was a lobby. I lived here. I was outside of my apartment by myself and nothing was happening.

Jackson entered the building. He started toward the check-in desk, nodding to a woman who pushed a stroller.

Then his eyes locked with mine, and he slowed his pace. The concern there propelled my feet forward until I was walking as steadily as he was to meet at the awkward chairs in the middle of the lobby.

Jackson reached out, gripping my arm gently. "What are you doing down here?"

My chin wobbled. I told him honestly, "I wanted to see you."

His breath rushed out, and he wrapped his arms around me. "Are you okay? Should we go upstairs?"

I eased back, but Jackson kept one arm firm around my back, giving me tingles. I glanced to the elevator, unsure. "I don't know."

In my fantasy world, we ran away hand in hand, losing ourselves on a paper vacation.

He lifted his eyebrows. "You want to stay down here?" He looked around the lobby as if searching for somewhere safe. "We can sit."

"Here?" I stared at the slick leather chairs in the middle of the space.

He smiled. I melted. "Why not?"

"It's…in the middle. Everyone can see us."

"You think anyone cares what we're doing? Here, let's ask this nice old guy if he cares what we're doing. Excuse me—"

"No, Jackson. Please." I pulled on his arm, trying to turn him back to me. "Please don't."

"You're scary strong, Zoe. Okay, how about…" He pointed to the courtyard. "There? It looks quiet. And empty."

"Good. Yes."

I started in that direction, but Jackson captured my hand and walked with me. Some of my worries from last night slid away. Jackson was here. He wasn't judging me. Maybe he could understand.

In the courtyard, a fountain spouted water from a stone fish, and matching concrete benches surrounded dozens of planters. I'd never been here before.

When I saw that no one else sat outside, the knot in my stomach eased. Jackson led us to a bench near the fountain, close enough that water splattered onto the stone beside him, which he seemed to find amusing.

Good thing. I had no idea what to say to him. No. Wrong. I knew exactly what I wanted to say, I was just too afraid to say it.

Jackson scratched his chin. "Let's start with how…I'm grateful you told me what you did last night, even if I acted surprised."

"Surprised," I said. More like shocked.

His eyes crinkled. "You'd just told me that basically people are your kryptonite. That doesn't bode well for me."

I laughed. "Yeah, I guess…you could look at it that way."

"How do you choose to look at it?"

"Like…" I ducked my chin. Jackson's fingers linked with mine, the strength and warmth of them giving me an extra boost of confidence. "Like there's more for me than this. But also like…" *Pretend you're talking to BlackKNIGHT.* "Like it's okay to be me."

"I really like this Zoe," Jackson whispered. "But I see what you're saying. You want to be yourself, but be able to do the things that scare you, too. Be a Zoe who sees the world, who lives in it." He smiles. "And still be you."

My breath caught in my throat. So, he did understand.

"Yes." I looked up at him. Eye contact. "Will you help me?"

36.

JACKSON

"Of course," I told her. I wanted to help Zoe. I wanted to help her fix this. "I'll do whatever you need me to do. Why did you and Mae fight?"

Zoe stared at our entwined fingers. "She was—she was mad at me because I was scared to…" Her shoulders moved in a shrug. "Scared to talk to you. Or to do anything, really, and that I didn't understand her side of all this. How things have b-been for her. I…" Zoe looked up, eyes sad. "She's right. It hasn't been fair. And—and if I don't fix this, I won't be able to go to her graduation. And there's this paper exhibit at the art museum, but…"

Her cheeks turned red. "I'm babbling."

"You're talking." I wiggled her hand so she'd look at me. "People do that sometimes. It's called venting. It's actually therapeutic."

"I'd have to check with my therapist on that."

I nodded. "What do you think they'd say?"

"She'd say, 'Jackson's right, Zoe. It's okay to talk about your problems. We all have them.'"

"I have to say, I agree completely. What else does your

therapist say?"

"I n-need to take steps."

When she said it like that, it reminded me of my dad, of the steps he was supposedly taking to get his life back together. But I had far more faith in Zoe than I had in my dad, which was why I hadn't called him back yet.

"What kind of steps?" I asked gently.

She squirmed in her seat, pulling her hand away and brushing the bangs from her forehead. "Check the mail. Dumb, huh? *Do* things with people."

"So, I'm just an assignment. A step."

Her eyes flashed to mine. "No. Oh God, Jackson, that's not—"

"I was just joking," I said, giving her a smile. "Sorry. Was that one of your steps? Asking me to stay last night for the movie?"

Her fingers twined together. "I w-wanted you to stay."

"I believe you. I wanted to stay. I want…" I shoved my hand through my hair. I wanted more than that. I wanted a relationship with Zoe. I wanted her to know I was BlackKNIGHT. Then it would make sense why I already felt so close to her. I felt like I knew parts of her she was too afraid to share with me in person.

Zoe's eyes lingered on my face, wide behind her glasses.

I reached up and touched the rims. "I like these."

"Oh. It's—I forgot to put in my contacts. I…"

"I like them," I repeated. "So, steps. I like the idea of steps, too."

"Why? Steps are scary."

"Steps are exciting. Especially if you let me help. I get to…" I grinned. "I get to take you places. Outside."

"Oh, no…I don't know…" She stood from the stone bench, hair in her eyes again. "You saw what happened when I checked the mail."

"And then you still came down here to meet me in the lobby, which was incredibly brave, and it hasn't resulted in disaster yet."

"Yet."

I grabbed her hand as she started to back up, pulling her closer. She took small footsteps, stopping just an inch from my shoes.

"It might not be a disaster at all, you know." I took her other hand. "We might actually stay here longer without anything terrible happening. And then we might go back upstairs and make plans for those steps you were talking about. And when you clam up on me, we might play a game of chess to get you to relax again."

Her mouth parted, bottom lip jutting out farther than the top. Enough to distract me from trying to distract her. "You…"

I eased her closer, tempted to pull her into my lap. "What?"

"You're trying to make me nervous."

"I absolutely am not."

"Then what are you trying to do?"

"I'm trying to be straightforward with you. So you know how I feel. So you *won't* be nervous."

"It's hard."

"It'll be easier the more time you spend around me. Can I ask you something?"

She blinked. "What?"

"How did all this start? The anxiety?"

Her cheeks reddened. Her voice turned small when she said, "It's stupid. I—I always used to be nervous about things. My dad would always make me and Mae be in his car commercials—the producers said little kids help sell things. Mae loved it, but I was always doing it wrong and I *hated* it. I'd always feel sick beforehand and freeze up when the camera was on me. Anyway, I was supposed to do the last one halfway through the school day, but I had to go to school first because I had a speech to give—which I was already nervous about. I *hated* speeches, too."

I nodded, able to relate. "I hear you. Speeches suck."

"When I got out of Mae's car at school, I got my skirt caught in the door and it ripped a little. Mom was busy and couldn't come bring me a new one until later, so I had to safety pin it. It was so obvious. And then—then at lunch, I spilled orange juice all over my clothes—right before I was supposed to give my speech. I freaked out and found Mae to see if she'd let me borrow her shirt and she could just wear her cheerleading stuff, but I was so stressed and worried about the—the speech and the commercial that I had a panic attack right in the hallway. It was the first time, but it scared me to death. Mae, too."

"Zoe," I said softly. "I'm sorry."

"It's—it sounds dumb, but sometimes after that, when I was nervous about something, I'd have a panic attack. Or I'd worry so much about having a panic attack whenever I went somewhere, I'd have one before I even left. After a while, it was just easier not to go anywhere."

"Not dumb," I assured her. "Kind of a snowball effect, right?"

She nodded.

I opened my mouth to tell her I understood about things being overwhelming. Then I shoved away the image of my dad staggering through the house with a bottle of Jack in one hand. That wasn't something I could talk about now.

Her eyes dashed across my face, and then she jumped when she heard her phone beep. She pulled it out and frowned at the message.

"It's my mom," she said. "She's worried. I didn't tell her I was coming down here."

I stood with a nod. "We can go up."

Zoe glanced around the courtyard. "I'm not sure I want to."

Her words encouraged me. "That's a good thing. But, still, it was your mom. Is that okay? If I come up? We can make plans to go out again. Somewhere safe."

Her shoulders relaxed at the words. Safe. That was key for her. Somewhere she wasn't overwhelmed. It would be a good starting point.

Zoe let me take her hand easily this time, and we went upstairs together.

I stood in her study while she hunted down her chessboard. She'd added to her paper wall and the ceiling. Some of the shooting stars hung so low, they almost touched my head.

When Zoe returned, I pulled out my phone. "Can I take a picture?"

Her eyes widened.

"Of the wall."

"Oh. I guess. I mean, it's just a wall. It's—"

"Badass."

I took a few pictures, making sure I got a close-up of Saturn. It was my favorite. She'd even gotten the colors right.

"What else can you make?"

Zoe set the chessboard on the window seat in the sunshine and started setting up. "Lots of origami. Stars and boxes and birds and frogs."

"Will you make me something?"

She stopped placing the pieces. "If you want me to."

I nodded.

She walked to her paper stand and pulled out a red sheet. At her desk, she wound her hair up and shoved a pencil through it, exposing her long neck. I never wanted to leave this room again.

Then she straightened. "You're watching."

I pulled off my glasses and the room went blurry around me. I could still see Zoe's smile, though.

"Can you just…turn around?"

I obliged, replacing my glasses and studying the rest of the wall. "You think you're going to keep working on this? Or maybe try a new project?"

"Well…I want to finish all the planets, and I haven't done Earth yet. But I got really sidetracked with the…the meteors because they were fun…" Her voice trailed off in concentration. But, distracted enough not to notice how much she was talking, she continued without me prompting her. "But I'd *love* to do something big. A huge project. Like the Eiffel Tower or something. It'd be so hard, and I'd need tons of paper but…it would be fun."

So was listening to her talk. Her voice was light and high, like an adult telling a story to a child. I just needed to keep her comfortable so she'd talk to me like this all the time.

But how? Never look at her?

"Okay," Zoe said. "It's done."

I turned around, and she placed a small paper heart in my hand.

She blushed. "It's not—I mean, it's just because I just learned how to do it. Make a heart, I mean."

"I like it."

"If you—if you blow in the end, it'll pop open. You know, 3-D heart."

When I looked at the paper, uncertain, she plucked it from my hand and pressed the small hole at the end to her lips. She blew softly and the paper expanded. The heart filled with air.

She gave it back.

"That was really cool. You think I could do that?"

"Make a paper heart? Sure. There are a lot of steps, but once you figure them out, it's not too hard."

"You'll show me then. One day," I decided. "Can I keep this?"

"Sure."

I compressed the heart and stuck it in my wallet so I could keep it with me.

"Now, we play chess."

That seemed to relieve her. We sat on opposite sides of the chessboard, me at black and her at white. Just like how we always played on *Chess Challenge*, and my original inspiration for using the name BlackKNIGHT. More than once I opened my mouth to tell her I knew she was Rogue, and that I was BlackKNIGHT. More than once, I stopped myself.

"I didn't know you played chess so well," she said.

"You inspired me." I smiled when she made her first move. "That day on the bleachers."

"Really?"

"You were…committed." I moved a pawn and saw her smile. It was the same opening we'd just done on our last match. "Kind of like your paper wall. You don't do things halfway. You grab on and commit yourself to doing the best you can. Nothing less than dazzling."

"Nothing less than dazzling," she murmured, cheeks reddening. "That was kind of poetic."

"Just another kind of art. Like your wall. Like the heart."

She laughed, amused. "Rhyming, too? Now I'm impressed."

"I didn't mean to rhyme, but it worked. I think we should go to the museum and see the art exhibit. I saw a brochure at the library."

She knocked over one of her knights, then scrambled to pick it up. "You know how many people go to the museum?"

"A healthy number."

She choked on a laugh. "A healthy number? Jackson, you—"

"Wait, stop."

She froze, her fingers still on her knight. "What?"

"You don't say my name often. Just wanted to savor it."

"Oh God," she whispered under her breath. She moved her pawn.

I grinned. "Do it again."

"No."

Just like Rogue.

"Zoe. Say my name."

She ducked her chin. "Jackson."

"Will you look at me when you say it?"

"Demanding," she muttered, fingers plucking at a stray piece of lint on the window cushion.

"Please?"

Zoe took a deep breath, lifted her chin, and met my eyes. Her perfect lips formed one word. "Jackson."

"You're *very* good at that."

She looked away, blushing again. "I can't even be around you. I—I say things I shouldn't and you—you think this is normal for me. It's not. It's..."

"Life would be awfully boring if we were all the same. All 'normal.' That's what my mom always used to say, and she was right. I like that you're different. I like that I can tell you how I feel, because it doesn't make me self-conscious. And I don't care if you do things differently."

"Your mom sounds like she was cool."

"She was."

And she would have liked Zoe.

Zoe took the pencil from her hair, and it fell, straight and shiny, to her shoulders. "What about your dad?"

I was picturing reaching out to touch her hair, so her question caught me off guard. "My dad?"

She nodded, dropping her eyes again. "You don't talk about him much."

"No, I don't."

"Is he…is he like your mom?"

I moved another pawn. Not the best strategy, but I couldn't focus on the game now. "No."

"I'm sorry," she whispered. "We don't have to talk about him. How about your house? What's your house like?"

Shit. I didn't want to lie to her. Not after I just told her I liked that she was different. Not after she confided in me about her nerves. It wasn't fair.

"It's not…like yours."

She waited for me to continue.

"I just…don't have a good relationship with my dad." I watched her fingers brush the head of her rook before choosing her bishop.

Her lips pressed together, and she angled her head. Probably trying to make sense of what I'd said. Probably brimming with a dozen other questions she was either too polite or too scared to ask.

I reached out and took her hand, brushing my thumb across her knuckles. "After my mom died, my dad couldn't handle it. He started drinking—drinking *more*, I guess—and doing drugs."

"Jackson," she whispered.

I gave her a strained smile. "I liked it better when you said my name before. This feels like a pity 'Jackson.'"

"It's not a pity 'Jackson.' It's a…my heart hurts for you."

I thought of the little red heart in my wallet and wished

mine could be tucked away that easily, so I didn't have to feel.

But not now. Not with Zoe looking at me with wide eyes that could tear over at any moment. She cared.

It was right there. The words I was keeping from everyone but Rogue. *I moved out of my house. I'm homeless.* But I couldn't do it.

"Is it bad?" she asked.

I swallowed and looked away. "It has been. I try to stay away from the house as much as possible. I don't see him much."

Her lips parted. She glanced at the door, as if certain her mom would walk through right that moment and tell her what to say.

"I'd feel better if you don't tell anyone," I said. Then the whole truth *would* come out.

Zoe stood. "But this isn't right. I mean, it's not your fault. But your dad—"

"Zoe, shh. Please. Just…" I sighed and stood as well, so much taller than her I had to look down to meet her eyes. "Can we just keep this between us for now?"

"This makes me sad. Jackson…"

"That's better. I liked it better that time when you said it."

She looked up at me, eyes swimming. "I don't think it's funny."

"If this is going to be a problem, I can leave. I'm sorry."

"No. Damn." I smiled when she cursed, and she did it again. "Stop. I'm trying to think."

"You're cute when you think."

She backed up. "Don't say that. You distract me. Maybe… we could tell someone? My parents? They'd understand. Then maybe you wouldn't have to be there—"

"Zoe." She had no idea I'd already fixed that problem.

She stared at my feet. "This isn't good. Stop looking at

me like that."

"Close your eyes."

She glanced up. "What?"

"I don't want you to be so nervous. Not when we're talking about this. Not when I tell you what I want to tell you. Close your eyes."

She blew out a breath and shut her eyes. I took a step closer, touching her jaw. She stiffened, but her lips parted, almost like she thought I was going to kiss her.

I almost did.

But instead, I lifted her chin so I could see the sun on her face. "Zoe."

"Yes?"

"I like you. A lot. I want to keep tutoring you, and see the meteor shower with you, and take you to the museum. I don't want to talk about things we have no control over."

"But—"

"So, for now, let's forget this conversation."

"You can stay here. I'm sure my mom won't mind. At least—"

I put my hand over her mouth. "That's the opposite of forgetting. If I'd known I could get you to talk this much, I would've tried a new tactic earlier."

Her cheeks flushed. I stepped one foot closer, enough to feel her heart race against mine, and the warmth of her breath through my T-shirt. "I'll figure it out eventually. I will. But for now…just hold on."

So, she did. She wrapped her arms around my waist, and I kept more secrets from her because, for the first time, I wanted to live in Zoe's little paper world as badly as she did.

37.

BlackKNIGHT: It's been a while.

    Rogue2015: I've been busy.

BlackKNIGHT: Playing chess with other people?

BlackKNIGHT. Your lack of response indicates I'm correct.

Rogue2015: It doesn't indicate anything. Only that I've been busy. Like I said.

BlackKNIGHT: Playing chess with other people.

Rogue2015: Playing chess with regular people.

BlackKNIGHT: But not me, the irregular one.

Rogue2015: I *mean*, playing chess the regular amount with people I typically play chess with. For the most part.

BlackKNIGHT: Ahhh…

Rogue2015: This distraction technique might work on

most people, but it still isn't going to win you the match.

BlackKNIGHT: Sometimes I just want to talk.

Rogue2015: Then why are you on *Chess Challenge*? There's this thing called Facebook. And another thing called Twitter. In fact, I can think of a lot of places you could go to talk.

BlackKNIGHT: If I log onto Facebook, will you talk to me there?

Rogue2015: No. I can't. I'm here. Playing chess. But you don't have to play with me if you don't want to. I can start a new match with someone else.

BlackKNIGHT: I don't want that. There, I made my move. Now, talk to me, Rogue.

Rogue2015: That was a decent move.

BlackKNIGHT: Maybe the chess club at my school will win our state championship and then we'll have to play your school. Then we could meet.

Rogue2015: You're part of the chess club at your school?

BlackKNIGHT: Yes. Are you?

Rogue2015: I don't go to school. I'm homeschooled. It's your turn.

BlackKNIGHT: Oh. You must be smart. Like Chess Champion smart. ☺

Rogue2015: Not really. I'm terrible at math. I have a tutor. Still your turn, or I'm letting you loose on Facebook.

BlackKNIGHT: Okay. I went. A tutor, huh? Old guy with glasses?

Rogue2015: Old guy: no. Glasses: yes.

BlackKNIGHT. Ah, a young guy. Is he cute?

Rogue2015: Why? You interested? I could give you his number.

BlackKNIGHT: You have his number?

Rogue2015: This really is a Facebook conversation.

BlackKNIGHT: Okay, sorry. I'm focusing. It's just…I think you're kind of great.

Rogue2015: I think you're kind of great, too.

BlackKNIGHT: Great. All right. Your turn.

38.

ZOE

"Progress is scary," Gina said, "but good."

"I'm not sure… No, I don't think I agree about the good part."

She paced in front of the paper wall, one hand fluffing her hot pink scarf. "I don't see why not. If I would have told you last week or the week before you'd be leaving your apartment almost every day, you wouldn't have believed me."

"Just because I'm doing it doesn't mean it's progress. I don't even leave the lobby."

"You see other people. You watched a movie with your friends—"

"Mae's friends."

"Did it feel like they were her friends or did it feel like you were all friends?" She glanced over with a smile. "In a friendly environment?"

"Yes."

"To which?"

"Friendly environment," I mumbled.

"See? Progress. And I bet her graduation doesn't feel quite so scary now."

I debated this, but I had to agree. I could actually picture myself going there without having a panic attack.

"You're even more comfortable talking with me," Gina said.

"That's how it works." I pulled my legs up on the window seat with me. "Almost everything is easier once I get more comfortable."

"Precisely my point." She stopped pacing and faced me. "Going outside will become more comfortable. Leaving the building and talking to strangers will be more comfortable. Keep at it, and some of these things will start to come naturally."

I picked at the sleeve of my hoodie. "I guess."

Gina sat at the desk and folded her hands. "What else would you like to talk about?"

"Can't think of anything."

"I think we should talk about Jackson."

My head whipped up. Jackson. What did she know about Jackson?

"Tell me what that was all about," Gina said.

"Wh—what?"

"Your expression when I said his name. Your mom says you've been spending a lot of time together."

I couldn't stop thinking about what Jackson had told me earlier in the week. About his dad being an alcoholic. And maybe a drug addict. It was so unfair. Worse, I wanted to help him fix it and he didn't even want to talk about it.

It sounded like he and BlackKNIGHT had a lot in common. Maybe I just attracted people who were as messed up as me.

"He's tutoring me."

"Outside of your tutoring sessions. Evenings sometimes."

"I…" Yes, evenings, and phone calls at other times. Daily visits. Texts.

How was I supposed to answer this? I *loved* how much Jackson was here. He'd become as much of a safety blanket as my paper room. But was that a bad thing?

"Sometimes," I said.

"Are you happy to be spending so much time with Jackson?"

My mind went blank. What did she want me to say? What was the right answer here?

Gina smiled. "Zoe. Why do I always feel like you're trying to give me the answer I want to hear?"

"There's an answer you want to hear?"

"Clever. I think you know what I mean. There is no right or wrong answer, just your feelings." She smiled and snapped her fingers. "Let's play a game."

I tucked my knees up under my chin, narrowing my eyes. "What kind of game?"

"The yes or no answer game, where I ask a question and you answer as quickly as possible with your first, gut reaction."

"Sounds dangerous."

She grinned. "Sometimes honesty is. You want to play?"

Not really. And yes. "Okay."

She tapped her fingers against her lips, thinking, and then she nodded. "We'll start easy. Do you like math?"

"No. And yes."

"Hmmm."

"Well, I like—"

"No, you don't have to explain. Just give the first answer that comes to you. The most honest answer. Does going to school scare you?"

"Yes."

"Do you want to go to school?"

"Yes."

She continued without even blinking, even though I'd just admitted something that was probably better kept secret.

"Do you love playing chess?"

"Yes."

"Are you jealous of Mae?"

"Yes." I frowned. Damn it.

"Do you like Jackson as your tutor?"

"Yes."

"Does he make it easier for you to spend time with other people—including him?"

"I...I don't understand."

"Does he push you out of your comfort zone?"

I nodded. "Yes."

"Is it getting easier to step outside of your comfort zone?"

"Yes."

"Do you want to go to graduation?"

"Yes."

"Are you happy?"

"Ye—what?"

She smiled. "It's okay. You can think about that one. Lots of yeses, though. You're making progress. I think you should keep taking those steps. And if you are considering the idea of school, I think it would be smart to talk to your mom."

I stood up, my hands tucked into my sleeves. "I... School is a big step."

"These are all really big steps. And also steps I think you're capable of."

Some of them, yes. But I couldn't help but think of her other question. *Are you happy?* I was. I felt happy. Because of a lot of things in my life, not just the big steps. Part of me was starting to realize that I would never be the world's version of normal, and that was okay. I needed to take steps for the things *I* wanted to do, not what everyone else thought I should be doing.

Gina smiled again. Why did she keep doing that? "You're

making progress. I think it's time to leave the building."

"And go where?"

"Wherever you want. Go grocery shopping with your mom."

"Yuck."

"Yeah, but you need to trade off. Do mundane tasks, and then something you like. Go to the grocery store and then go to the art museum. Take a trip to the post office and then visit the library."

"Can I go with someone else?"

"Jackson?"

Why'd she say that? Maybe because she could see right through me.

She laughed. "Yes. But don't only rely on him. Go with other people, too. And soon…you can do it on your own."

"All by myself?"

"Anywhere Mae would normally go by herself, you should, too. This is great, Zoe." She nodded when I looked doubtful. "It means you're trying. It means you could be in school soon. It means you'll have your senior year if you want it, maybe even the rest of your junior year." Her smile widened. "Graduation. And prom."

"Yeah, I figured you'd say that."

After Gina left, I sat in the window seat in my study. Prom? Was she kidding me?

But part of me, the part that was getting used to trying new things, could almost picture it. I'd spent a lot of time worrying about things. Obsessing over them. But not much time really enjoying myself. Not at school, not with my family, and not with Jackson.

It was time I did something to change that.

39.

JACKSON

"Foul," Robert said. "That was a foul."

I laughed. "You wish. That was a fair point. Just accept it—don't be a sore loser."

Robert grinned and flipped me off before tossing from the three-point line. The basketball went in the net with a smooth swoosh, and then he cheered. "That would have tied it."

"In your dreams."

I scooped the ball from the floor to return it to the cart, dodging a few other players who were finishing up their own practice.

"You in a hurry?" Robert asked as he followed me to the locker room.

I deliberately slowed my pace. "No."

I didn't have to be at Zoe's until later, but I still wanted a shower and a chance to clean up. I also wanted to talk with Rogue on *Chess Challenge*. I wasn't sure why I still kept them separate—but mostly it was because we had different relationships. Rogue could be herself with me. Zoe couldn't. Zoe was there, real flesh and blood, and I wanted to get to know her, and Rogue was in cyberspace. I wanted both of them.

Robert punched my shoulder. "Liar. You're going to see her, right?"

"Her? Who?"

"Zoe."

"Later," I said with a shrug. We passed one of the billboards where I'd put a flyer for tutoring. I checked to see how many people had taken the number and nodded to myself.

Three.

Maybe one out of the three would call. But those weren't the only flyers I'd put up, so there was still hope. I needed the tutoring gig with Zoe for my scholarship, but I still needed others to save up more money.

"Uh…" Robert stopped at his locker and ran his hand on the back of his neck. "My cousin…he's not doing so well with math. Maybe—"

"It's fine," I said quickly, embarrassed that Robert had noticed me looking at the flyer. "I've got it figured out."

"No, really. He's failing and his parents are about to send him off to some military school or something because they don't know how to get him to bring up his grades." Robert shrugged, just as I had earlier, and dug through his locker so he wouldn't have to meet my eyes. "I thought if anyone could get through to him, you could. I know it's just eighth grade math or whatever, but it'd be a job, and it'd help out my aunt and uncle…"

I snagged a towel with a nod. "Sure. If it'd help them out."

"Good," Robert said. "I'll let them know."

That still didn't stop me from checking the rest of the flyers around the school before I left. Freshly showered and a little more sober from my conversation with Robert, I drove to Starbucks to use the wifi.

My stomach grumbled when I stepped inside and spotted the items in the pastry case. I didn't care so much about the coffee, but the banana bread used to be one of my favorites. I allowed myself to mentally tabulate how much spending money I had before steering myself to one of the tables well out of view of the pastries.

Spending money? I laughed to myself. What was that? Since when did I think I was allowed spending money? Besides, Mrs. King would probably have a whole counter full of food when I got there, and I'd make my stomach hurt from eating it all.

I still pulled a granola bar from my backpack, though, and tried to pretend it was banana bread as I set up my laptop. The *Chess Challenge* site came up, making me smile. It was something Zoe and I shared, even if she didn't know it.

Then my mom's voice popped up in my head telling me to be honest. To be a man.

She kept telling me other things, too.

You should call your dad. Let him know you got his message.

You should tell Zoe about being homeless. Then you won't be alone.

I know things are hard, but you can get through it.

She was a lot more optimistic than I felt sometimes.

When I saw Zoe was online, I tried to let that relax me.

Rogue2015 has initiated a match. Would you like to play?

I accepted the match and marveled how every move she made seemed to have a purpose. That's what chess was all about, wasn't it? I still had a lot to learn from Zoe. I didn't think it was so much that I didn't understand the technique. I think it was more about patience. I was so eager to watch it play out on the board, I didn't want to wait the three or five or ten turns it took to see it. But Zoe had that patience. She could see the bigger picture.

Call him.

It was my mom's voice again, nagging me about my dad. And damn, she was hard to ignore. I respected her. If she was telling me to call him, she was probably right that I should. But that didn't change how I felt toward him.

"I don't know how that's going to help the bigger picture," I mumbled, making another move on my virtual chessboard.

The lady from the next table over cast me a strained smile. One that said she was worried about sitting so close to a crazy person. She didn't have to worry about me. It was just one voice in my head, and it was perfectly sane.

Call him.

I fished my phone out of my pocket and stared at the screen for a long moment. When the lady continued to stare at me, I returned her smile. "Girlfriend troubles."

That made her smile widen. For a moment, I thought she might try to engage in a conversation, to help me fix my troubles. But after a second, she went back to her book.

With a deep breath, I pulled up my dad's number and pressed send before I could change my mind. The longer it rang, the more relieved I got. If he didn't answer, it wasn't my fault. I tried, it didn't work. Time to move on.

Then the phone clicked and I heard a voice. *His* voice.

"Hello?"

I opened my mouth but nothing came out. I couldn't think of anything I wanted to say to him, not even how angry I was with him.

"Hello?" I heard his breathing for a long moment. "Jackson?"

When he said my name, I hung up. My heart raced, making me glance around like everyone else might notice as well.

The lady next to me offered another smile. This time it

was sympathetic.

"I couldn't do it," I told her.

She nodded, probably assuming I was talking about my girlfriend.

"Give it time," she said.

I summoned a nod. Time. That's what my mom would say. Give it time. Keep trying. But right now, I didn't want to think about any of that. I wanted to be with Zoe.

When she started a conversation with me, I didn't hesitate to answer her. To put the world around me on hold. Not too much longer and I could go see her.

After another few moves, I turned to the lady next to me. "Can you watch my computer while I use the restroom?"

"Of course."

I took my backpack with me, winding around the line of people as baristas called out names for completed orders. Inside the bathroom, there was one man washing his hands. I nodded at him and waited until he was finished before propping my backpack on the sink.

Once I had the bathroom to myself, I pulled out my toothbrush and hurried to put paste on it. I stared at myself in the mirror as I brushed.

I'd called my dad. I'd taken that step. It was a start. I could say to my mom I'd done what she wanted. Sure, I'd frozen up, but it was still a step.

The door opened mid-brush. My eyes locked with the man who walked in. I was frozen just like I'd been hearing my dad's voice on the phone.

The guy lifted his eyebrows, and all I could do was stare. He knew. He knew I was homeless. And if he knew, who else did?

I gave myself a mental shake. No. This guy had no idea what was going on, and neither did anyone else. I'd covered my bases, hadn't I? I'd been careful.

I spit in the sink and tried to shrug like it was no big deal. "I'm going to see my girlfriend after this."

The man chuckled and disappeared into a stall. I finished my teeth quickly, zipped my backpack, and stepped into the hallway.

That was the second time I'd used a girlfriend as an excuse. Zoe. Is that what we were? A couple? I had no idea. All I knew was that I wanted to see her more often than not. And I planned on enjoying myself this evening despite the setbacks of the day.

I didn't have to hear my mom's voice to know that she was on board with that decision.

All except for the part about me keeping secrets from Zoe. But tonight was about enjoying the evening, right? Even the truth could be put on hold sometimes.

I stopped at the bulletin board to add one of my flyers and then returned to the table, where my laptop was sitting safe and sound. I thanked the woman and made one more move before I shut down the game to head to Zoe's house.

40.

Rogue2015: Where are you?

BlackKNIGHT: What?

Rogue2015: Where are you? I'm in my room, looking out the window. I always wonder where you are when we play.

BlackKNIGHT: I like to people watch, so I go somewhere with free wifi. And you're extra inquisitive today.

Rogue2015: Just curious. But you're right, it's none of my business. It's your move.

BlackKNIGHT: I didn't say it wasn't any of your business. I like when you ask questions. Then we're more than just robots playing a game. ☺

Rogue2015: It feels like that sometimes, doesn't it? But other times… Okay, where do you people watch?

BlackKNIGHT: I really want to know what you were going to say. Sometimes it feels like we're robots to me, too. But others…

Rogue2015: It's like talking to someone who knows you better than anyone else.

BlackKNIGHT: Exactly. I agree.

Rogue2015: Are you people watching now?

BlackKNIGHT: A little.

Rogue2015: Where?

BlackKNIGHT: Starbucks.

Rogue2015: Oh. You like their coffee?

BlackKNIGHT: Uh…actually, no. It's strange.

Rogue2015: Strange? Their coffee is strange?

BlackKNIGHT: Not *their* coffee. All coffee. I don't really like it. But their banana bread is killer.

Rogue2015: Wait, you sit in Starbucks and people watch, and use their free wifi, but you don't drink their coffee?

BlackKNIGHT: I exert my patronage in other ways. Hello, banana bread.

Rogue2015: LOL. Exert your patronage. Back to being a robot, I guess.

BlackKNIGHT: Did you ever think I might talk like that in real life?

Rogue2015: A 17-year-old boy talking like that? Never heard of it.

BlackKNIGHT: I'm extremely cultured. You have no idea.

And I practically live at the library, so you know, I'm surrounded by books all day. I can't help but be smart.

Rogue2015: A 17-year-old boy who practically lives at the library? Now I'm convinced you're a robot. Only a robot would say things like that and actually think I'd believe they were true.

BlackKNIGHT: Oh ye of little faith. One day you'll believe me.

Rogue2015: Maybe. Maybe not. But in the meantime… I'm about two moves away from checkmate. Although if you were a robot, you'd already know that.

BlackKNIGHT: I had no clue. You believe I'm not a robot now?

Rogue2015: Not yet. That was a bad move.

BlackKNIGHT: Okay, do you believe me now?

Rogue2015: LOL. I'm thinking about it.

BlackKNIGHT: You think, I'll people watch. And eat banana bread.

Rogue2015: I might have to try some sometime. Just to see if you're really telling the truth.

BlackKNIGHT: You do that and let me know.

41.

ZOE

When the elevator *ding*ed, I felt it in my stomach, too—a mix of fear and excitement, part of me dying to see Jackson and the other part afraid something would go wrong. But still, it was getting easier.

"Is that Jackson?" Mom called from the kitchen.

The doors opened to reveal Jackson carrying his worn backpack and giving a warm smile when he saw me. Every part of me responded to that smile. All the times I'd watched him from the other room when Mae had invited him over, even the times I'd watched him play basketball when I still went to school—all those moments bubbled to the surface. Jackson was here. For me.

"Am I late?" he asked, still smiling as he stepped into the lobby.

"No."

He toed off his sneakers and lined them up along with the others. They were out of place, old and dirty, but somehow they fit. Like they belonged. Like Jackson belonged here with us.

Mom peered out of the kitchen. "Jackson." She smiled.

"I wasn't expecting you."

I ducked my chin. That's because he wasn't usually here this late.

"Worksheets," Jackson said smoothly. "I have *lots* of practice worksheets for Zoe."

I held in a grimace. Exactly what I didn't want. More homework. More real life.

Then Jackson grinned at me, and I didn't care how many worksheets he had in his backpack, I was just glad he was here.

"Worksheets are good," Mom said. She beckoned us into the kitchen. "Snacks for the hard workers."

We followed her into the kitchen and loaded up our plates with snacks, making my mom happy. Jackson didn't even blink when she piled more food on top of what he already had. With his dad the way he was, he probably didn't get many home-cooked meals. And it made sense he'd rather be here than there.

By the time Mom finally let us leave the kitchen, we'd amassed enough food for a small army. I was fairly certain Jackson would eat it all and go back for seconds.

I turned on the lights in the study, illuminating the colored sheets of the sun. Outside the window, the sky was a flat shade of gray, but in here, it was a sea of color. A new meteor shot by Saturn, and I'd created another of Jupiter's moons.

Jackson set his plate of food on the desk, and I considered it a huge compliment that he wanted to look at my paper art more than he wanted to eat. He walked to Jupiter and studied it, then angled his head at the moons. Long enough to make me self-conscious.

"I really don't know how you do it," he murmured.

I set my plate down as well and walked closer. "Do what?"

"Make it look so real. Up close, you can see all the pieces and parts and how much time it took to make each piece, but from far away, you just see a galaxy. A galaxy that looks a lot like the real thing."

"I do a lot of research before I make each piece."

Jackson turned to me, a question in his eyes. Oh God. He knew. He knew I was a stalker and that I made this solar system because of him. "You could make a job out of this," he said. "I saw some pictures of the paper art at the museum. Yours is just as good."

My cheeks warmed. I'd seen the pictures, too. I'd been looking at the website almost every day, trying to build up the courage to go. My art was nowhere near as good as what I'd seen, but the more I practiced, the better I'd get. Visiting the museum and seeing the pieces in person would help.

"What got you so interested in astronomy?" I asked.

Jackson's jaw clenched, and for a moment, I thought he wasn't going to answer. Then, finally, he said, "My mom."

"Oh."

Something he didn't want to talk about. I grabbed my plate for a distraction and brought it to the window seat. Jackson joined me, balancing his plate on his knees.

"She always used to talk about space and how much else was out there," Jackson said. "She said it made our problems seem less significant, that they were something that we shouldn't worry about so much in the grand scheme of things."

I ate a carrot and waited, afraid to say anything. I didn't want him to stop talking.

"When we moved here," Jackson continued, "I wasn't happy about having to switch schools. And the very first thing we did that same night in our new house was go out back and look at the stars."

I smiled at him. "Your mom got through life by looking at the stars, and mine gets through it by feeding people."

Jackson laughed. The sound relieved me. "Yeah. We all

have different ways of coping with things."

I nodded. We did. Jackson was only too familiar with my coping technique.

He ate a few more bites of food, still staring at the stars and planets. He looked relaxed, too relaxed for me to ask about his dad. To bring up more stressors. But what else could I say?

"How many worksheets do you have?"

He grinned. "Worksheets?"

"Yeah, you told my mom…" I trailed off when he kept smiling. "Were you just making that up?"

"Completely. I mean, I *could* write up some worksheets if you want—"

"No. No," I said more calmly when his grin widened. "I'm good. I need a break from worksheets. I just want to…"

"What?"

I shrugged. "Spend time with you."

He set aside his plate and linked his fingers with mine. "This is why I made up the not-so-elaborate story of worksheets. So we'd have plenty of time."

I jumped at the soft knock on the door, guiltily pulling my hand from Jackson's.

Mom peeked her head inside. "There's a lot more food out there."

Jackson smirked.

I stood with a nod. "I know. We'll come get more soon."

"Come get more now," she said. "Then I can put it away and start regrouting that tile for my channel."

Jackson coughed, his eyes locking on mine. *Regrouting tile?* he mouthed. I held in laughter as I stood. Mom was into her home improvement phase and documenting every step on YouTube.

"I'll get us another plate," I said to appease my mom. And

because I needed to breathe. Jackson wouldn't stop looking at me.

His fingers were so warm. Sometimes he'd glance at my mouth and I thought he was going to kiss me, and then I'd find something to distract me because I was nervous.

I left Jackson in the study, munching on his plate of food, and followed Mom to the kitchen. Mae was there, eating celery. When she saw me, she launched into song.

"Z-oe has comp-any," she crooned off-key. "Jack-son is in the stuuuuuuudy!"

"You need professional help," I told her as Mom handed me another plate.

She leaned in, close enough Mom couldn't hear what she was whispering. "Are you really doing homework in there?"

"Mae."

When Mom turned to the refrigerator to put food away, Mae nudged my arm with her elbow. "Is he a good kisser?"

I choked on my response, ready to chide her again.

"You *have* kissed him, haven't you?" Mae asked, her eyes amused. "Because if not, I can keep Mom busy for you. Just pull him over to Mercury and say something about gravity not working or something then kind of *fall* into him…with your lips."

A laugh gurgled out, and Mae covered her grin when Mom turned around.

"What are you whispering about?" Mom asked.

"Gravity," Mae and I said immediately.

"Physics," I added.

"Right." Mae nodded. "Physics."

I brought the full plate back to the study and found Jackson leaning over at the desk. I closed the door and walked up behind him.

"What are you doing?" I asked.

"Massacring this piece of paper."

I scooted around to see the piece of paper he had in front of him. It was full of creases and looked about to rip in two.

"Why? Red is hard to find sometimes."

He lifted his phone and showed me a picture. A paper heart, similar to the one I made. "I wanted to make one for you, but it's harder than it looks."

"Lots of steps."

He nodded, putting his phone away. "I'm a good student."

I set the plate aside and went for more paper. Pink this time. "You want me to show you?"

"I do. If you show me how to do it, you'll have to sit really close, right?"

I blushed. "I can show you without being *that* close."

"How close is that?" He stood and stepped forward so there was only a foot of space between us. "*This* close?"

"Probably, uh…" I stared at his chest. The words slipped out before I could help it. *Gravity.* "Closer than that."

Amusement tinged his voice when he settled his hand on my hip. "*This* close?"

I lifted my chin, Mae's words bolstering my courage. "Closer."

His lips found mine without hesitation. They were warm, like his hands, and softer than I expected. Gentle. My mouth parted, ready to say his name, but he took it as an invitation to press even closer, so his hand slid up my back and the other found my cheek with those same warm fingers.

"Close your eyes," he murmured.

They dropped shut, blocking out everything but Jackson. His tongue touched mine, and I shivered. Was I doing this right? Was Jackson disappointed?

He eased back, breath hot on my cheek. "You're analyzing."

"I'm sorry."

"No. God, it seems like I always say the wrong thing."

"Isn't that my line?"

He laughed, touching my cheek again. "That wasn't scary, was it?"

"Terrifying." Not that I'd never kissed someone before, but there was always that doubt.

"Maybe we should work on it. Practice."

My heart thudded, beating against his. "I'm not surprised you said that."

"Practice makes perfect."

That was definitely something I could get behind. When he pressed his mouth to mine again, I let myself go. My heart beat out of control as his breath whispered against my lips. A soft sigh slipped out, and I laughed, keeping my eyes closed.

I was right, Jackson was a great kisser, and I never wanted him to stop.

42.

JACKSON

I watched as Zoe showed me all the steps to make a paper heart. And I sat really close, because Zoe smelled good and now that I'd kissed her it was hard to think of doing anything else.

I'd never felt lips so soft, never knew what it was like to have someone trust me so completely. I could have kissed her the entire afternoon—if only her mom would stop bringing us food.

It was the first time in a long time I didn't care about food.

"You have to get a really good crease here," she said, head bowed over the partial heart.

"Here?" I asked.

I could see what she was doing perfectly well, but that didn't mean I didn't want her to scoot a little closer for instruction.

"On this fold," she said, voice dropping low.

Her fingers brushed mine and lingered. I shifted in my seat a little so our knees touched. I could feel the heat coming off her, feel the warmth of her skin through her jeans and mine.

"There." She blinked up at me. "You've got it now."

I breathed out, wishing this was it. That there was nothing else between us but this moment. Instead, there was the reality that she never left her house. There was the reality that I didn't have a house.

And *Chess Challenge*.

Tell her. My mom's voice bloomed in my head as Zoe went on to explain the heart. We'd already been at it for twenty minutes, and I didn't think I'd retained a word she'd said. Not when she sat so close.

Get it out in the open. Clear the air. She deserves to know.

My mom was right. Zoe did deserve to know.

I looked over at her, her tiny fingers forming another fold in the heart, and froze inside. I couldn't say anything.

"Got it?" Zoe asked.

I hurried to make another fold, knowing I'd already messed it up beyond repair. Zoe was a patient teacher, but she had to know my heart wasn't going to stand up to hers.

She only smiled at me. "Looks good."

"Liar."

She chuckled. "Trust me. My first one looked pretty horrible. And the second one…and the tenth one." She shifted in her seat, then glanced at me. "Do you go to the library a lot?"

My breath caught. I managed to keep my fingers steady on the paper heart, but my real heart wasn't as steady.

"The library?" I asked, like I had no clue what she was talking about, even though I was pretty sure this was a BlackKNIGHT reference.

Zoe nodded. "Yeah. It's just—I have a friend…I mean, Mae's friend…who said he went to the library a lot. And we—we were joking that boys his age *never* go to the library. But—but—" She broke off and shook her head. "It was just a joke."

I tried to relax in my seat. She didn't suspect I was BlackKNIGHT, did she?

But this would be the perfect time to tell her.

I swallowed. The perfect time to ruin the whole evening.

"I go sometimes," I said, hating that I had to lie. I practically lived at the library. Wasn't that what I'd said as BlackKNIGHT?

"Well, of course *you* do." Zoe smiled. "Because you like to read. But normal kids your age..." She shrugged. "It's nothing. Never mind."

Before I could open my mouth again, she swiveled to face me. She held up the heart. "See? That's the last step."

I frowned at my paper. "Mine doesn't look like yours."

"Practice," she said. "Remember? You said practice makes perfect."

I grinned. "You know exactly what I was talking about."

Her cheeks turned red. "Jackson."

"Show me."

Zoe's eyes widened. "What?"

I laughed, realizing she thought I meant the kissing thing. I pointed to her heart. "Show me how you do the 3-D part."

"Oh." She almost dropped the heart then gave a nervous laugh. "You just open this end up a little..."

She put her lips to the microscopic hole in the end of her heart and blew. It inflated and formed a 3-D pink heart, as perfect as the one she'd given me.

"I'm not sure I'm ever going to be able to do that," I said.

"You will. It takes time."

The understanding in her eyes, how calm she seemed right now, boosted my courage. I'd tell her right now. I'd explain how I had no idea she was Rogue in the beginning, and that it was just a coincidence. A crazy coincidence my mom would say was meant to be. I was meant to meet Zoe.

And then she'd ask about me being homeless, and the

whole universe would come crumbling down on me.

I opened my mouth, but another knock sounded at the door. Zoe rolled her eyes.

This time it was Mae who came in, balancing two plates of what looked and smelled like brownies.

"Mom wanted me to deliver these to you and tell you— like you didn't already know—there are a lot more in the kitchen," Mae said.

She set the plates on the desk with us, then gave me a sly smile. "Have you checked out Mercury yet?"

My gaze shot automatically to the planet, and then to Zoe when she stood and gave Mae a playful shove. "Thanks for the brownies."

Mae caught my eye again with a grin. "I think Zoe was wondering what the gravity on Mercury was like—"

"I already *asked* him that," Zoe said, shoving Mae toward the door.

Mae slapped a hand over her mouth, and then stumbled out the door when Zoe pushed her again. She started to say something else, but Zoe shut the door in her face.

"Did I miss something?" I asked.

"No." But Zoe blushed anyway. "Mae was just joking. Brownies," she blurted. "I bet they're really good."

My bubble of courage burst. I couldn't tell her now. We were talking paper hearts and brownies and planets, not serious things like our real identities.

I pointed to the speaker I'd heard her call Cyclops before lifting the brownie to my mouth. "What kind of music are you supposed to listen to when you make paper hearts?"

She smiled. "Something without catchy lyrics. Because then you get distracted and focus more on the song than the heart."

"So, boring music?" I waved my hand toward her wall and

the ceiling. "You listened to boring music to make all this?"

"Not boring music. And I listened to different music for almost everything. You—you can't just cut and fold paper and get a masterpiece. It takes time, and the right atmosphere." She pointed to the sun. "Alternative rock. Because I needed energy for all those pieces. And because, well—it's the sun. But Earth. That was some indie stuff. More mellow. Earth was fun."

"Was Uranus country?" I asked. "Because personally, I've never been a fan of that planet. It leaves a lot to be desired."

Her laughter warmed me, and I fought off any more urges I had to tell her about BlackKNIGHT. What was the point if it was just going to screw things up anyway?

"Maybe you can help me with a meteor," she said, standing and stretching.

"Right now?"

"Another time, maybe. After all this food, I need to get up and move around." She glanced at the window, a frown tugging at the corners of her lips. "I wish we could go for a walk."

I moved aside my plate. "We could." I reached for her hand, locking my fingers with hers. "Something short, close by."

Doubt registered on her face.

"We could go get coffee or something, and then drink it on our walk."

Her mouth opened. I thought, for a moment, she might say yes.

"There's a Starbucks just down the street," I told her, in case she didn't already know. I'd even been there once or twice after leaving Zoe's house.

She nodded. "I hear they have really good banana bread."

Another jolt went through me. "They do," I answered carefully.

Her eyes met mine. "I'm…I want to, but I'm not there yet. I need a little more time."

I tried not to show my disappointment. I got it. She needed to take her steps and work up to it.

I nodded and squeezed her hand. "Another time, maybe. But…the meteor shower. Maybe we can plan for that?"

I almost held my breath. This was a big deal for her. These were important steps.

"I think…" She exhaled. "I think that would be good."

I pulled her into my arms and rested my hand on her hair, the soft strands tickling my fingers. "It'll be fun," I told her. "And I'll be there the whole time."

I'd make it fun for her. I wanted to show her life outside her apartment was worth living.

You should tell her now.

I continued to hold on to Zoe, and for the first time, I ignored my mom's voice.

43.

BlackKNIGHT: I'm pretty sure I'm at chess master status now.

Rogue2015: Why do you say that?

BlackKNIGHT: Because I beat you two out of the last three games.

Rogue2015: Bragging is strictly forbidden in the game of chess.

BlackKNIGHT: Did you just make up that rule?

Rogue2015: No. Everyone knows that rule. So, clearly, you aren't at chess master status yet.

BlackKNIGHT: What other rules am I missing?

Rogue2015: If you lose five games in a row, you're locked out of the site for a whole week so you can study up on technique and do better.

BlackKNIGHT: Really? I think I might've lost that many

games in a row before.

Rogue2015: And if you win five games in a row, you get to play with the golden chess set.

BlackKNIGHT: Really? Is that what you're playing on?

Rogue2015: Yep, you just don't get to see it from your side.

BlackKNIGHT: That's not fair.

Rogue2015: And if you win ten games in a row, you get a personal email from the chess master himself, Rupert Flintlock.

BlackKNIGHT: I don't think I've heard of him. I'm Googling that right now.

Rogue2015: LOL. You do that.

BlackKNIGHT: Wait…are you just messing with me? About Rupert Flintlock?

Rogue2015: Maybe.

BlackKNIGHT: About everything?

Rogue2015: What? You don't think I'm playing on a golden chessboard?

BlackKNIGHT: No, I don't. I think you made it all up. I bet you just broke a dozen chess rules right there.

Rogue2015: How would you know? Maybe you should look it up. ☺

BlackKNIGHT: What I'm *going* to do is beat you at this game, just to show you how funny I think your joking is.

Rogue2015: Judging by how you're playing this game so far, you think it's pretty funny.

BlackKNIGHT: Be prepared to lose your number one ranking.

Rogue2015: We'll see about that.

BlackKNIGHT: Hey, Rogue.

Rogue2015: Yeah?

BlackKNIGHT: Do you think sometimes it's better to keep a secret instead of telling someone if you think it'll hurt them? Or you?

Rogue2015: That's a serious question.

BlackKNIGHT: I know. But there's someone I don't want to hurt.

Rogue2015: When you care about someone, I think it's better to do what you think is best for them. And for yourself. For both of you.

BlackKNIGHT: That makes me feel better. I don't like hurting people.

Rogue2015: Me, either. But it seems like we do it no matter how hard we try sometimes, huh?

BlackKNIGHT: We do. But not this time.

Rogue2015: You're smart. And nice. I'm sure you're doing the right thing.

BlackKNIGHT: Thank you. I hope so.

44.

ZOE

"I can't do this. I'm nervous."

"We're not doing anything yet. Just math," Jackson said, eyes smiling.

"It doesn't matter."

"Why?"

Always endlessly asking why. That was Jackson. He wanted the answer to everything, even when the answer didn't make sense.

I squeezed the pencil I was holding. "We're going out of the house this afternoon. I know it, and my stomach knows it. It—it makes me nervous. *Really* nervous, even if it isn't happening for a while." I ventured a glance up at him. "That's sort of how it works."

Jackson tapped the paper in front of me. "This is supposed to distract you."

"Seriously? Math?" I glared at the problems he'd written down as a sort of pretest. "Other things distract me. Math just tortures me and makes me feel worse."

"Other things," Jackson said. When I glanced over again, he smiled. "What other things?"

Fire burned in my cheeks. I focused intently on the math problems. "No other things."

"Zoe, Zoe, why?"

I wouldn't look at him. "Why what?"

"Why won't you just accept it?"

My breath wheezed out. "Accept...what?"

His arm slid over, brushing the paper aside. He grasped my hand before I could move it, fingers entwining with mine. "Accept your feelings. You like having me here."

The world spun around me like a merry-go-round. Like the moons of Saturn when I'd spin them so they'd orbit the planet.

"Accept it," Jackson continued. "Accept it, and then kiss me, so I know you feel the same way as I do."

I suffocated on my own shock.

"Breathe, Zoe."

I shook my head, heart hammering, mind zooming with amazement, whole body thrumming with possibilities and the need to simply be near him. How come Gina hadn't told me this might happen, or Mae, so I could be prepared? Kissing Jackson was like the dreams I used to have about flying. Exhilarating. And now he wanted more of it.

"Otherwise I'll have to do CPR," Jackson said.

With a laugh, I squeezed my fingers around his.

"Talk to me," he said.

"I can't believe you just said that. Who talks like that?"

"I do."

"I..." Glancing up at him, I gave an apologetic look. "That's a lot of pressure."

"I just made you more nervous. Okay, one step at a time. First, you do this math test so I can see how you're progressing. Then, we get the others and go shopping for meteor shower supplies. And then...then there won't be pressure."

"There's always pressure."

"If we were never anxious about anything, some things wouldn't mean quite as much as they do when they happen." He brushed my hair off my cheek. "Right?"

A flicker of frustration raced through me. Even Jackson wanted more from me—wanted me to leave the house. In this way, I kind of wished he were more like BlackKNIGHT. That he'd just accept me as I was.

His phone rang before I could answer. He pulled it out of his pocket, peeked at the screen, and frowned. When he returned the phone without answering, I looked up at him.

"It was your dad, wasn't it?"

His jaw flexed. He pulled off his glasses and cleaned them on his shirt. "He keeps calling."

"And you don't answer?"

"I don't... No, I don't answer." He returned his glasses to his face. "Ready for your test?"

"What if it's something important?"

"He left a message. It's nothing urgent."

"Urgent and important aren't the same thing." Carefully and slowly, I reached out and placed both hands on his chest. "You're helping me. I want to help you."

His eyes searched mine, a depth of understanding there I hadn't expected. "You are one of the most important people I know. But I need time."

I blinked back moisture. It wasn't my place to be sad about this—he didn't seem to be. But I couldn't help it. Why couldn't he understand that he needed more than an alcoholic parent who was never there for him?

He needed family.

He needed a good home.

That made me think of BlackKNIGHT and his words that night he'd stepped away from our match. How he'd talked about his bright side being home. Why did I keep thinking about BlackKNIGHT when I was around Jackson, and the other way around?

"I'll do my test," I said, turning to the desk.

Jackson sighed. "I'm sorry."

"Me, too. It's none of my business. Ready to time me?"

"I'm ready," he said, resignation in his voice. "Go."

I put pencil to paper and focused. I could do this. I understood this. I did the first four problems without a hitch. Jackson wandered to the window and stared out at the sunny day.

Then I got lost in another problem and forgot about the time. I just kept working. My mind circled around all the concepts Jackson had taught me the last several days. When I couldn't figure something out, I'd close my eyes and visualize, and see Jackson calmly explaining the process in a reasonable voice. In a reasonable way.

Once I finished the last problem, I looked at Jackson. He'd turned around and he was staring at me.

He grinned. "Are you finished?"

I held up the test. "Easy peasy."

"We'll see." He walked over, took the paper, and settled into a relaxed stance. He propped his hip on the desk and read through the problems, making noises under his breath. "Nice handwriting."

"Keep grading."

"You show your work in neat little columns," he said, eyes on the paper. "Your numbers are like soldiers, perfectly lined up."

I lifted my eyebrows.

"You only missed one," he said.

"Really?"

"A hard one. We'll go over it next week so you're prepared.

You did good."

"You're a good teacher."

"I am?" Jackson moved closer so our shoes were touching. "Care to show some gratitude?"

My heart raced. I froze for nearly five seconds, afraid to make the move. Then I stepped forward so our bodies touched.

His arms came around me, hands locked behind my back, and I lifted my arms to wrap around his neck.

Jackson exhaled, like he was releasing a day's worth of stress. His breath touched my lips, but before I could move, his mouth was on mine. It was slower, sweeter than the first time. I shut off my brain, even though it wanted to analyze.

Jackson made it easy. He let his fingers wander, dancing up my spine and then winding into my hair. A shiver ran through me as he pressed closer.

"You're getting really good at this," he murmured against my lips.

I released a quiet laugh. I didn't agree, but right now I didn't care. Jackson felt too good. Everything I was feeling right now was good.

And then Jackson pointed to the door. "Are you ready for this?"

My heart clutched. "Outside?"

"Don't focus on the scary things." He brushed his lips against mine, distracting me from his words. "Focus on the good things. All the things you get to see. All the people you get to walk past. Focus on me."

Even though nerves fluttered through me, I was excited. For once, I was looking forward to leaving the house. As long as Jackson was with me, I felt like I could go anywhere and do anything.

What would Gina say? That I could do this. That I was making progress. But then…then she'd say I needed to try to do this on my own.

That meant not being able to lean on Jackson.

I wasn't sure I was ready for that yet.

45.

JACKSON

I watched her closely, her slender fingers touching items in the aisle as we loaded up our baskets with food for tonight. We'd walked to the local market because Zoe and Mae agreed taking the bus to the grocery store was a panic attack waiting to happen.

But I kept her hand locked in mine the whole way and tried to point out everything I could that might make her smile. Which she seemed to be doing a lot.

I found a pair of sunglasses on a rack nearby and handed them to her. "Try these on."

She jumped, and then laughed, and then blushed, and then took the glasses. "Sorry."

I only smiled. "Please?"

She put the glasses on. They were large, Audrey Hepburn style, engulfing half her face. Like the ones my mom used to wear to block out as much sun as possible.

"These would be good. You'll need something when you go out."

She pulled off the glasses and rolled her brown eyes. "I'm sure I have a pair of sunglasses somewhere at home. Probably."

"And if you don't?" I plucked the sunglasses from her hand and set them in my basket. "I'm buying these for you."

Her humor faded. "Jackson."

"I want to."

She tried to grab my basket, but I held it out of her reach. "I'll buy the glasses."

With a laugh, I held it higher. "No."

"Yes. I'll buy all that. Just…" She glanced around and then clutched her hand at her chest like her heart was aching.

"It's just a few things for tonight and one thing for you. I want to contribute to the cause. Are you okay?"

Her hands squeezed together tightly, turning white, and she ignored the question. "I'm…trying."

I stepped forward to take her hand. "It's okay. This is a happy day. You're doing good."

"You—you keep doing that."

"What?"

"Trying to make me feel better. Trying to help me. But you won't let me help you." When I didn't answer, she frowned, making wrinkle lines appear on her forehead. "Jackson."

"You are *so* good at that."

"Stop it."

I laughed. "Feisty. I like it."

Startled when she lunged for the basket, I yanked it back too hard, and all our stuff fell on the floor. Zoe's eyes widened.

"Oh God." She dropped to her knees to grab the items.

Mae came around the corner with Robert.

"Children," he said. "Playtime isn't until later."

I laughed until I noticed the panic on Zoe's face. Her cheeks burned red, and she scrambled across the floor to grab the sunglasses.

Setting the basket down, I joined her on my knees. "No big deal. Deep breath."

She eased back on her heels, breathing in deeply.

Mae smiled at her. "It looks like you guys are doing more playing than buying."

Zoe nodded, her face appearing calm even though her hands were curled into fists. "It's just…Jackson isn't cooperating."

I met her eyes, willing her not to say anything.

"Cooperating with what?" Kelly asked.

Zoe clutched all the items she'd gathered to her chest and forced a smile. "He keeps putting things in our basket we don't need. I mean, Twinkies? For a meteor shower?"

"Hell yes, we need Twinkies," Robert said.

She grabbed the basket, keeping her grip tight on it so I wouldn't try to take it away. She stood. "I guess we'd better grab the Twinkies, then."

Before she could make her way down the aisle, I snagged her waist.

"Don't you dare touch my basket," she said, cheeks still flushed.

"I wouldn't dream of it."

"You're very frustrating sometimes, you know?"

I kissed her on the lips, right there in the middle of the store. She stood still like a statue, eyes wide.

"I know I'm frustrating," I said.

She shook her head, eyes sad. "I have lots of things I want to say, but it's hard."

"You can say anything to me."

She bit her lip, hand clenched tight on the basket handle. "Twinkies."

"That's what you want to say?"

"I don't know what else to say."

"How you feel. You can tell me how you feel."

I expected her to say embarrassed. Or nervous. Or maybe

even surprised this trip outside her apartment seemed to be working out so well.

"I'm sad. I want you to…" She ducked her chin. "I want you to call your dad. I want to help. I want you to talk to me."

I stood still a long moment, as surprised by her words as she seemed to be.

"I'm sorry," she whispered, and turned to the front of the store.

I watched as she joined her sister, both of them combining the items in their baskets. Zoe smiled at something Mae said, and it sent a shock of longing through me. She'd stepped out of her comfort zone even though it terrified her. She was brave.

I couldn't even talk to her about my father.

I couldn't call him back.

Maybe she wasn't the one who needed help. Maybe it was me.

We didn't see the first meteor shoot across the sky until well after midnight. But it was dazzling—a long, hot green tail that trailed behind the bright light. It was worth it to see Zoe's face. The wonder there. She'd been able to relax the rest of the evening after we'd returned to her apartment building and brought our meteor viewing party to the rooftop.

I grabbed two more sodas from the cooler and brought one to Zoe on the blanket we'd set out. She lay on her back, head propped on one of the pillows her mom sent up with us.

"Drink?" I asked her.

"I'm so full, I don't think I can. Thanks, though." Another star shot across the sky. "That's thirty-three."

"You're counting them?"

Even in the dimness of the evening, our area only lit by small lanterns, I could see her blush.

I reclined and reached for her hand. "I used to do the same thing."

"How many times have you done this?"

"What?"

"Watched a meteor shower."

"Two dozen maybe."

She didn't answer. I wasn't sure I wanted to know what she was thinking. I watched so many meteor showers because sometimes I had nothing else to do with my night. And I was outside anyway—or in my car, at least. But she didn't know that part.

"I watched my first one with my mom," I said.

She shifted onto her side so she could face me. The rest of the group chatted on another blanket. I heard the wrapper of a Twinkie and Kelly's infectious laugh.

I reached out, taking Zoe's hand again, and saw another star fly past. "Thirty-four. We did it just like this, with blankets on the ground in our backyard. Drinks and candy—enough to make us sick—but I loved it."

"How old were you?"

"Six. I counted the meteors that night, too. Only twenty-six, though. I got tired and couldn't stay up longer. Plus, Mom had to work the next day. But after that, it became a tradition until…"

"I'm sorry," she whispered.

I nodded.

"I'm glad you have so many good memories of her, though."

"I listened to my dad's message."

Her lips parted.

I cleared my throat. "Yeah, it was just…it wasn't anything important."

"Oh."

"He wanted to remind me about the meteor shower, actually."

She squeezed my hand. "I think you should call him."

I didn't tell her that I already had. And that I'd hung up. "I wonder if…he's really ready to take this step. I mean, we've been here before. He went to rehab once, and it was fine for a few months. But it didn't last any longer than that."

She bit her lip, and then lay on her back to stare at the sky again. "Thirty-five."

"Zoe."

She didn't answer.

I leaned over her. "Tell me what you're thinking."

She had her glasses on, and I could see stars and the moon reflected in the lenses. But I couldn't see her eyes behind them or tell what was going on in her head.

"Zoe," I prompted. "The truth, right? It's okay to tell me how you feel."

"I'm angry."

"Oh."

"I don't want you to have to deal with this. I want you to go be okay with your dad, or be able to go somewhere else if that doesn't work out. I want to feel like I'm worth giving advice on this."

"You *are*. Your opinion is important to me."

"I know I haven't lived outside a lot. I know I haven't made an impression on a lot of people, but—"

"That's not true."

Her words caught when she spoke again. "I know you're trying to be nice, but it is true, and it's about time I grew up and realized I need to do more than hide in my apartment every day."

"You *are* growing up and doing more," I said. I pointed at

the rooftop. "Look. We're outside. You're outside, Zoe. And we went to the store today, too. And it was good."

"I was with you," she murmured.

"That's okay, right?"

Zoe removed her glasses and rubbed her eyes. "It's…okay. But not the best. Not ideal."

She sounded like a therapist. Not ideal? Why not? "These are steps, right? What we talked about."

She put her glasses on again before glancing at me. "They're *our* steps. Not mine."

"I can still be there for you," I said.

"I have to try to do some things on my own," she whispered.

"I know. And I can help."

She made a noise of disagreement and then fell quiet. The night pressed in around us, and I wished I knew what to say.

It felt like walking on a tightrope. The truth was always what came to mind, but only because there seemed to be a lot left unsaid between us. Now Zoe knew all my secrets, which meant I should tell her the truth about *Chess Challenge*. But then she'd make comments like what she'd just said, and I realized how much I could lose if I told her the truth. How she might just back away for good because I knew who she really was in secret and in person. What else could I do to bridge the gap between us? To make her understand I wasn't trying to take over, just trying to be here for her?

I reached for her hand, and she let me. We both kept silent while we counted the stars shooting over our heads. Normally it made me feel better to sit under the night sky, but tonight it made me feel like I was missing something before it ever started.

46.

Rogue2015: You ever feel like playing chess is just a way to escape the real world?

BlackKNIGHT: That's okay, right? I mean, sometimes we all need a break from reality.

Rogue2015: Yeah, but then when you get back to reality, you realize how hard it is. All you want is to go back to the game.

BlackKNIGHT: A safe zone. I can understand that. I kind of like to escape here, too.

Rogue2015: From what?

BlackKNIGHT: Reality. Like you said. But when I go back to reality, I feel refreshed. Like I'm ready to face the world head on.

Rogue2015: I wish it worked that way for me. Instead I feel like I'm stepping out of my comfort zone.

BlackKNIGHT: We all have to do that sometimes. Even those of us who *like* reality. ☺

Rogue2015: I guess I should work on it.

BlackKNIGHT: How are you going to do that?

Rogue2015: I don't know. I guess I'll let you know when I figure it out.

BlackKNIGHT: I'll be here.

Rogue2015: ☺ I know you will.

BlackKNIGHT: And for what it's worth, I like you just the way you are.

Rogue2015: Thanks.

47.

ZOE

He would. BlackKNIGHT would be there, just like my safe room, waiting for me to return. I wasn't even being myself on *Chess Challenge*. BlackKNIGHT thought I was some regular girl from a cornfield somewhere, when really, I was hiding. Pretending to have a life. Was Jackson just another way to hide, too?

I couldn't tell whether I was falling for him because I felt safe with him or because we had something more, beyond the comfortable bubble he was building.

"Zoe, do you still have the same goal for our sessions?" Gina asked as we talked in the study this morning.

"You mean to go to Mae's graduation?"

"Yes."

"Yeah, I still want that." I shifted in my seat, unable to get my mind off my conversation with BlackKNIGHT. Or my conversation with Jackson last night. *That's* what really brought all this on. Knowing I was only stepping out of my comfort zone because of him. "And I want…"

"What do you want?"

"I don't know."

"Do you want to go to graduation?"

"Yes."

"Because she expects you to?"

"No."

"Because you said you would?"

"Yes. And no."

"Explain."

"That's not a yes or no question."

She smiled. "We're not playing the yes or no question game this time. Explain your answer to me—this is important."

"I want to go because…because it's important to her. I promised I'd go, but I want to do it because I want to, not because I have to fulfill a promise. Because I…"

"Yes?"

"I'm tired of being scared."

"And making decisions because of how scared you are."

"Yes. I want…I don't want to be defined by my fears anymore."

Gina sat back in her seat and smiled. Really smiled. That's when it hit me. I couldn't rely on anyone to change my circumstances but me. Not even Jackson.

Once Gina left, I had to escape my study. My stomach churned with the realization of what I'd told Gina. I was the only one who could change my life. It felt freeing and terrifying at the same time. But I'd already started. I'd left the house this week. I'd gone grocery shopping and watched meteors, and I hadn't had one panic attack.

Feeling empowered, I walked into the kitchen.

Mom looked up from her recipe book. "Hi. You want lunch?" Mom asked. "Udon or sushi. Or I could make California rolls."

"That's a lot of work."

She looked hopeful. "Pizza?"

With a laugh, I sat on the stool across from her at the counter. "No, thanks."

She shut her recipe book. "We could…go get something."

I automatically opened my mouth to tell her no, but then stopped. I had to do this, right? Not on everyone else's terms, though. On mine.

"Like go pick something up and bring it back here?" I asked.

"Or—or I could go and bring it back."

"Or we could eat there," I said.

She blinked then patted her shiny black hair. "Eat there."

Like it was a foreign concept.

"I'm trying to…have a life." Even if I wished Jackson were the one taking me to lunch. I missed him already, even though I'd seen him last night.

"I want a cheeseburger," I said.

Mom smiled. "Cheeseburger. Yes. French fries. There's a place a few blocks down. Mae and I used to go there after her practices all the time. Ooh! Girls' lunch. We could go get manicures, too."

My stomach rolled.

Mom gave me a gentle smile. "One thing at a time, right?"

I tried to take Gina's advice. No stressing about going out because I couldn't control what happened when I did. I'd keep telling myself it was just like taking a stroll around the house. I'd be fine.

Until my phone *ding*ed with a message. I have a new test for you to take. Is it still okay to come by for tutoring after school?

Mom pointed at my phone. "Jackson?"

I nodded. "He was asking about tutoring. But I can just tell him we won't be back in time. I think I understand algebra pretty well now. I think I'll be okay for my test."

"Zoe."

"What?"

"Are you avoiding him?"

I squeezed my palms around my phone. "What? Why would I do that?"

"You usually answer his texts right away. Did something happen?"

"No. I'm being my own person," I said. If I answered his text right away, that just showed how much I relied on him, right?

My mom's lips turned down at the corners. "Jackson is a good boy."

He *was* good. But he was more than that. He was more than my mother saw, and yet everyone was still trying to change *me*. It wasn't their responsibility. It was mine.

"We should go. So we can walk and enjoy the sun," I told my mom.

She gave me a wide-eyed look. "Are you going to answer Jackson?"

I stared at my phone. I should. I didn't want to be rude, but I didn't know what to say. I wrote a quick answer and pressed send before I could change my mind. Another test sounds good.

Once I did this test, once I made sure I understood math enough, we could stop tutoring. It was for the best, right? I couldn't depend on Jackson anymore.

I swallowed down the fear that jumped into my throat. I'd left the house for Jackson. I'd pretended like I was a regular teenager, but it was only because Jackson gave me the strength. I had to find that strength somewhere within myself, or I was never going to be able to live my life how I wanted.

Jackson's message appeared. Looking forward to it.

Pocketing my phone, I put on a brave smile for my mom. "Let's go."

• • •

Lunch went better than I thought. Mom let me pick the restaurant and the table, and was fine with leaving early because things started to get hard. I realized if I kept taking steps like this, stepping out of my comfort zone but doing it in a way that worked for me, I might actually make it to Mae's graduation. Only three weeks to go.

When we returned from lunch, carrying our leftovers, Jackson was in the lobby, sitting in the hideous middle chairs and looking completely comfortable while doing so. He stood when he saw us.

My feet stopped automatically. Jackson smiled when we joined him, his eyes crinkling. He had the same backpack he always carried and wore a T-shirt I often saw him in. I wondered where he went if he wasn't at home much. Or was that why he always wanted to be here?

I kept quiet as we rode the elevator, my stomach protesting the whole way up. Jackson glanced at me more than once, but all I could manage was a weak smile. It was me trying to be strong when I really had no idea how.

Mostly, I just wanted to reach out and take his hand and go about our business like usual. But something had to change.

Upstairs, after putting my leftovers in the fridge, I walked with Jackson to the study. He took his shoes off by the door like we always did, but I still heard his quiet footsteps behind me. I still felt the warmth from his body as he stepped inside the door, close enough I could touch his hand.

I heard his breath release when I moved away.

"My test is next week," I said.

Jackson lowered his backpack to the floor by the desk. "Which is why I made another test for you. I think you're really getting this."

I nodded. Smiled. Good. He was sticking to math. I could handle that.

"I think I am, too. If I can do this test of yours, I should be ready. Physics is going well, too."

He smiled, pulling papers out of his backpack. "I know."

"So, after this…I'll probably be done with tutoring."

He stopped taking out papers. "I can still help."

Then it occurred to me that I should have talked to Mom first. I shouldn't have said anything at all. Jackson was doing this for the money, and maybe even to be away from his dad, so it wasn't my place to get in the way of that.

"Of—of course you can. I didn't—I mean, I know you have to do this. I'm sorry. Yes, tutoring—"

"Zoe."

"No, not 'Zoe' again. Don't say my name. I'm sorry. This is your job, and I'm—it's not my place to say anything. Let's do the test—"

"Please wait." He stood and walked to me, with those expressive eyes and studious glasses, making me want to forget all about tests and worries.

"It's fine. Forget I said anything." I forced a smile as I turned to the desk. "You know me, I don't think before I talk, and I babble—I'm babbling now, so…"

I blew out a breath and grabbed a pencil so I could do my test.

"You're not babbling. You're being honest. You're being Zoe."

"I'm not—that's not who I am anymore. I have to grow up and *deal* with things. Really deal with them."

I sealed my lips shut, afraid to say anything else. I was terrified of growing up and being in the real world on my own. But I had to. Mae was going to college this fall. My mom had her own stuff, too, and I had nothing.

I felt him behind me before I heard him. His hand touched my arm.

I turned around, staring at his shirt for a long moment before lifting my gaze. He'd taken off his glasses and looked so vulnerable without them that an ache bloomed inside of me. His eyes were tired, and it broke my heart to think he'd gone home to an empty house last night, or hadn't talked with his dad at all, even though they lived in the same place. It broke my heart to think of him being so alone.

My lip trembled, and I bit it.

"I'm trying really hard to understand where you're coming from," Jackson said. "I know you want to do things on your own, and I can step back if that's what you need. But I still want a chance with you."

The words struck me hard. A chance with me? All I'd wanted since I met Jackson was a chance with him. And now I had it. I felt my resolve crumbling. "I still want a chance with you, too."

"Really?"

"Yes. But—"

"No, don't take it back. You have to at least let me enjoy it for a few minutes."

I wrapped my arms around his waist, letting him have his moment. "Okay, two minutes."

He chuckled, but his voice was still cautious when he spoke again. "Are you sure this is what you want?"

"Yes."

"Then…" He eased back. "Why did you say 'but'?"

"I'm trying to, uh…" I dropped my eyes. "I'm trying to do this—this thing where I step out of my comfort zone. And I thought I was. I thought I had the—the meteor shower and the grocery store. But all that was you. I can't prove to myself I can do this if you're such a big part of it. Does that make sense?"

When he didn't answer, I looked up to see conflict raging on his face. "It does. But that doesn't mean we can't spend time together, right? I can tutor you if you need it, we can play chess like normal people. We can go places, too."

"But I…" I wanted to say yes. Just because I had to figure out who I really was didn't mean Jackson couldn't be a small part of that.

"It'll work. People do it all the time."

I laughed. "What do you mean?"

"You know, there's a girl who's ridiculously cute with her too-long bangs, and she's awesome at chess and she likes to fold paper. And there's this boy who's completely screwed up, who needs new glasses because he slept on them last night—"

"Oh, Jackson."

He grinned. "And he meets this girl and thinks she's amazing and he wants to be there for her. As a friend. As a boyfriend. Without stepping on her toes."

"How does that work?" I asked, my heart thumping. Boyfriend. How did a paper girl get a boyfriend as amazing as Jackson?

"I hang out with you. I take you places. You hang out with me, and you take me places or play chess with me. An even balance. Stepping out of our comfort zones."

"I see how I'll be stepping out of my comfort zone, but what about you?"

This time he looked away, throat working in a difficult swallow. "I'm…I'm going to talk to my dad. And I could really use your support. Like, just…be there for me. If I need to talk, or vent, or bang my head against the wall or something."

"Sure. Of—of course. Absolutely." An even balance. That sounded good.

He kissed me before I could say anything else, lips warm on mine. I closed my eyes automatically. His hand moved in slow circles on my back, and I shivered in anticipation. Wrapping my arms around his neck, I let him turn me to lean against the desk.

His fingers slid up my spine, making my world tilt.

"I feel dizzy," I whispered.

"Sick?"

"No, in a good way."

"See? We're practicing physics."

I glanced to the door. "I don't think my mom would agree."

He straightened abruptly, looking in the same direction. He shoved a hand through his hair and blew out a breath. "God, Zoe, I thought you meant she was standing right there."

Laughing, I brushed my bangs from my eyes. My lips still tingled from his kiss. If I hadn't been so embarrassed, I would have pulled him to me again.

"You need to get your glasses replaced."

Jackson shrugged. "I can see you just fine."

"And you can't—I mean, you should maybe talk to someone about your dad if he's still drinking or—"

"One thing at a time," he suggested, returning to his backpack.

"Please don't brush this off."

He glanced up, surprise on his face. "I'm not. I promise. If you can do what you're doing, and face the world even though it scares you, I should be able to talk to my dad, right?"

"Yes."

"Test first, then. And you could get just a *few* wrong, you know, to give me an excuse to tutor you longer."

I grinned. "Don't let my mom hear you say that."

"You know she loves feeding me. It's a win-win." He came

back and touched my cheek. "We're working on fixing things, right?"

"Right." I gave a firm nod. We were both working on ourselves, and it would be okay. "All right, time me."

"Ready. Set. Go."

48.

JACKSON

I wasn't sure how I'd ended up at the library instead of at my dad's house, but here I was. Dale's shift must have been over, because he wasn't in any of the aisles.

But when I reached my table, there was a book with a banana set on top. I glanced around, assuming someone had claimed my spot. But when I saw what the book was, I smiled.

It was an origami book. It had to be from Dale. Same with the banana.

I sat down and pushed the banana aside. Normally, I would have eaten it right there, but I wasn't hungry. In fact, I was so full my stomach ached. Zoe made me eat at her house. And when her mom saw how much I'd eaten, she'd happily packed me leftovers from the night before so I could "take them home to my dad."

That's where I was supposed to be. I'd promised Zoe, and I didn't intend to break that promise. But I couldn't do it. Not yet. He could be at work. He could be there doing drugs.

Any excuse I could think of to not go there, I had it

I opened the origami book and searched the table of contents for shapes. I grinned when I found one for a heart, and turned the page. It looked more complicated than the one I'd already tried. How did Zoe do it?

Tiny hands. That had to be part of it.

Mine were too big and clumsy to make anything that delicate.

My phone buzzed. My stomach clenched, thinking it might be my dad. But when I looked at the screen, I relaxed.

It was Zoe. Good luck.

Before I knew it, I was calling her number, waiting for her voice on the other end.

She answered after two rings. "Hi."

"Hi."

"Did I interrupt?"

"With your text? No, I'm not…I'm at the library."

She didn't answer, but I could hear her breathing on the other end.

"I promise I'm going," I said. "I just need a pep talk."

"You'll be fine, I know it. You have to do this. You have to try to work this out. No matter what happens, I'm here for you. Just go over there, try to talk to him and see how it goes. The worst thing that happens is you have to leave, and I'll be here for you. My whole family will, if that's what it takes."

I swallowed. "You're right."

"You can do this."

"Thank you."

"Do you feel better?"

"I want to talk to you more," I said, paging through the book.

"Jackson."

"I love when you do that. Say my name with a sigh. Or say my name. Or just—"

"I won't do it again unless you do what you're supposed to."

I smiled and took note of a page that had a basic origami

flower on it. I might be able to do that. For Zoe. "Are you threatening me?"

"Do I sound scary? I can use my serious voice."

Laughing, I said, "Yes, do that."

"Young man, you get your butt over there and do what you're supposed to. Now."

"Very good. But I like your exasperated voice better. You kind of angle your head when you say my name, and it's like the weight of the world is on you. And I just want to fix it."

She was silent for a long moment.

"Zoe? Talk to me."

"It's not your job to fix my problems."

"It's my job to support you like you're supporting me. Please let me."

"I'm trying."

I shut the book and stretched my legs out under the table. "I want to take you somewhere tomorrow."

"Where?"

"Nowhere scary. On an art tour. We can walk, and I can show you all my favorite spots."

She hesitated. "Is it close?"

"Yes. Don't stress about it. That's part of the rules, right? To try not to stress about things before they happen. You'll make yourself feel sick."

"I try not to, you know. And I can distract myself sometimes, but then I start thinking again, and I worry and worry and worry until it seems so overwhelming I don't know what to do. Except worry."

"What's the worst that can happen?" I asked, using her line. "It rains on us? Then I get to give you my jacket and treat you special, and it's actually a good thing instead of a bad one."

"A panic attack is what could happen," she said softly. Then she released a breath. "But I know it seems bigger and scarier than it is, and that's what I need to understand. It's just…it's not one specific thing I expect to go wrong. It's not knowing. It's all the things that could happen that I won't be prepared for."

"I'll be there. The whole time."

"Which means I'm depending on you again," she said with a sigh. "It's a big contradiction. I want to have someone there, and I need to do it on my own. But…"

"I can come over."

"What? Now? No! You have something to do. Ignore me. I'm not talking about this anymore."

"I love when you talk."

"You need a better hobby, then."

With a grin, I put the banana in my backpack. She sounded just like Rogue. How had I ever doubted they were the same person?

"I like this one just fine," I said. "Tell you what. I'll take you out tomorrow, and you can plan something for next time. By yourself."

"Pressure," she murmured.

"I know how you feel."

"I know. I'm sorry. Go see your dad."

"You should do something to distract yourself so you won't think about tomorrow."

"I was thinking about maybe working on an asteroid belt."

"Oh God, you make that sound sexy."

"Jackson."

"I need to come over there right now."

"Jackson."

"You can't deter me. I'm on my way."

"Don't you dare."

I took the origami book downstairs to find my holds. "But, Zoe."

"No arguing."

I gave an exaggerated sigh. "If you say so."

"Really, Jackson. You can do this."

The house looked empty when I got there. No car in the driveway, no weather-beaten chairs out on the patio. Of course, they'd been falling apart anyway. Maybe Dad had put them out with the trash.

There *was* a big pile on the curb. The chairs weren't there, but there were boxes and two trash cans, and a broken shelf— one I remembered used to be in the main bathroom.

I sat in the car for a long time, staring at the trash, making up scenarios about why my dad actually wanted me here. He was moving. He'd gotten a job across the country. He'd gotten taken to jail, and someone else now owned the house.

Anything was more likely than he simply wanted me to visit. That he'd gotten his life together. That he wanted to be a father again.

Zoe's words jumped into my mind, pumping me full of purpose. *You can do this.*

She was right. What did I have to lose?

I opened the door and stepped out. The sky had become overcast with dark billowy clouds that hovered above the city, trapping in the heat. It felt like it was weighing me down, making it harder and harder to take each step.

When I arrived at the curb, the trash cans in front of me, I found another way to distract myself. There were dozens of papers in a bag, mostly shredded, but just underneath I could see an amber bottle.

Gritting my teeth, I lifted the bag out, staring at the contents of the trash can. A handful of alcohol bottles. Beer in cans, Jack Daniel's bottles, even wine coolers. More than half the trash can was full of liquor.

Of course. This was his world. Why had I thought he might have changed?

I shoved the bag back inside and peeked into the other can. This one didn't have any bottles, but it held something even worse.

Clothes. My mother's clothes. Two bags of them, and even some loose items like an old jacket and a pair of boots. Her favorite pair. Granted, they had holes in them, but they were still her favorite.

What an ass! How dare he throw her stuff in the trash.

The sound of the screen door opening caught my attention. Dad walked out, wearing jeans and a ball cap. "Jackson?"

"What is this?" I said.

He descended two steps and paused. His gaze swept to the house across the street, and I noticed someone looking out the window. Probably wondering why I was going through the garbage. Maybe even ready to call the cops because I was scavenging. After all, most of the neighbors probably had no idea who I was, since I'd been gone for so long.

Dad moved closer. He squinted, looking pained. "It's not what it looks like."

"It looks like you had a party. It looks like the same thing it always looks like around here."

"That's not—"

"I don't want to hear it."

"They're full," Austin said. "Most of the bottles, all the beers. They're not empty cans or things I've drunk. See? I can show you—I'm getting rid of them."

His words struck a chord, but I was already on a roll. "And Mom's stuff? You figured you'd toss that out, too?"

"Just her old stuff. Stuff no one else would want."

"Not even me?" Pain pierced my heart. He was getting rid of everything from the past.

When the screen door opened again, a woman with blond hair walked out. I stared dumbly at her, trying not to put the pieces into place.

I reached into the trash can and grabbed Mom's jacket, clutching it close to my chest. "I get it," I whispered, already turning. "You've replaced Mom. You just needed to throw her stuff out."

"No, that's not—"

"Don't talk to me!" I shouted, starting across the street. My voice broke when I said the words, and my eyes blurred with the rage of tears I was embarrassed and mortified to be on the verge of shedding.

Why would I expect anything different? This was Dad. This was what he did.

"Jackson, wait!"

I got into my car, slammed the door, and shoved my keys in the ignition. When the car wouldn't start, I pounded the steering wheel and cranked the keys again.

Dad started toward my car, waving his hands as if to make me stop. The car sputtered to life, shuddering once before I whipped around the cul-de-sac, driving from my home as the first raindrops started to fall.

49.

Rogue2015: Hey. You're not really going to let me win this one, are you?

BlackKNIGHT: It looks pretty hopeless from my end.

Rogue2015: Hopeless? We've only made five moves.

BlackKNIGHT: Still.

Rogue2015: Are you okay?

BlackKNIGHT: Rough day.

Rogue2105: You want to talk about it?

BlackKNIGHT: I really want to, but I should probably go. It's getting late.

Rogue2015: I'm here if you need me.

BlackKNIGHT: I know.

50.

ZOE

Worry ate away my stomach lining. I couldn't sleep at all last night. Jackson hadn't called after he went to visit his dad, and hadn't answered my call when I tried to get in touch with him later in the evening. When I tried Jackson's phone again this morning, there was still no answer.

He was probably busy with school, that's all. He couldn't get back to me because it was a school day.

But that didn't help. He texted me all the time when he was at school.

I didn't know what else to do but talk to my parents. They'd be able to figure it out. But I'd told Jackson I wouldn't say anything. I was trying really hard lately to keep my promises.

But I couldn't even talk to BlackKNIGHT about it. He'd had a rough day, too. Something twisted in my gut—an idea. A fear. Jackson and BlackKNIGHT…there were so many similarities.

I paced in front of my paper wall, for once not thinking about planets or asteroids or chess. My mind was jumbled. I couldn't stop putting Jackson and BlackKNIGHT together as the same person. And worse, I couldn't stop worrying that something had happened to Jackson. That his dad had been drunk when he'd gone over there. Or he'd gotten violent.

Gina wasn't coming until tomorrow, but I seriously considered calling her. I could tell her about Jackson and she couldn't say anything. She had to keep it confidential. But maybe she'd give me some advice. She'd help me figure out what to do.

Mom popped her head in the room. "Did you do it yet?"

"Huh?"

"Your math test."

I glanced to my computer. I'd told Mom I was going to take my final test early, and I'd completely forgotten.

"I…" I shook my head. "No."

"You should do it now before Jackson gets here. Then you won't worry about it later. You're going out tonight, right?"

She looked hopeful. I couldn't infuse that same hope into the smile I gave her. Jackson said he'd be here, but I didn't know for sure. He wouldn't even talk to me.

What if something had happened to him?

"Zoe?"

I blinked, realizing I was staring at her but not really seeing her. "The test. Right. I'll do it now."

Instead of leaving, Mom walked into the room. She looked up at my wall with a smile. "You added more."

"Yeah."

"I like Venus," she said, pointing. "That's Venus, right?"

"Yes. I like that one, too."

"Nice colors." Her smile was strained when she looked at me. "Are you okay? You seem…distracted."

I shrugged.

"No." She frowned. "Not just distracted. Worried."

"It's…" My math test came up on the screen. All I had to do was click the box and the timer would start.

"Did something happen with Jackson?" Mom pressed.

I practically forced him to talk to his dad last night, even though his dad could be dangerous, and now I haven't heard anything from him. I'm scared.

"I'm nervous, that's all," I told her.

"For today?"

I nodded. "And Friday. I'm going to take Jackson to the museum for that art exhibit."

Mom brightened. "Really?"

"I already bought tickets."

She smiled. "I'm really proud of you. And the exhibit looks fun. You'll have to tell me about it."

"I will."

I hadn't given Jackson's secret away. But now I felt worse. I wasn't helping him by lying about his situation.

"I'm going to do my test."

She set a hand on my shoulder before leaving the room. I forced myself to focus on math and think about Jackson later.

Twenty minutes before Jackson was supposed to be here, I found my mom in her workroom, answering comments on her YouTube page. Her fingers flew over the keyboard, showing how comfortable she felt with answering questions and keeping her fans happy.

"I'm getting ready to go," I said.

She turned around, hand clasping the back of her chair. "I didn't hear the elevator. Is Jackson here?"

"I'm going to meet him downstairs."

A range of emotions traveled across her face before she settled on a smile. "Okay. Just check in later, okay? And let me know when you'll be back. And be safe."

I hugged her. "We will."

But something about the moment made me linger. Maybe it was the blue kimono she had hanging on the wall, or the way she lined up all her note cards on her desk—like something I would do. Maybe it was the concern in her eyes or the detailed barrette she'd put in her hair. Something about that moment made her more real. Like a person instead of a mom.

"Something wrong?" she asked.

"Were you nervous when you came here?"

Mom flexed her fingers on the back of the chair. "Here? Our apartment?"

"No…here. America."

"Oh." She laughed, then released a breath that deflated her shoulders. "Yes. *So* nervous. I had to start middle school, which wasn't anything like school back at home. My English was—" She wobbled her hand back and forth. "So-so. I thought I was going to throw up in my first class."

"But you didn't."

She shook her head, eyes turning wistful. "No. I was actually sort of a novelty. It was fun. I just—I had to give it a try. I locked myself in the bathroom that morning, you know. With my shoes on and everything, which really annoyed my mom." She grinned. "It took my parents twenty minutes to convince me to come out. I was almost late to school."

"I'm glad it was good for you," I said. I could picture her clearly. A shorter, more petite version of my already tiny mom, heading off to school with a backpack and a belly full of butterflies. Even scarier than when I went to school.

"Life is full of adventures." She nodded as if in approval of her own words. "Try to think of it like that. An adventure."

I swallowed my fear and guilt and said, "Can I talk to you about something?"

"Of course."

Before I could stop myself, I spilled it all. Everything about my worries and about Jackson. I needed an adult—someone who knew how to deal with the situation.

Mom listened to the entire thing, and then said she'd talk with Dad. It was the best I could do right now. I'd see Jackson today and maybe he'd give me good news. Maybe everything would be fine.

After giving Mom another hug, I walked to the elevator and slipped my shoes on, pretending this was something I did all the time. Getting the mail, going to school, going out with friends. An adventure.

Checking for the third time to make sure I had my key card and my wallet in my purse, I pressed the elevator button and rode to the lobby. The man at the desk greeted me like he'd taken to doing when I'd started coming out of my apartment more and more.

I smiled, made myself say hi, and walked across the lobby one tile at a time. No Jackson yet. That was okay. I was a few minutes early. Though, he usually was, too.

I stopped in front of the revolving door, staring out at the overcast afternoon. I hadn't been outside of the building (besides the rooftop and balcony) since I went to lunch with Mom. The thrill that ran through my body was tinged with terror. How was it possible to want something so much and be so afraid of it?

My chest started to get tight, and panic clogged my throat. No, no, no...

Then Jackson appeared outside the door, hands in his pockets, and all my worries melted away. He stared up at the building, his face thoughtful, then lowered his gaze. His eyes met mine through the glass.

He smiled.

Heart fluttering, I walked through the revolving door and joined him on the sidewalk. A breeze blew by, and I tugged my cardigan tighter around my body.

"I missed you," Jackson said, drawing me close.

I went into his arms, for a moment forgetting what happened yesterday. "I missed you, too."

"You look nice in that color."

"It's Mae's," I said.

He eased back to look at my outfit again. "I like it better on you."

Laughing, I dropped my chin. His shoes were scuffed, almost worn through on the big toe. My stomach somersaulted. "Jackson…"

"Zoe."

The smile in his voice made me look up. "I thought maybe you weren't coming."

He clasped his hand around mine. "Why wouldn't I come?"

"Did something happen with your dad?"

He shifted from one foot to the next, the corners of his mouth turning down in a frown. Someone bumped me from behind, and I stumbled, my cheeks flushing. "Sorry."

My heart squeezed in my chest, warning me this was the real world I stood in, not my safe room.

"Zoe," Jackson said. "Look at me."

I exhaled and met his eyes.

"Are you okay?" he asked.

It felt colder than it had a minute ago. I shivered.

"Do you need to go back inside?"

Yes. No. I shook my head, but the pressure in my chest wouldn't stop. It wasn't just because I was outside. It was Jackson, and me worrying about him, and the fact that I'd actually told Gina I might go to school. And graduation was less than three weeks away. It hit me all at once. It was too much.

But that wasn't Jackson's problem. He already had so much to deal with.

"Close your eyes," Jackson said.

I glanced around. People walked everywhere, crossing streets, talking, laughing, shouting. "I don't—"

"Who cares about them?"

He set his hands on my arms, thumbs brushing lightly on my sweater. "Close your eyes. No one is looking at us, no one cares."

Sure. If you were Jackson. I was Zoe. I was hyperaware of everything, even if it wasn't my problem.

I did as he said and closed my eyes. I was supposed to be making him feel better and instead, he was helping me.

"Good," he said. "Whatever you're worried about, we'll fix it."

"But—"

"No arguments." There was laughter in his voice. And then, as if reading my mind, he said, "Don't worry about me."

I shivered when I felt his lips touch mine. "You can't stop me."

He kissed me again, one hand brushing my cheek so softly I could barely tell it was there.

I opened my eyes to find him staring at me. "What happened with your dad yesterday?"

"I don't want to ruin the day."

"I want you to stay with us. Or Robert, maybe—"

"Why does this have to be a big deal?"

"Because I really care about you. A lot."

And it was growing into something more. Something I was afraid to even think about.

The moment the words registered on his face, I ducked my chin. My shoes looked brand new. Clean. No frayed laces or scuff marks. My heart slammed into my ribs. The air thinned, no longer reaching my lungs.

"I really care about you, too," Jackson said.

The world stilled around me. For once, I didn't care who was looking, who stood near me, who heard me.

He pulled me close in a hug, breath touching my hair. "This is a good thing."

It was. It felt like us against the world, and we would come out on top.

When I looked up, Jackson smiled at me. "Let's enjoy the day."

Because I didn't want him to stop smiling, I set aside what I wanted to say about his dad. I didn't want to ruin what we'd just said to each other.

51.

JACKSON

I took Zoe to the art museum first. I knew how much she wanted to see it. She stood there for a full minute, looking up at the building, staring at the strange industrial lines of it. Trying to make sense of the shape.

It made me feel better than I'd felt all day. I'd managed to make it through a day of school, but it wasn't easy. I kept thinking about my dad. I'd avoided Mae and Robert because I didn't want to talk to anyone. But by the end of the day, I knew meeting with Zoe would help get my mind off all the stress.

Next, I showed Zoe another one of my favorite pieces of art, a giant dustpan with a broom attached. It reminded me of Horse on Chair. You could take it literally or find all sorts of hidden meanings while staring at it.

Then she turned to futuristic Stonehenge, her head angled. "This is interesting."

She had a better eye for art than I did, so I didn't say anything about how I thought it was weird. But none of that mattered because Zoe was out here. With me.

And she'd told me how much she cared for me. How did that even make sense?

All this time, I'd been playing chess with a girl who barely knew me, trying to find a way into her world. And now I had.

Even the shit with my dad yesterday couldn't ruin that.

Zoe touched the stone, rubbing her hand on the smooth surface. "It's kind of creepy."

I laughed and wrapped my arms around her waist from behind, dropping my chin to her neck. "It *is* creepy. I like the one on the other side better."

She settled her hand over mine, our fingers entwining. "Show me."

"As you wish." I released her and gestured. "This way."

We walked around the building, passing kids on the sidewalk and a bus full of tourists who'd stopped to see the library.

"The building is like art," she said, dodging someone who had pulled out his camera. "Can we go inside?"

"Of course. I'll show you my favorite spot after we see *Yearling*."

"What's *Yearling*?"

I pointed to the sculpture.

She stopped walking and laughed. "That's a horse on a chair."

"Right."

Grinning, she said, "I like it."

"Me, too. I can show you more. There's so much to see. The whole world."

"Maybe we'll stick to our art tour today. But…"

"What?"

"You're right. There's a lot out here to see."

Taking her hand, I led her into the library. I didn't miss the way she watched everyone else as they walked by, or how she grimaced when a group of teenagers exited the front doors, surrounding us.

"One minute," she said.

I stopped by her, alarmed. "What?"

She pointed to the corner, away from people. "Can I just have…one minute?"

It sounded like she was having trouble breathing. I quickly walked to the corner with her, wishing there was something I could do. But being quiet seemed like my best bet. I waited, listening to her breathing, but kept my gaze averted so she could compose herself.

"It's… Sorry," she whispered.

I looked back. "Are you okay?"

She clutched one hand at her chest but nodded. "I'm okay."

"You sure? We can go back."

"No. No way." She smiled at me, and even though it wobbled some, it was sincere. "I want to do this. I'm *going* to do this."

"Okay. Anything you want."

After another moment, she took my hand. "That's better."

"You're good?" I asked.

She glanced around. Probably to see if anyone had been watching. No one even looked at us.

"This is just…a lot." She lifted her chin. "Yes, I'm good."

I squeezed her hand and led her into the library, vowing to try to keep her distracted so she'd have less to worry about.

"If you could go anywhere in the world, where would it be?" I asked.

She lifted her head, staring at the tall ceiling as we entered. "I don't know. Maybe Japan, to visit my family. It would be cool to make a paper village of an old Japanese town. Pagodas and temples, fishing boats, and—" She broke off, blushing.

"Don't stop. Keep talking," I said, squeezing her hand again. I led her to the second floor, walking through the aisles of books and watching her face as she took it all in. "You'd visit Japan. Where else?"

"Maybe, uh…college somewhere."

I grinned at her. "Boulder has lots of good hiking close by. I went there a few times with my mom."

And, of course, that's where I was going for college. I kind of liked the idea of Zoe being there in the future.

"I could take all the astronomy classes you're going to take," she said. "I bet they have huge telescopes you can see Saturn with."

She made it sound magical. I reminded myself how lucky I was to be able to go. Even with all the hard things standing in my way, I had a chance to start over there. I needed to do it.

"You should start with high school," I told her, changing the conversation.

She stopped in one of the aisles, tracing her hand over the spine of a book. "I talked to Gina about that. Maybe starting this fall. It's going to be overwhelming."

"I'll help you. Zoe, this is…"

"Scary."

I put my hands up on the shelves, on either side of her shoulders. "Scary. Intimidating. Wonderful. An adventure. You could do it, I know you could."

"It's just an idea. And I know what you just did there."

"What?"

"Changed the subject."

I leaned in to kiss her, loving the way her eyes automatically dropped shut. Like she was waiting for something she knew would change her day. Her week. Her life.

"It's because I want you to go to school," I murmured.

She slid her arms around my waist. Her head barely came up to my chin. Her phone buzzed with a text, and she released me. She pulled it out of her pocket, looking at the message.

"Everything okay?" I asked when she frowned.

"Just Mae. She was asking if you were with me."

"Oh." I frowned. "What for?"

"I don't know."

I took her hand, trying to ignore the twist of worry in my gut. "Let's keep doing our tour. I'll show you my favorite spot to sit."

We spent more than an hour in the library, scanning all the books, sitting in the children's pavilion where my mom would read to the kids. Once my stomach started grumbling, Zoe insisted we go back to her apartment for dinner instead of eating somewhere outside of the house.

"Unless you have to go home," she said.

I shook my head. Even if I *were* living with my dad, which I wasn't, I was right where I wanted to be for the moment.

We rode the elevator up and stepped inside. After removing our shoes, we walked into the kitchen. Zoe's mom had written a note on the counter about going out for dinner, which left us alone in the huge apartment.

"We have subs left over from lunch," she said, leaning into the refrigerator. "Or I could make something. Spaghetti? Anything you want."

"Subs are fine."

She turned around, body backlit by the refrigerator. "Are you sure? Because I could make something. Or we could order something. What sounds good to you?"

"Subs are fine," I repeated. "You don't have to go out of your way."

She turned away, pulling the sandwiches out of the refrigerator. When she went for another cupboard, probably to grab plates, I caught her hand.

"What's wrong?"

She shook her head, forcing a smile in my direction even though I could see the tears in her eyes.

"Please, stop for a minute. Come sit down and talk to me."

"Aren't you hungry?"

"Come talk to me."

She followed me to the couch in the living room, with only the low light of a lamp to guide us. Outside the bank of windows, the sun was setting, and I could already see a few stars and the full moon.

When she tried to walk past me on the couch, I pulled her into my lap. Her breath caught, and her arms came around my neck.

"I know you're worried for me," I said, realizing how many times today I'd brushed off her concern.

"Why won't you let me do anything to help?"

"Because it's not your problem."

She frowned. "Neither is my anxiety. I mean, it's not *your* problem."

I sighed, not wanting to see her point. "That's different."

"No, it's not."

"Who's being stubborn now?"

To my surprise, she reached out to touch my cheek, meeting my eyes. "I'm not being stubborn. I said—I said I care about you, and…I meant it."

My humor vanished. She was right. She meant it. I could see it in her eyes. I could see everything. Worry, fear, hope, longing. All I wanted in that moment was to be near her. To forget about the world and pretend there was nothing weighing us down.

I closed my lips over hers, letting my hands slide down to her waist. She shifted in my lap to straddle my legs, and I let out a groan, surprised at her boldness.

"Zoe."

"What?" she whispered, easing back. "Did I hurt you?"

"No. I don't want you…"

"You don't want me?"

I choked on a laugh. "No, I absolutely want you. I don't want you to feel like I expect anything is all."

She swallowed, her cheeks reddening. "I don't expect anything, and I don't feel like you do, either. I just…I've missed out on so much, Jackson. I'm afraid I'm going to run out of chances before I'm brave enough to try everything I want to do."

My chest moved up and down in a few deep breaths, trying to sort through her words. "Zoe…"

She pressed her hands over her face. "God, this is embarrassing. I didn't mean *that*. I meant—I'm sorry. I shouldn't have said anything. I'm really sorry."

She moved as if to get up, but I held her in place. "Don't apologize. Let's just…don't think. Don't assume. Don't *worry*."

I pulled her hands away again and kissed her before she could even take a breath. I'd let her set the pace, I'd let her do what she wanted, and I'd show her that I'd respect whatever or wherever we ended up.

Her tongue touched mine tentatively, and my hands squeezed her hips. She felt like a feather, so light I could barely tell she was there except for her mouth against mine, her soft breaths tickling my checks, and her hands making their way up my chest.

Her name was on my lips. I slid my fingers under the hem of her shirt, touching bare skin. I froze when her breath stalled in her throat.

With her mouth still fused to mine, she ran her hands under my T-shirt, and it was all I could do to sit still. Zoe was the bravest person I knew, and she was bringing me to my knees.

The elevator *ding*ed, startling both of us. Zoe was off me faster than I could blink. She stood in a rush, starting in the direction of the elevator as we heard her family's voices. I ran a hand over my face as I walked to the kitchen, and patted my hair to make sure it looked normal. Then I yanked down the front hem of my shirt to cover the effect Zoe had on me.

"We got back about ten minutes ago," Zoe was saying as they all joined me in the kitchen. "We're going to eat your subs from lunch."

Yoko smiled when she saw me, but it didn't have her usual pep. "Of course. Jackson, I can fix something else if you want. You don't have to have a sandwich."

She sounded just like Zoe. Zoe, who stood in the doorway to the kitchen, her cheeks flushed, wringing her hands.

I gave her a wry smile and focused on the sandwiches. But after a moment, with Yoko still staring at me, I looked up.

"Everything okay?"

Yoko fidgeted, also like Zoe, and Mr. King shrugged out of his jacket. "We want you to know you're welcome over here any time."

I swallowed, gripping the edge of the counter. Uh oh… did they suspect something just happened between me and Zoe? "I know that. I appreciate it."

Zoe's mouth hung open, but nothing came out. I didn't have to look hard to see the apology in her eyes.

Yoko stepped forward, looking first at the sandwiches, and then me. "Jackson, if you need somewhere to stay…"

The meaning behind her words slammed into me, killing my appetite. I turned to Zoe. "You told them?"

Mae's eyes were wide, but she only watched the exchange silently.

Zoe wrung her hands in front of her. "Jackson—"

"We're concerned about you," Yoko said. "We want you to be safe."

I had a bad taste in my mouth, and my heart beat hard, blood rushing in my ears. Zoe had told them about my dad, which meant they'd figure out I was homeless eventually. Were the Kings going to tell social services?

"Why don't we sit down and talk this through." Mr. King turned, as if to go for the kitchen table. "We'll figure this out."

"I can't," I said, panic gripping me. "I should go. It—I should check on my dad."

A lie. But what else was I supposed to say? I couldn't be here anymore. I had to get out.

"Jackson," Zoe said, following me to the elevator. "Please don't go."

I shoved my feet into my sneakers. "I have to figure this out."

"I know. I can help. My parents understand—"

"I can't believe you told them."

Her face was stricken, tears threatening to spill over. "I'm worried about you. Please don't go."

"Worried about *me*?"

"Yes. Why won't you let me help?"

I choked on a painful laugh. "Let *you* help? What about you? I've been *trying* to help you, too. You're perfectly fine listening to me online, but in person, you're the exact same way. You don't want any help."

"Online? Jackson…" Her cheeks paled. "What do you mean?"

"Rogue," I said, my voice sinking low. But the moment the word was out of my mouth, I felt a twinge in my stomach. Especially when her mouth dropped open. But she'd hurt *me,* and she was trying to tell me what to do, so I powered on. "You're Rogue, from *Chess Challenge.* I know because I'm

BlackKNIGHT. I've known for a while."

She jerked in a sharp breath, and then shook her head, like she didn't believe I was telling the truth. "How long?"

"Who cares?" I asked, tying my laces. "It sucks to believe in someone and have them not be who you really thought they were."

Hurt flashed in her eyes, but I turned to the elevator.

"Jackson, wait—" Her voice came out choked. "Black-KNIGHT—he said he was homeless."

I froze, realization zooming through me. Now she knew everything. The whole truth—and the real reason I never went home. "It's not like that—I mean, you can't—"

"Please don't go," she whispered. "You can stay here. Or call Robert. You don't have anywhere to go."

"I'll be fine," I said. "Just…ask your parents not to say anything. It's not a problem. I'm almost eighteen. It's not—not a big deal."

"They won't say anything. I promise. Please, stay."

I couldn't. I was worried about the future. I could be in trouble. I might have to go home, or else deal with the consequences. Consequences meant a foster home most likely, or staying with my dad until I was eighteen and could be emancipated. Consequences meant everyone else would know what had gone on, too.

I pressed the elevator button and got in the moment the doors opened. Zoe watched with tears in her eyes until the elevator shut and I couldn't see her anymore.

52.

Rogue2015: I haven't heard from you for a while. Everything okay?

Rogue2015: I discovered a new chess move. I'll try it on you when we start another match.

Rogue2015: Okay, so…good night.

53.

ZOE

Gina sat across from me at the kitchen table. Mom insisted we eat muffins during our session. She'd been feeding me a lot since Jackson left two days ago. When in doubt, feed your children. Pretty sure that was her motto.

It wasn't helping. I picked at my muffin. I understood why Jackson was worried; I just didn't know why he wouldn't talk to me about it. It's not like he was going to get in trouble because of what his dad had done—or for leaving his dad's house.

Then my cheeks flamed. Besides, he wasn't the only one who'd had secrets revealed. As Rogue, I'd told him everything. I'd even told him about this boy I like and how I was coming across like some kind of stalker. He had to know it was him. I'd sounded like such an idiot.

"Your mom said you passed your math test. Ninety-eight percent."

I nodded.

"That's great. Congratulations."

"I hate math."

She laughed. "Okay."

"Sorry. I'm tired."

I hadn't slept at all last night. I kept checking my phone to see if Jackson had called or texted. I was supposed to take him to the museum tonight, and I had no idea where he was.

"You want to talk about it?" Gina asked.

Did I? Yes and no. My heart hurt for Jackson. For once I wasn't thinking about how scary it was to leave the apartment. I was thinking about how hard it was for Jackson to deal with this, without knowing what was going to happen to him. And part of me…just a small part, was angry for the lies he'd told.

"I don't…" I shook my head. "I don't think so."

"What about school? Your mom said she stopped by the school—"

"What?" I dropped muffin crumbs on my plate. "What for?"

"She had to at least go in and talk to them in case you decided to enroll this fall. Which I think you should."

My stomach clenched. Now, after everything that had happened, school seemed like such a huge step. Normally I'd talk to BK about it. Or even Jackson. But then…I had no idea when I'd see him again.

I straightened. Maybe this was a sign that I needed to start dealing with things alone. The thought made a jolt of fear shoot straight to my belly. But alone was good, right? Alone was…independent.

The house was quiet. Mae was at cheerleading practice, Dad at work, and Mom making another YouTube video about the perfect hostess gift. There was comfort in the silence. But I kind of missed the noise, the people. At school, out *there*, I'd have noise. I'd have new adventures like both my mom and Jackson had said.

Gina smiled. "These are really good muffins."

I couldn't help but laugh. "Mom's good with muffins."

She dusted her hands together and pushed the plate

aside. "Seriously, I think you're ready for this. You've built up momentum. You're coping with things. You're dealing. You're taking steps, and that's great progress. If you keep this up, the world is yours."

The world is yours.

It sounded like something Jackson would say. And dammit, I had to stop thinking about him! This was one of those things Dr. Edwards would tell me to let go. Right now, there was nothing I could do, and making myself sick because of it wasn't going to fix the problem.

"Stick to the plan," Gina said. "Whatever you were planning on doing, do it. Stick to it. Even if life tries to set you back."

"You sound more like a motivational speaker than a therapist."

"Kind of the same thing, right? I'm here to encourage you to move on from things. To work through things. To find your place and hold on tight to it because this won't be the first or the last time life tries to knock you on your ass."

"You're right."

My throat grew thick with emotion. The tickets I'd bought for the art exhibit were in my pocket, and I thought about not using them and what it would mean. I'd miss out. If I didn't start school, I might not do it at all. And I'd miss out.

And graduation…it would kill Mae if I didn't go.

Everything with Jackson had made me realize how much I needed my life to change. But not for everyone else. For me.

The first planet hurt. As I removed it from the ceiling, my heart physically ached. I'd spent months and months folding and cutting and planning my solar system.

But it was time to let it go. It was time for something new.

I'd let my paper room become my reason for living, my comfort. At first, it helped. But now…it seemed like it was stopping me from moving on.

So I pulled planet after planet apart, stuffing the paper into trash bags. I sniffled by the time I reached the third bag, and sat at my computer.

Right about now I'd message BK and have a conversation that would calm me down and make me feel better. Or I'd text Jackson, and he'd make me feel better.

I curled my fist around a stray piece of paper, crushing it. They were the same person. Whichever one I got in touch with, the other would know.

Just like the paper wall, Jackson/BlackKNIGHT had become my safety net. With new determination, I stood and ripped more paper off the wall. Then off the ceiling. I threw it on the floor and yanked another piece down.

Jackson had lied to me, which meant BlackKNIGHT had lied to me, and I was *still* trying to do what everyone else wanted. I tossed Saturn toward the trash bags and went after Jupiter. No more. I needed to live my life for myself.

It took six large black trash bags to get rid of the entire universe. Jupiter was gone. Cassiopeia had vanished. There was no trace of the asteroid belt I'd started only last week, or my favorite dwarf planet, Pluto. All gone.

All I could do was stand and stare at the bare, white wall.

I heard Mae's gasp before I saw her in the doorway of the study.

"You took it down," she said.

I did. I did it, and part of me didn't regret it.

Mae walked into the room, eyeing the bags on the floor, all filled with paper. "Why?"

I shrugged. "I needed new scenery."

"Did you just do that to make something new?"

Did I? I glanced at all my unused pieces of paper. Every color of the rainbow. My fingers itched to get my hands on them, to create a whole new world in my room. Something that made me happy. I'd considered Paris.

But then I'd shot down the idea.

Mae folded her arms, still standing directly in the doorway. "I thought you were going to school."

"I don't know," I said, still staring at the wall. "I'm figuring it out."

"But Mom said she went in to talk to them. You can start in the fall."

"I like being homeschooled," I said. It was true, I did like it. But it wasn't a substitute for all the things I wanted to do.

"Liar."

"Mae."

"I don't think you do. I think you're scared. Especially without Jackson."

My gaze whipped to hers.

Her eyes went soft. "I'm sorry about what happened. I think Jackson just needs some time. But you can't wait for him to do everything you want to do."

"Who said I wanted to go to school?"

"*You* did! When we talked last week, you said you wanted to go to school, even if it was scary. Guess what? It *is* scary. For all of us. So what? Deal with it!"

Tears filled my eyes. "You don't understand."

"I don't. Just like you don't understand all the things I'm dealing with, either. But you can't hide in here with your paper all the time. And Mom's letting you!" She stared at the paper stand, shaking her head. "She got you all this paper—almost like she wants you to stay in here."

"That's not how it is."

"It isn't?"

"She just…she feels bad."

Mae walked to me, lips pressed in a firm line. "You can't stay in here every day."

"I'm not—"

"You are. You were doing good. You were trying…"

"I *am* trying."

Mae grabbed a handful of papers. I reached out, trying to take them gently from her.

"Be careful—"

"This isn't living." She waved the papers around, crumpling them in her grip. "It's a hobby."

"Stop! My papers!"

"I want my sister back."

I froze, her words so heavy they almost knocked me over.

Her cheeks turned red—whether from embarrassment or exertion or anger, I wasn't sure. She dropped the papers on my desk and stalked out of the room.

A sob rose in my throat. Stuffing it down, I picked up my papers, smoothed out the edges, and returned them to their correct slots. Mae's words ran over and over in my mind, a roar of accusation.

And the tickets to the museum were still in my pocket. Waiting. Proving her right. I was still waiting to hear from Jackson, still hoping he'd want to go.

But I hadn't heard anything from him.

54.

JACKSON

Sitting in my car across the street from my dad's house, I held my mother's worn jacket on my lap. It smelled musty.

It was my fault for not bringing a few things with me when I'd left home the first time. But I'd been in a hurry. And after that…going back wasn't an option. Until now.

I had to get this dealt with so I didn't get in trouble for living on my own. Once I knew Dad wasn't going to tell anyone, that our secret was safe—or safe enough, now that Zoe and her family knew—I could get on with my life. And he could get on with his.

Stepping out of the car, I stared at the front door. Maybe he wasn't home. Then I'd have a few more hours.

But part of me, the part that was tired and aching and longing to go sit with Zoe in her safe room, wanted this to be done for good.

I walked up the front steps and knocked on the door. It opened almost right away, my dad standing with a pair of glasses on and looking nothing like the day I'd left.

"Jackson. Are you okay?"

"I'm fine."

"This is your house, too. You don't have to knock. I didn't change the locks, just in case, but — " Dad broke off, shaking his head. "I was wondering when you were going to come up here. You've been sitting out there for almost an hour."

I had. In that hour, I'd almost texted Zoe three times, but I didn't know what to say to her.

"You want to come in?" he asked.

His jeans hung on his frame, but he looked clean. Healthy for the most part. His eyes weren't red rimmed like they had often been in the past. He even looked rested.

"I'm still deciding." My feet were glued to the porch. What was I supposed to do? This was the moment to fix it all — or to end it.

I needed to do something. Zoe's parents knew about my dad, and Zoe knew about me being homeless. If I didn't fix this, everything — my future, especially — could go wrong.

"I…went to visit your mom," Dad said. "In fact, I go a lot to bring her flowers."

The daisies at her gravesite flashed through my mind. My dad had been the one who brought the flowers? He'd remembered how much she loved daisies?

Dad rubbed the back of his neck. "It's like…it's like she's closer to me when I go. Like I can hear her talking to me. Telling me how hard this was for you, but that I still have to try. I…I'd really like it if you came in for a bit to talk."

Struck silent, I followed him numbly into the house.

"You want something to drink?" Dad asked.

I shadowed him to the kitchen, so distracted by the cleanliness of the living room, I almost ran into the wall. It looked like he'd hired a maid to come in and straighten it all up, though I doubted he had money for that.

"I don't have much," Dad said, peering into the fridge. "A soda. Orange juice. Water."

"Water is fine."

He filled a glass with ice and tap water. I resisted the urge to hold the glass up to the light to make sure it was clean. If the rest of the kitchen was any indication, it had been washed recently.

Dad gestured to the round table by the window. "I could fix you a sandwich, or there's some leftover lasagna Cathy brought over."

"Cathy? You mean Mom's friend Cathy?" I vaguely remembered a chubby blonde who always smiled and brought me suckers.

I sat at the table. Dad joined me, but he couldn't seem to sit still. It looked like he was nervous.

"Cathy. Right. She was here when you…dropped by the other day."

"That was Cathy?"

Dad smiled, tapping his fingers on the table. "Yeah, she looks different. Lost a lot of weight. She…she wanted to help."

"Help?" I frowned. What the hell was that supposed to mean?

Dad stood, walking to the pantry. He pulled out a bag of pretzels and set them on the table between us. "Yes, help. I—I needed to clean out the house."

"Mom's stuff."

"No. I mean, not just that." Dad pulled off his glasses and rubbed his hands over his face. "It's…" He sat again. "Everything else."

The alcohol. All the bottles in the trash.

"I still had everything in the house, and it seemed smart to get rid of it. I—I've been sober for six months, but I thought it might be a good idea to have someone here when I threw it all out. So I wouldn't be tempted. I should have done it a long time ago. I was supposed to, but it was my own kind of test. Like…if I could be around all that shit and still say no, then…I was making progress."

His words sank in. It was true that most of the bottles in the trash didn't seem to be open or weren't missing much, but that didn't mean anything. He could have gone out afterward and gotten more. He could have more in the house right now.

"I'm sorry you had to see that. I was hoping it would all be out of here if you—you know, if you decided to come back."

He opened the bag of pretzels and pushed them in my direction. "I can make you that sandwich, too, if you want."

"I'm fine. I can eat later."

Or I'd take the bag of pretzels with me. That would be good enough for the rest of the evening.

"Uh…" Dad tapped his fingers again, seemed to realize what he was doing, and set his hands flat on the table. "That's what I wanted to talk to you about. Not—eating. I mean…" He looked at me, a mirror image of hazel eyes behind identical glasses. "I've been calling because I wanted to see if you wanted to come home."

I laughed, but it came out rough. Short. Painful. "Come home? Why would I do that?"

"Because I—I have a plan. I got a job."

"You got a job?" He'd said that in his voicemail, hadn't he? But I hadn't believed it.

"It's nights right now because I've only been there for five months. But they said maybe after a year I could switch to daytime. Anyway, nights work better because I make more. So I can—you know, pay the bills. Catch up. I've been saving money for you, for college."

"You paid my insurance payment. And my phone bill."

Dad nodded. "That's my job."

"It hasn't been for the last two years."

"I wasn't doing my job for the last two years, and I'm sorry for that. Your mom—" His hands curled slowly into fists and then relaxed. "She always took care of that. And—and, once she was gone, I was lost. It—I couldn't deal. It's not an excuse. Really. Just…that's what it was. And it was my fault. You dealt. I didn't. And I'm sorry. I couldn't even be there when she died. I let her down." His eyes lowered to the table. "I let you down."

His words made my throat ache. I grabbed a handful of pretzels to give myself something to do. This wasn't Dad. No, it wasn't the dad from after my mother's death. It was the guy I knew when I was younger. Sure, he didn't play with me a lot or take me places, but he was there.

And now he was here. Trying.

"I've been working on fixing things, though," Dad said, standing before I could swallow my bite. "Here, I'll show you."

He vanished down the hallway, so I followed along to the opposite side of the house, where his bedroom and mine both were. Bags sat in a pile in the spare room, and he pointed to them. "Your mom's stuff. Not all of it, because there were things I wanted to keep. But Cathy said maybe it was time to donate some of her clothes. We only got rid of the stuff that was too old or holey to fix."

Like the jacket I had in my car.

"I kept the rest. I thought you might want to look through it or whatever." Dad shoved a hand through his hair. "I didn't want to get rid of it or donate it or anything until you had a say."

Words jammed in the back of my mouth. Then Dad was turning again, walking to my room.

He gripped the handle on the door. "I fixed the lock," he said, looking embarrassed. It was the lock he'd broken the day I'd stolen all his Johnny Walker Black and hidden it under my bed, sick of him getting drunk and yelling about Mom. "So you can have privacy or whatever."

I scanned the small space. It looked just like I had left it, but cleaner. And there was a poster of the solar system above my bed.

Dad ducked his head. "I know you're not a kid anymore. But I found it in the crawl space, and it was one your mom had bought. I can take it down."

"No," I said, so quietly I wasn't sure he heard me. "You can leave it up."

"Yeah." Dad ran a hand through his hair again. "So... you're almost eighteen now."

This summer. By the Fourth of July, I'd be legal. I wouldn't have to pretend I wasn't homeless when I was.

"You don't have to stay here, but I want you to. I want to... fix this, Jackson." Dad scuffed the toe of one of his boots on the other one. "I opened an account for you for college or whatever you want. So once you turn eighteen, if this doesn't work out—or...or before that—you can take the money and do what you need to. But I hope it doesn't come to that. It's about time I got my shit together."

He was right. It was about time. And what was I supposed to say to that?

"You don't have to pay for college," I mumbled. I'd figure it out. I was *already* figuring it out.

"Of course I do. It's my job."

I didn't answer.

"Jackson. You're supposed to have this opportunity. I'm working hard—extra shifts to save money. You deserve this chance. And if it's not what you want, I'll support you. If you want to work at Wal-Mart, that's fine. You can stay here while you figure out what you want to do. But...I saw your grades. You're kind of at the top of your class."

"Kind of," I said with a laugh.

Dad joined with a short laugh of his own. "Not kind of. You *are* at the top of your class. It's—God, you're just like your mom. She would have wanted you to go to college. Or do whatever it is that makes you happy. And it's my job to help give you that chance."

"Since when do you talk so much?" I asked gruffly, feeling sentimental and awkward and surprised all at the same time.

"Yeah." Dad chuckled. "It's the meetings. They're like, 'Don't hold back your feelings. You need to be able to talk. You can't build up anger or resentment.' All that…emotional sh—stuff. It's—it's strange. But they helped me get a job, and sometimes I eat other things besides TV dinners, so I'm not totally defective."

I blew out another laugh. "Sounds like."

"You can decide," Dad said. "You don't have to stay here. I won't say a word if you don't. I'll pretend everything's fine. But I want you to give it a try. For yourself. For me." He shrugged. "For your mom."

When I hesitated, Dad tried again. "We could get the internet."

Which made me laugh again. We stood there awkwardly for several seconds. I didn't know what to say, only that I needed time. Dad seemed to sense that.

"So, listen, I have to get to work soon. You're welcome to stay here, think about things, find some grub in the kitchen. I'm off at one in the morning, so if you'd rather not be here when I get back, well…that's when I'll be here."

He almost looked like he was going to step forward for a hug, so I nodded and said, "Thanks."

Dad stepped back, putting his hands in his pockets. "Sure." He turned to the hallway, and then back. "So…I'm glad you're here."

I waited until he left to say, "Me, too."

55.

BlackKNIGHT: I saw your messages. I want to see your new chess move. Actually, I'd really just like to talk to you…

56.

ZOE

Jackson texted me Friday afternoon, and I was so relieved to hear from him I stopped thinking about Mae's words and the waves of hurt that kept rolling over me. I just needed to know he was okay.

When he asked if he could drop by, I said it was fine and waited in my study. I turned in a complete circle in my now paper-free room. I couldn't tell if it looked clean and new or sad and lonely. Or maybe a mix—just like how I felt inside.

I gathered my school papers and turned on the computer in case he wanted to work on math or physics. My stomach was coiled too tightly to think about either of those things, but that's what we were supposed to be doing. Jackson was my tutor, and at least that was normal. Something that could distract us from the mess that was going on.

But when I heard the elevator and, soon after, Jackson walked into the room, those thoughts immediately vanished.

"Are you okay?" I asked, my voice coming out so soft it was a whisper.

He smiled, a genuine smile that relaxed every bone in my body. "I'm okay."

"You're not in trouble, are you? I mean, my parents didn't say anything to anyone—but still—"

"Everything is fine…" He ventured a step closer, but his words trailed off when he saw the empty wall.

His gaze traveled to the ceiling and then the wall again, as if he couldn't understand what it was about the room that looked so different.

"Your galaxy." His eyes met mine, a flash of conflict traveling through them. "You took it down."

I nodded, not sure what to say. It had felt like it was time, but now it just seemed rash. I couldn't believe I hadn't saved some of it. Or talked to Jackson first. But that was the problem, wasn't it? I shouldn't have to talk to Jackson or Mae or Gina about everything I did. I needed to make choices and deal with consequences on my own.

Mae was right. This wasn't living.

Jackson looked like he was choosing his words carefully. I stayed where I was, though my whole body itched to reach out to him.

"I talked to my dad," he said finally.

"You did?"

"Yesterday. It needed to be done."

I blew out a breath. "I'm glad."

He looked at the bare wall again. "I should have told you the truth. I mean, the whole truth about my dad."

Before I could convince myself to back down, I said through gritted teeth. "What about *Chess Challenge*?"

His jaw clenched. "Yeah, I should have told you the truth about that, too. But then you'd know that I was homeless and…"

A flash of hurt flickered in his eyes, and my heart softened again. "And you were worried about someone finding out."

He nodded.

"Then I told my parents," I said, understanding. He'd been trying hard to keep a secret, a secret he thought would get him in trouble, and that's exactly what had happened. "I'm sorry."

He swallowed, leaning against the wall. Part of me wanted to go to him, to take his hand, to hug him. But I stayed where I was.

"I was doing what I thought was right," I said, lifting my chin. "I was worried your dad might be…dangerous to be around."

Jackson met my eyes. "I understand. I really do. But things are okay between us now. He's been sober for a while."

"Really?"

"Really. I'm thinking…I don't know. I'm thinking I might move back in with him."

I angled my head, worried. "Are you sure that's a good idea?"

"I think it is. It seems like he has his stuff together. And if not…I'll try to handle things better."

His words relieved me. Even though he was being cautious, he seemed less stressed.

"I'm sorry for the other day," he said.

"Me, too."

After a few moments of silence, after we'd both stared at the blank wall long enough, he asked, "How was your test?"

A little part of me puffed up, proud of how well I'd done. "I got a ninety-eight percent."

"Zoe, that's great. I knew you'd do well." He smiled, and I took that as an invitation to step closer. Just so I could feel him near me.

"So…*Chess Challenge*," he said.

My heart twisted. "Yeah, I'd kind of like to know about that."

"Remember that day at school when we talked about

chess?" he asked. "I liked how you were so into it—so focused. Zugzwang, remember?"

Zugzwang. I *had* said that to him way back then. I'd said that to BlackKNIGHT, too. I nodded mutely.

"So I went online and found this site. *Chess Challenge.* And I started playing with this girl. Rogue. I had no idea it was you."

My cheeks burned. God, I'd told him so many things. So many personal, private things. He had to be thinking how big an idiot I was. Acting like a little girl with a crush on a boy but *talking* to him online like I knew what I was doing. Like I knew what life was like outside my four walls.

"You told me about your comics and about places you wanted to go," Jackson continued. "I finally put it all together."

I drew in a sharp breath. This was probably where he told me it was over between us.

Jackson walked a foot closer. "I think this is a good thing."

I almost choked on the question. "How?"

"We have so much in common. Rogue was like...my best friend. And you're—you're more than that."

Which was exactly how I felt then. And exactly why I felt so conflicted now, maybe a little like I was losing my best friend.

Jackson scratched his cheek and walked even closer, so our shoes were almost touching. "I really hope this is okay. I know it was a shock, and I didn't mean to tell you that way. But I still want..."

"What?" I asked, voice barely above a whisper.

"I still want us."

It didn't take me long to answer. "Me, too."

"So this is okay?" He reached up to brush my bangs out of my eyes.

Was it okay? I thought I had two new people in my life, but they turned out to be the same one.

"I'm glad it's you," I said, and it was the truth. Now they were both in my life, and it felt right. My mind ridiculously went to math problems. Zoe + (Jackson + BlackKNIGHT) = <3.

"Good." Jackson leaned in close enough I could feel his breath on my lips. "I'm glad."

I swallowed. "But…"

He froze.

I replayed Mae's words in my mind. *This isn't living. You can't stay in here all day.*

"I know what you're thinking," Jackson said before I could tell him. "That this is your comfort zone. I get that. I promise. Let's talk about it. We're supposed to go to the museum tonight, right?"

I reached into my pocket, feeling the worn ends of my tickets, waiting to be used. "I can't."

"What?"

I shook my head. "I can't go to the museum with you." I felt my resolve build brick by brick inside of me until I was sure. "I need to do this alone."

"But, it's outside. It's not that close."

"I know." I drummed up a smile, forcing confidence in my words. "I can do it. I *need* to do it."

"Zoe…"

I watched the struggle on his face, and it only made me feel more empowered. He was everything. I'd let him— Jackson and BlackKNIGHT—take up my whole world, and I couldn't do that anymore.

"At least let me walk you. I can wait outside, or—"

"No. I'm going to go on my own." I pulled out the tickets. "I'm going tonight."

"Are you sure?"

"I'm sure."

Jackson opened his mouth again, looking like he was going to argue. I challenged him with my eyes. I was determined to do this—to finally prove I was taking steps to move on.

And this time I wasn't going to let Jackson *or* BlackKNIGHT have a say in it.

57.

JACKSON

I almost typed a message to Zoe in *Chess Challenge*, but it felt so strange to talk to her that way now. She said it was okay that I was BlackKNIGHT, but I saw the terrified look in her eyes. Like everything she thought she knew was wrong.

Instead of *Chess Challenge*, I pulled up our series of texts and sent her a quick note. I wish I could be there with you. I can still come if you want.

I sent the message before I could change my mind, and sat at the table in my dad's kitchen. No, *our* kitchen. It could be ours again, even though it felt so foreign.

My stomach grumbled, and I almost ignored it. Like usual. I looked at the refrigerator, debating. Dad said to help myself. This wasn't like Robert's house where I had to be careful what I used. I could eat an entire bag of chips and not feel like I was wasting food or being irresponsible.

Still no response from Zoe. Had she really gone all the way to the museum by herself? I got that she felt she needed to do this, but it was a huge step. Huge.

I still felt like I should be there. Not just because I wanted to support her, but because I cared for Zoe. A lot. In fact, it was a kind of like I'd never felt with someone before.

Love.

Which is what made sitting here doing nothing even worse.

I stood and walked to the refrigerator, surprised when I actually found fruit and yogurt inside. No trace of beer or any kind of alcohol. I opened the freezer to check there, too, but all I found was a pint of mint chocolate chip ice cream. I snagged that and pulled a spoon from the same drawer we always used to keep them in. In fact, hardly anything had changed. No, I took that back. Hardly anything had changed from when my *mom* was still here. This looked like *her* house.

The thought hit me so hard I put the ice cream back. It used to be her favorite. Pocketing my phone, I wandered through the kitchen, down the hallway, and to my dad's room. I listened for his car for a minute, afraid he'd pull up and catch me in here.

Silence.

I flipped on the light switch and stared. It was like being thrown back in time, to when my mom used to make the bed every day and put her favorite quilt at the bottom. There weren't clothes on the floor or piles of junk mail on the end tables.

I should have been happier about that. It meant Dad had gotten his shit together, right? But that also meant he'd probably thrown away most of the other stuff around here he saw as junk. With a sigh, I turned for the door, but stopped when I spotted a book on his dresser. No, not a book. A photo album.

Curious, I walked across the room and lifted the book. It wasn't an album I'd seen before. In fact, the last time I'd seen an album in this house was when my dad got drunk one night and decided to "remodel" the house—which involved tearing up all the pictures of our family. Maybe it was because he couldn't stand Mom being gone, or maybe he'd just been out of his mind. But that had been the last straw.

All those pictures I thought were gone were in the book. Pictures of me as a baby, pictures of Mom and Dad when they got married, and more. Some of the photos were creased from where they'd been crumpled. Some had been taped several times to cover tears. I sat on Dad's bed, my heart in my throat.

Mom smiled back at me from those pictures. Full of life, full of hope. I felt like I should have done more for her, *been* there more or made things easier for her. Now I just felt hollow. I hadn't been able to save her.

And now it looked like I might be letting Zoe down, too.

Swallowing the lump in my throat, I set the album back on my dad's dresser and quietly left the room. Still no message from Zoe.

I rubbed my hand over my eyes and wandered through the house, searching for inspiration. Something to get me out of my funk. I stopped at the end of the bed in my room. The poster of the solar system was still there, a reminder of what my mom and I had shared, of what I'd wanted to do with my life. College. That's what she wanted for me.

I could do that much. Whether things worked out with my dad or not, I could do this. I *had* to. Everyone kept telling Zoe to live her life, but no one ever said that to me. And why? I was just as stuck as she was—scared of the what-ifs.

Grabbing my backpack and computer, I decided to go to the library. Sure, it was right next door to the museum, and it would be convenient if Zoe texted me back. Maybe she'd want to meet up afterward. Then she could tell me all about the museum.

Then I could tell her about my feelings for her.

But either way, I wanted to study up on the University of Colorado. Zoe was getting her life on track; I had to do the same.

58.

BlackKNIGHT: I know it was a shock to find out who I really am. It surprised me when I found out you were Zoe, too. We can use our real names on here if you want. Or play chess in real life instead. In the meantime…I'll make another move. Hope you have fun at the museum.

59.

ZOE

I got to the art museum late because I couldn't force myself to ride the bus. There were so many people. And what if I missed my stop? I'd freak.

So I walked. In the cool, cloudy late afternoon, I walked all the way to the art museum by myself, counting every pair of shoes I passed.

And I hadn't had a panic attack yet.

No, I *wouldn't* have a panic attack. I could handle this—as long as I focused on shoes. Shoes were safe.

I forced myself to make eye contact with the lady at the front as I passed my ticket over. When I stepped through the doors for the special exhibit, all I could do was stare. Paper spilled into the room, an elaborate chandelier of butterflies flowing down over me. The Eiffel Tower stood tall in a roped off area in the middle of the space. I smiled at the small renditions of people at the base of the tower.

It was far better than what I'd pictured for my paper wall at home. Jackson was missing this.

But I wasn't.

I gave myself ample time at every display, focusing on

the technique of each piece so I wouldn't think about the people around me. There was folded paper, textured paper, thick paper, thin paper. It was a wonderland of paper, nothing like I'd ever imagined.

I took pictures and made notes for my designs at home. By the time I'd made one circuit around the exhibit, I wanted to do it all over again. My heart beat fast, and it was awkward being by myself, but once I got going, it was easy to pretend it was only me alone in the museum. Me and the paper.

A voice came over the loud speaker, announcing the museum would be closing in thirty minutes. I checked my watch. The museum stayed open until eight p.m. on Fridays, which meant I'd been here for nearly three hours.

Keeping calm, I took one last look at the paper house I stood in front of before folding my pamphlet and stuffing it in my purse. I checked my phone, surprised to find two messages. One from Jackson and one from Mae.

I read Jackson's first. I wish I could be there with you. I can still come if you want.

My heart clenched. Someone bumped me from behind. Flushing, I apologized and made my way to the exit. Outside, the sun was sinking lower, touching the tips of the mountains. I stepped to the side of the entrance and read the message again. I can still come if you want...

I almost called him. But no, we both needed time. Besides, I was committed to this adventure. I was here at the museum, on my own, and I was doing it.

Mae's message was just as brief. Mom said you went to the museum. Are you okay?

I didn't answer her. I could do this myself. Maybe I'd take my time walking home—get a hot dog or snack from a vendor on the street. It's something Mae would have done.

I turned to the street and then froze when I saw Jackson.

He had one strap of his backpack over his shoulder, and he gave me an almost sheepish grin.

"Hey," he said, lifting his chin.

A flash of anger raced through me. What was he doing? He knew why I was here. He knew that I needed to do this by myself. Instead of answering, I stared straight ahead and passed him without a word.

I halfway expected him to call out or to catch up with me, but he didn't. And I was glad. How was I supposed to take these steps and move out of my comfort zone if Jackson didn't give me the space to do it? If Mae thought she needed to check on me?

With a huff, I crossed the street alongside a group of people also leaving the museum. I got swept up in the crowd, and part of me wanted to throw it in Jackson's face. See? I was one of them. The people out in the world.

When I got to the other side, I turned left automatically. That's the way I came from, right? Of course it was. And it's not like I couldn't turn around if I went the wrong way.

With long, sure strides, I kept walking until I started to doubt myself again. What if I'd gone the wrong way? I didn't recognize some of these buildings…

Panic crawled up my throat. *Calm down*. I could do this. I had to. If I could do this, that proved I could go to school, and that's what I really wanted.

But another few blocks went by, and I knew I was going the wrong way. I stopped, looking at the street signs. I should have stayed on 16th instead of straying off course. I needed to turn around.

Now it felt like a long way back. My anger had taken me a lot farther than I'd expected.

My chest tightened. It was getting dark. Really dark. And I was so far away.

The bus. I could take the bus. Mae did it all the time. I crossed the street again and waited for the bus to stop. I stood at the back of the line and got on after everyone else.

I sat in the very front, so it'd be easy to get off when I needed to. But after a few stops, I realized I barely knew where I was.

My phone buzzed, and this time I pulled it out, grateful for the contact. It was another text from Mae, asking if I was okay.

I texted her back, I'm on my way home, and almost asked what stop I was supposed to get off at. But then she'd know. She'd know I couldn't do this on my own.

Pressing a hand to my chest, I glanced up at the next stop. Was I supposed to get off here? Or at the last one?

I stayed on for two more stops, afraid I'd still be too far away from home. But at the next one, I realized I'd gone too far. My chest squeezed painfully.

No. Not here. I couldn't have a panic attack on the bus.

I hurried to get off, almost pushing a man aside to get to the sidewalk. There were streetlights, but I felt alone out here. Nothing was familiar and there was barely anyone walking by. At least not anyone who looked friendly.

My breathing grew shallow, and I let a sob slip out. Clutching my phone to my chest, I found a bench and forced myself to sit down. I needed to close my eyes, to calm down, but I was too afraid to do it.

This is why you stay at home, Zoe. This is why it's safer not to go anywhere.

I tried counting to make the breathing easier, but I was practically hyperventilating. Why had I ever decided to do this?

"Mae," I whispered. I should have asked her to come with me. Or Jackson.

But I'd brushed them both off. I'd chosen this. And now

I didn't know what to do.

A woman walked past, giving me a concerned look. I couldn't smile back. I couldn't even breathe.

My fingers shook as I wrote a text to my mom. **Please come get me.**

I gave her the streets I was on and waited for her answer, my hand clenched tight on my phone as if it were a lifeline. I stared at my shoes, afraid to look up. The world crashed in on me, and all I could do was sit there with my head down, trying to breathe in and out. Trying not to panic.

And failing.

At home, I stumbled inside from the elevator, forgetting to take off my shoes as I headed for my room.

"Zoe?" Mom followed me, worry straining her voice.

"I'm going to lie down," I mumbled, not waiting for her to answer.

In my room, I curled up in my bed with my shoes still on, facing the wall. I barely remembered the ride back home. My chest was still tight, and there was still that horrible voice in my head telling me how badly I'd failed.

If I couldn't go to the museum, how was I supposed to go to graduation?

I tried to ignore the knock at the door and Mae's voice calling my name.

She came in. "Zoe?"

"I'm asleep," I said, even though there was no way I was going to be able to sleep anytime soon.

I heard her footsteps as they approached the bed. "I know you're not."

Go away. That's what I wanted to tell her. "Don't you have a date or cheerleading practice or something?"

She sighed and touched my leg over the covers. "I want to be here with you."

"I'm fine."

"I don't believe you."

I shifted, considering turning over to face her. "Why?"

"Because…" Her voice lowered. She sat on the bed, jostling me. Instead of irritating me, it made my throat ache. She used to do this all the time, sit on my bed while I tried to sleep. "Mom's making you homemade hot chocolate, so I know you're not okay."

Of course Mom was. She was probably making a chocolate cake, too.

"You wanted me to grow up," I whispered. "I did."

"Oh, Zoe." She touched my back. "I'm sorry. I shouldn't have said anything. You don't have to go out there ever again. What do you need? Paper? I can bring you paper—"

"No, I'm fine. I don't need anything. Good night."

She hesitated a long moment before standing. "I'm sorry," she whispered before walking out of my room and closing the door.

I squeezed my eyes shut tight. I was sorry, too. If I hadn't gone off on my own, maybe this wouldn't have happened.

I'd tried, and I'd failed. I should have stayed here in my paper room where it was safe.

60.

JACKSON

I sat with Robert and Kelly for lunch at school on Monday, feeling like things were finally getting back to normal. I'd spent the whole weekend at my dad's house. No, *my* house. And nothing had gone wrong.

Yet.

No, nothing *would* go wrong. If Dad slipped, there wasn't anything I could do. But I was trying to keep faith in him.

Things with Dad were going well, but things with Zoe…

As I bit into my piece of pizza, I remembered her face when she'd seen me outside of the library after her visit to the museum. I'd never seen her so frustrated. And I understood why. I was making it hard for her to take her steps.

But that didn't mean I didn't want to be a part of her life.

I had to fix this.

"Things are cool, right?" Robert asked. "With your dad."

I nodded. It was such a relief not having to lie anymore. I still couldn't believe Dad was saving money for me. He used to be unable to save money for himself. Now he was working double shifts, not just to make up for the debt he'd created, but to give me some kind of future. And even better,

I had a home again.

Zoe. I had to tell her.

I pulled out my phone and checked *Chess Challenge*. She hadn't made a move in our current match, and she hadn't responded to my messages. I checked my texts and saw the same thing. She hadn't answered.

"If you're checking in on Zoe, she's probably not going to answer," Robert said.

"Why not?" She couldn't be that mad at me, could she?

"Mae said the museum thing didn't go well."

I glanced around. "Where is Mae?"

"She stayed home today. She said she wanted to be with Zoe."

My gut clenched. "What happened?"

"I don't know. Just…Mae said she won't leave her apartment."

Guilt washed over me. Something must have happened. Zoe had gone alone to the museum because of everything that had happened with us, and I hadn't been there for her. And something had happened.

I sent Zoe another text, but heard nothing. Damn it. Why hadn't Mae called me if something serious had happened? I needed to know what was going on.

It almost killed me to wait until school was over to get away. But the instant the last bell rang, I got into my car and headed in the direction of the King household.

My stomach churned the whole way. I should have been there with Zoe—watching out for her.

Inside at the front desk, the clerk greeted me.

"Can you call? See if it's okay if I go up?"

"Of course," he said.

He rang the Kings and announced that I was here. He listened for a moment, nodded, and said, "Of course. Have a good day."

I waited, but he only smiled apologetically.

"Sorry, Mrs. King said they don't want any visitors right now."

"But…"

"Sorry."

I backed away from the counter, lost. I needed to see Zoe. I needed to know she was okay. I pulled out my phone and texted her again.

Zoe? I'm downstairs. Are you okay?

Clenching my phone tightly in my hand, I waited at the chairs Zoe hated. I had a clear view of the elevators from there. But she didn't appear and she didn't answer my text.

Unable to think of another way to see her, I turned for the exit, feeling useless. Then the elevator opened behind me, and I whipped around.

Mae walked out, saw me, and headed straight over. "She's not coming down."

"Is she okay?"

Mae sighed and turned to the courtyard. We walked out together, both silent until we sat next to the spitting fountain.

"What happened?" I asked.

"She went to the art museum by herself," Mae said. She stared at her hands. "They had a paper exhibit."

I reached out, hesitantly touching her arm.

"I was frustrated with her because she just…" Mae sniffled. "She was upset about what was going on with you, and I saw her paper wall and all this new paper Mom got for her, and I was angry. I was angry and I took it out on her. So she went out by herself. She went to the museum to prove to me she was still living her life, and then she got lost on the way home and had a panic attack. It really scared her."

I rubbed my hands over my face, realizing how much of a setback this could be for Zoe.

"She's fine, she just doesn't want to leave the apartment now. She was doing good and now she just wants to stay in her room."

I stood, unable to sit still. "Maybe if I could talk to her—"

"She doesn't want to talk. She won't talk to me, either."

"I could try. I could—"

"Mom won't let you up. She doesn't want to upset Zoe. It's nothing against you, but I know she doesn't want to see Zoe hurt."

"I understand."

But what was I supposed to do? I couldn't leave, not without seeing Zoe.

Mae stood. "I'm sorry. Maybe you'd better just go home… or wherever…and let things cool down."

I didn't try to explain to her I'd moved back home. I only nodded and watched as she went back inside.

I wanted to run after her and hop into the elevator, but that would only make things worse. So I left the courtyard and walked to the revolving doors, leaving Zoe's building without any clue how I was going to fix this. Or if I even could.

61.

BlackKNIGHT: I learned something new today.

    BlackKNIGHT: You're the bravest person I know. My mom would have loved you.

62.

ZOE

I knew Mom was really freaked out by my behavior when she asked Gina to come for a session this morning even though I wasn't supposed to see her for a few days.

"It's just a check-in," Mom said as we waited for her to come up in the elevator. "In case you need to talk."

Talk? I wasn't sure how talking was going to help. But I guess if it made Mom feel better, and made her stop baking pounds of cookies and banana bread, then I'd do it. She'd even brought home more paper even though I hadn't touched the last batch she gave me.

Gina entered with her typical smile, though I swear there was pity behind it.

"Should we get to it?" she asked right away.

"Absolutely," Mom said.

"How about your study?"

I sighed and led Gina to my study. She wore a simple pair of jeans and red Converse, kind of like she hadn't been expecting to meet with anyone. Her scarf was bright blue — the kind of color that made her stand out. That made people stare.

"You took down your paper wall," Gina said, her eyes raking over the bare space.

"It was time for something new."

Her eyes flicked to the wall again. It looked plain and sad, like a blank piece of paper.

I picked at the sleeve of my sweater, waiting for her to say something.

"Your mom told me what happened," Gina said. "How are you doing?"

"Fine."

"Really fine, or are you just saying that?"

I frowned but wouldn't meet her gaze. "I'm really fine in here."

"And outside?" Gina asked, walking to the window.

"Haven't been outside since last week."

"I can see why," she said. "It makes sense to stay in here."

When she didn't continue, I looked up. She seemed to be enjoying the view outside the window, relaxed despite my discomfort.

"That's all?" I asked. "No, 'Zoe, you can't let this stop you from living your life. There's a whole world out there. It's just one minor setback.'"

Gina smiled at me. "Is that what you think? This shouldn't stop you from living your life?"

"In theory," I mumbled.

"Ah…" Gina sighed. "In theory, life should be so much different. In theory, if we understand we legitimately can't solve a problem, or it's not our fault, we shouldn't worry about it, right? But that's not how life works."

I nodded.

"I have another coffee story," she said. "You want to hear it?"

"Sure."

"This was when I was in college, too. I went out for coffee with friends one Saturday night, and I had to cross the campus to get home," she continued. "Being the empowered young woman I was, I had my can of pepper spray ready just in case. And one of those whistles to blow for help. I took a self-defense class every year. But all that didn't stop me from being jumped from behind. He had a knife. I tried to fight, but…" Gina smiled at me, even while I stood frozen by the wall. She pushed aside her scarf to reveal a jagged scar that ran down her neck to her collarbone. "It almost killed me."

Mouth dry, I could only stare at the scar. It looked painful even this many years later. How had I not noticed it before? No wonder she always wore a scarf.

"In theory," she continued, "moving to another campus should have made me feel safe. Only going out during the day should have made me feel safe. Always walking places with someone else should have made me feel safe. But it wasn't enough. So, I quit school, and I didn't feel safe. It was a chain reaction of useless solutions. *In theory*, I should have been able to work through it and move on. But that's not how life works. So, screw *theories*."

She readjusted the scarf to cover the scar.

"How did you move on?" I asked.

She tapped her finger against her lips, thinking. "I had to take my life back. One day at a time. I made myself go to the store alone. I started school again. I made myself walk to my car at night. And so on. Things are going to happen no matter how much we prepare for the worst. But in the meantime, we're denying ourselves all the good we can have in our lives if we hide from it. Sounds cliché, but sometimes the simplest solution is to just keep going."

I thought about Jackson, and how he had kept going even after his mom had died. He was talking to his dad again, and

I was proud of him. But that was Jackson. He was stronger than me.

Gina gestured to my wall. "I think like…scenes from old monster movies would be awesome. You know, paper Frankenstein and some zombies. Nosferatu. The Thing."

I laughed. "Maybe…I'll take a break from the paper art for a while."

She smiled. "If that's what you think is best. And maybe next time we have a session, you can come to my office instead."

I blew out a slow breath. "I think I'd like to try that."

Later that night, I sat in my room with my laptop, staring at the screen. *Chess Challenge*. I had a few messages from BlackKNIGHT. He'd even made his next move on our match. But what was I supposed to say to him?

I'd pushed him away when what I really should have been doing was trying to find a balance. I wanted him in my life, and I couldn't just back off every single time he tried to be there for me. That's who Jackson was, and that's part of why I loved him.

My heart squeezed tight in my chest. Love. I loved Jackson.

A knock sounded at my door.

"Come in."

Mae walked in carrying a plate covered with slices of banana bread. "Mom made me bring it." She set the plate on the end table by my bed and lingered. "Do you want me to go?"

"You can stay," I said before even thinking about it. I missed Mae.

She smiled and sat on the bed. "I'm really sorry for what I said that day."

"You just told me how you felt."

"Yes, but still. I feel bad. So does Jackson. I kind of just want to stay home with you this year. We could homeschool together. College homeschool."

I blinked. "Really?"

"Yes. Then we could tease Mom all day and get fat on her scones. Make YouTube videos with funny voices and wait for them to go viral."

I laughed. "You don't want to do that. And you know what? Neither do I."

"You don't want to be homeschooled anymore?"

I swallowed, shaking my head. "I don't think so. I…can't stay in here all the time. You're right. I need to get…there. Wherever there is. I need to be me, and I have no idea who that is outside of this apartment. It would suck if I never found out."

"I think that's brave."

"So, I have…steps."

"More steps?"

I nodded and reached for my journal. Mae looked at me like I was crazy. She was used to seeing me with colored paper or copy paper. But this was just plain journal paper with all my ideas on it.

Mae read a few, then glanced up at me. "Go to a cheerleading event and hold up signs like you used to?"

"Yep."

She read another. "Go to the museum with Mae."

There were more. All things I wanted to do, things that made me who I am. Steps for *me*, so I could ease back into life on my own terms. Some were easy, some were scary, but they were all ways to get me where *I* wanted to go.

Mae stood, looking excited. "We have to find clothes. The perfect outfits for all your outings."

I laughed. "I'm not going to do all of them tomorrow. One at a time."

"Zoe?"

"Yeah?"

"I meant it. I think you're brave."

"I think you're brave, too," I said without hesitation.

In my fantasy world, I wouldn't have done anything different. This was life. Good, bad, and everything in between.

She laughed. "I'm working on it."

"Will you help me?" I asked.

"With your outfit? School?"

I grinned at her. "Those things, too."

"What else?"

I shoved my laptop aside. "I have a plan."

63.

JACKSON

It was the last month of school, and I wasn't sure what to do with myself. Normally I was organizing my clothes and trying to find books on sale and extra jobs to make sure I had money for the school year. But I'd been staying with my dad and things were going smoothly. No food worries, no money worries. My dad even suggested I take a break from work to focus on school.

Maybe Dad was trying a little *too* hard, but I couldn't blame him.

Even though I had wifi at home, I brought my laptop and backpack to the library to do more college research. It made me feel like myself—or maybe the person I'd become over the years. Independent. Free.

Inside, I grabbed my books on hold and rode the escalator to the second floor to sit in my favorite spot. The sun shone bright outside and part of me thought I should be out there enjoying the day. But the more I thought about it, the more I realized I had a lot of days to be out there, in the world, enjoying my life.

Even if I had to do it without Zoe.

I hadn't heard from her since I visited her apartment, and I hadn't tried to get in contact with her again. Maybe I needed the space just as much as Zoe did. Besides, I had to learn that there were some things that weren't my job to fix.

When I opened my computer, I frowned at the box in the corner with a notification. *Chess Challenge*. I opened up the app and stared at the screen. Zoe. No, Rogue2015. She'd left me a message.

Are you at the library?

I glanced around like I might find her standing right behind me. Then I laughed a little at myself. Of course she expected me to be here. Wasn't this where I always was?

My fingers hovered over the keyboard. I didn't know what I'd expected from Zoe. A hello maybe, a how are you. Maybe even "I'm sorry" because she'd shut me out and there was nothing I could do about it.

Finally, I lowered my fingers and wrote back. Yes.

When she didn't respond or make another move, I typed in, Where are you?

Probably at home. Maybe making more art for her paper wall. Her *new* paper wall, since she'd taken down the other one. I still had a picture of it on my phone, but it was nothing like the real thing.

I heard Dale's telltale shuffle and the sound of his cart rolling in my direction. I cast him a smile before turning back to my computer. But he didn't start stocking the shelves; he walked to my table instead. Without a word, he set something next to me.

An origami crane. Like something Zoe would make.

This time I physically turned around in my seat, sure she was behind me. I even stood and walked to the shelves, peering down each one, trying to find her. Nothing.

When I walked back to the table, I noticed writing on the

wing of the bird. Small, loopy writing. *Stonehenge.*

I released a breath. She was here. Or there. At Stonehenge. She hadn't talked to me in what felt like forever, and now she was here.

The hesitation lasted only a minute, then I gathered my computer and books and shoved them in my backpack. Still holding the crane, I stepped out into the sunshine and headed right, my stride a lot more casual than I felt. When I rounded the corner and saw the sculpture, but not her, I stopped.

No Zoe? Then why had she wanted me to come out here?

I shielded my eyes from the sun and walked until I reached the two tall structures. And there, right at the bottom of one, was another piece of origami.

A flower this time. It was made with colored paper. A purple flower, green stem, so intricate I knew only Zoe's tiny hands were capable of creating it.

No note this time, but I had an idea what she was doing. Taking me on a tour with her origami to the same places and sculptures I'd shown her. So, I walked to the dustpan and broom and collected an origami frog.

At the next one, the giant metal piece of art that kind of looked like a robotic spider, I found origami Yoda and laughed. I knew where she wanted me to go next. My favorite one, *Yearling.* Or Horse on Chair.

When I walked around the corner, the emerald lawn stretching to my right, I froze. She stood next to the giant red chair, with a colorful box in her hands.

She smiled as I made my way across the grass and to her.

"You're here," she said.

"*You're* here."

Her smile wobbled. "I wanted to see you. And—and give you this."

I took the box from her. I expected more origami, but this

looked like a gift. A gift wrapped in comic paper. "What is it?"

"Open it."

First, I wanted to hug her. To kiss her. To pull her close and make sure she was okay. But she looked okay. She looked great. A little nervous, maybe, but so alive.

"I'm really glad to see you," I said instead.

"I'm really glad to see you, too."

"Are you okay?" I had to ask.

"I am. I really am." She dropped her chin slightly before lifting it again and meeting my eyes. "And I'm sorry. I should have called you back or something. Anything." She touched my arm. "I was taking time and dealing with things I needed to deal with, but I wasn't being fair to you. I'm sorry."

The tension in my shoulders eased. That was all I needed. To understand what was going on and to know she was okay. "I forgive you."

She smiled again. "Thank you. You should open it."

I tore the wrapping to reveal a plain brown box with a lid. When I popped it open and spotted all the hearts, my laughter bubbled out. Origami hearts. Dozens of them.

"You made all these?" I asked.

She nodded. "There's, uh…something at the bottom."

I dug deeper, unable to help my grin. This must have taken her hours. I *still* couldn't make an origami heart, let alone dozens of them that looked so perfect. Underneath the mass of pink and red hearts, I spotted a white piece of paper folded in half.

When I read the words, my mind went blank. *Will you go to prom with me?*

My mouth opened, but nothing came out. Prom was a big deal. And it was also at school. My school. *Her* school, too, if she ever decided to go.

"I know it's kind of last minute, but I was hoping—"

I cut her off with a hard hug, nearly knocking her off her feet. "Yes. I'll go with you."

"Really?"

"Yes," I murmured again, lips against her ear. I let myself hope even more. "Are you sure?"

I heard the tremor in her voice when she said, "I'm sure." And then she laughed, and it was the best sound I'd heard in a week.

I wouldn't release her. She felt too good in my arms, and I missed being near her. Smelling jasmine and hearing her laughter.

She let me guide her to the benches, where we sat in the sunshine.

"I thought you weren't going to talk to me again. I'm so sorry about the museum, and—"

"It's okay. It's not your fault."

I dropped my chin, mumbling the words because I couldn't help it. "I feel like I let you down."

"No. Jackson. Jackson," she said again when I didn't look at her. "You made this right. You made me braver than I was—and made me see that there's a whole world out there I want to be part of. Both you *and* BlackKNIGHT helped with that."

I met her eyes, more hope seeping in.

When she smiled and said her next words, it nearly undid me. "Your mom would be so proud of you."

I swallowed hard, reaching for her hand. "So, you're okay? For real?"

"I'm okay."

Blowing out a breath I felt like I'd been holding for weeks, I said, "I was worried."

"That's my line," she whispered.

"You're not the same, Zoe. Look at you. You're out here. Wearing shoes." It relaxed me even further when she laughed.

"And we're going to prom. Really? Or did I just imagine that?"

"No, you didn't imagine that. I want to go with you." She looked around, watching people as they passed. "I've been taking steps. *My* steps. And it's been going well. I want to go to prom, and I want to go to school. And I definitely, definitely want to go to graduation."

I smiled at her. "I'm glad."

"I've been thinking about a lot of things, too. There's…" Her cheeks flushed, but she met my eyes. "There's something else I want to tell you."

"What?"

She pressed her lips together for a long moment, then said, "I love you."

The words nearly knocked me over. Since when was Zoe the brave one? I took her hand, my heart full. "I love you, too." I squeezed her fingers, letting the words sink in, amazed at how much had changed for me these last few weeks. "I have a lot to tell you."

"About your dad?"

"Yes."

"Are you living with him now?"

"Yes."

She smiled, eyes sparkling. "Let's start over."

"What?"

She held out her hand. "Hi, I'm Zoe. I like paper. And comics. And chess. And sometimes I hide in my apartment because I'm too scared to go outside."

"Hey, Zoe. Nice hair."

She smirked.

"I'm Jackson. I live with my dad—now—and I rock at chess. I love astronomy, and if you understand physics, you'll have the key to my heart."

"Good to know." She angled her head. "This really cool

guy I once met said that you learn something new every day."

"He sounds like a genius."

"Yeah. He thinks so. So, Jackson, what did you learn today?"

I brushed her bangs out of her eyes, thinking. I learned that Zoe was even more amazing than I knew. I learned that it was okay to trust people again. I learned that the world looked a whole lot brighter with her in it.

But I settled for something simple. "I learned that school goes really slow when you're about to graduate."

She kissed me. "I bet."

"Wait, what was that?"

"What?"

"That kiss? That was…not the best welcome back kiss."

"No?"

I brushed her cheek with my thumb, waiting while she debated. The old Zoe blushed. The new Zoe leaned in and kissed me with everything she had. My hand tangled in her hair, and I lost all train of thought.

Except for one. One thought.

My mom would be happy for me.

"I really missed you, Zoe."

"I missed you, too."

Her breath tickled my cheek and I kissed her again. "I want to go lots of places with you."

"Me, too. But let's start with school. You have to keep your grades up and prove to everyone else you're as much of a genius as I know you are."

I laughed. "All right. If you insist."

"So, what do you want to do today?"

"Anything. Everything. As long as we can do it together."

"Deal."

64.

BlackKNIGHT: Hey there. How's it going?

Rogue2015: You know how it's going. I just saw you 45 minutes ago.

BlackKNIGHT: True, but…well…

Rogue2015: What's wrong?

BlackKNIGHT: I think my girlfriend might be suspicious about us.

Rogue2015: Uh oh. What gave us away?

BlackKNIGHT: I keep talking about chess and how I have this really wonderful tutor who flirts with me all the time.

Rogue2015: I think you've got that backward.

BlackKNIGHT: ☺ You think I'm a wonderful tutor?

Rogue2015: No, I think you flirt with *me* all the time.

BlackKNIGHT: Ha! True, though. My girlfriend will be jealous.

Rogue2105: Better not tell her, then.

BlackKNIGHT: No can do. We don't keep secrets from each other.

Rogue2015: Don't know what to tell you. I guess no more chess for us.

BlackKNIGHT: Maybe I can convince her to sign up for *Chess Challenge*.

Rogue2015: What would her screen name be?

BlackKNIGHT: PaperGirl.

Rogue2015: That could work.

BlackKNIGHT: So, PaperGirl, I think we should hang out tonight. Watch a movie or something.

Rogue2015: I think I could manage that.

BlackKNIGHT: Are you nervous? Not about coming over. About graduation.

Rogue2015: A little. But excited nervous. Mae helped me with my outfit.

BlackKNIGHT: Is it made of paper? Because that would be really cool.

Rogue2015: Maybe next time.

BlackKNIGHT: You forgot to make your next move.

Rogue2015: Oh, right…how about that?

BlackKNIGHT: Perfect. Checkmate.

(BlackKNIGHT has passed Rogue2015 on the leaderboard)

Rogue2015: Seriously?

BlackKNIGHT: I. AM. AMAZING.

Rogue2015: Maybe we should just stick to playing chess in real life from now on.

BlackKNIGHT: Why's that? So you can distract me and I won't win? Fat chance. I learned from the best. There's no stopping me now.

Rogue2015: ☺ No, there isn't. You can do anything you want in life.

BlackKNIGHT: So can you.

Rogue2015: You know what? It took long enough, but I'm finally starting to believe it.

65.

ZOE

The stadium was full. It had been a long time since I'd seen this many people all in one place. It was full of excitement, and I tried to lose myself in it instead of being nervous.

I would get to see Mae graduate today. She was already here somewhere, getting ready, and I think she didn't believe I'd come. Before she left she told me it was okay if I couldn't make it.

But I did.

I sat next to Mom and Dad, watching while Mom dabbed her cheeks and Dad manned the camera. Mom had been baking all week, and Dad had been making sure he had work covered so he could take the day off.

I'd been preparing mentally. Which meant a lot of sessions with Gina to make sure I was ready. This was a huge step.

Once the ceremony got going, I relaxed even more. We were close to the back, but I could still see everyone. Robert and Kelly as they walked across the stage for their diplomas. Then Mae and Jackson.

I cheered extra hard for them even though I knew they couldn't see me all the way back here. Then Jackson stood to give his valedictory speech. I glanced across the aisle and saw his dad fumbling with his phone to take a picture. He nodded along with Jackson's words, looking like a proud father.

When Jackson finished his speech, I stole the program from my mom and set it in my lap.

I started folding it, which made her frown.

"Zoe, really," she said, dabbing her eyes.

I just smiled at her and folded the program into a paper airplane. Mom chuckled.

Up on stage, Jackson's voice was confident. "There are going to be a lot of things in life that we can't control. Things the world will make us think we can't handle. But it's those moments, the strength we show when we do our best to handle them, that show our true character."

He couldn't be more right. The things I'd been afraid of—the big ones and the little ones—were all the things that had helped me the most. That had made me into this new Zoe. The person I really wanted to be.

Cheers went up when Jackson finished speaking.

After the ceremony, I told Mom and Dad I was going to find Mae.

"Take your time," Dad said with a glance at Mom to see if she was listening. He lowered his voice. "She's going to make me help her steam clean the carpet when we get home." He shuddered. "And film it."

Laughing, I nodded and turned. Then I took a deep breath and walked down the aisle in search of Mae.

When I caught sight of her with her friends, I aimed the airplane and threw it at her. She spun around when it hit her shoulder.

I smiled when she saw me. She abandoned the paper airplane and ran in my direction. "Zoe!"

She nearly bowled me over with her hug. My cheeks

burned, but I held her tight. "Happy graduation."

Mae pulled back, still grinning. "You came."

"Of course I did."

She tugged my hair. "Of course you did."

Then she pulled me over to Robert and Kelly, and Jackson found us, and they all acted like I was meant to be there. Jackson wrapped his arms around me and gave me a kiss.

"I knew you'd be here," he said.

I nodded, for the first time not doubting myself. "I knew I would, too."

I'd made it to graduation on my own terms, which meant I had my whole life ahead of me, one step at a time.

ACKNOWLEDGMENTS

It's been a long and amazing writing journey to get to this point. Those of you closest to me and those of you who have been part of my journey know th's—and I want to take the chance to thank you. Writing can be a solitary effort but publishing and all the steps it takes to get there involves an army, and I'm lucky to have had some great support on that front.

Thank you to my awesome critique partner, Jessica Hoefer. Not only have you helped make my writing a million times better, you've been there through writing and life crises, and I appreciate it so much. Thank you also to other writers who have helped support me in various ways. Cara Bertrand, who read an early version of this book, the AMAZING Eighteeners—you guys are the best debut group a girl could ask for, and also Wendy Miller. You've been a great and important friend.

To my agent, Stacey Donaghy. It seems likc all of my books come to the world in strange ways, and they wouldn't get there without your help. You've been an amazing agent, and a friend when I needed you. Thank you.

To my editor, Stephen Morgan, for loving this story even when I wasn't sure about it. And for taking a chance on a new author. Thanks also to Lydia Sharp, who came along during this book's journey to help make it even better. I love it that much more because of you two. And thanks to the rest of the Entangled team for putting love and support behind this book.

Thanks to my family, especially my daughters Katelyn, Libby, and Brooklyn. You have no idea how much you've inspired and encouraged me. And more, you supported me through good times and bad times and gave me the chance to follow my dream of writing.

Finally, to the readers of this book. It means a lot to me that you get to see a story of my heart. It makes me so happy to be able to share it with you.

GRAB THE ENTANGLED TEEN RELEASES READERS ARE TALKING ABOUT!

VALIANT
BY MERRIE DESTEFANO

Earth is in shambles. Everyone, even the poorest among us, invested in the *Valiant*'s space mining mission in the hopes we'd be saved. But the second the ship leaves Earth's atmosphere, the alien invasion begins. They pour into cities, possessing humans, forcing us to kill one another. And for whatever reason, my brother is their number one target. Maybe if Justin and I can save my brother, we can save us all…

FREQUENCY
BY CHRISTOPHER KROVATIN

Fiona's not a kid anymore. She can handle the darkness she sees in the Pit Viper, a DJ whose wicked tattoos and hypnotic music seem to speak to every teen in town…except her. She can handle watching as each of her friends seems to be nearly possessed by the music. She can even handle her suspicion that the DJ is hell-bent on revenge. But she's not sure she can handle falling in love with him.

Illusions
by Madeline J. Reynolds

1898, London. Saverio, a magician's apprentice, is tasked with stealing another magician's secret behind his newest illusion. He befriends the man's apprentice, Thomas, with one goal. Get close. Learn the trick. Get out.

Then Sav discovers that Thomas performs *real* magic and is responsible for his master's "illusions." And worse, Sav has unexpectedly fallen for Thomas.

Their forbidden romance sets off a domino effect of dangerous consequences that could destroy their love—and their lives.

Toxic
by Lydia Kang

Hana isn't supposed to exist. She's grown up hidden in a secret room of the bioship *Cyclo* until the day the entire crew is simply gone. Fenn is supposed to die. He and a crew of hired mercenaries are there to monitor *Cyclo* as she expires, and his payment will mean Fenn's sister is able to live. But when he meets Hana, he's not sure how to save them both.

entangled teen

an imprint of Entangled Publishing LLC